LEGEND OF THE GALACTIC HEROES

VOLUME 5

MOBILIZATION

YOSHIKI TANAKA

HAIKA SORU

SAN FRANCISCO

LEGEND OF THE GALACTIC HEROES

VOLUME 5
MOBILIZATION

WRITTEN BY
YOSHIKI TANAKA

Translated by Tyran Grillo

Legend of the Galactic Heroes, Vol. 5, Mobilization
GINGA EIYU DENSETSU Vol.5
© 1985 by Yoshiki TANAKA
Cover Illustration © 2007 Yukinobu Hoshino
All rights reserved.

English translation © 2017 VIZ Media, LLC

Cover and interior design by Fawn Lau and Alice Lewis

HAIKASORU
Published by VIZ Media, LLC
P.O. Box 77010
San Francisco, CA 94107

www.haikasoru.com

Library of Congress Cataloging-in-Publication Data
Names: Tanaka, Yoshiki, 1952- author. | Huddleston, Daniel, translator.
Title: Legend of the galactic heroes / written by Yoshiki Tanaka ; translated
    by Daniel Huddleston and Tyran Grillo
Other titles: Ginga eiyu densetsu
Description: San Francisco : Haikasoru, [2016]
Identifiers: LCCN 2015044444| ISBN 9781421584942 (v. 1 : paperback) | ISBN
    9781421584959 (v. 2 : paperback) | ISBN 9781421584966(v. 3 paperback) | ISBN
9781421584973 (v.4: paperback) | 9781421584980 (v. 5: paperback)
    v. 1. Dawn -- v. 2. Ambition -- v. 3. Endurance – v. 4 Stratagem — v.5 Mobilization
Subjects: LCSH: Science fiction. | War stories. | BISAC: FICTION / Science
    Fiction / Space Opera. | FICTION / Science Fiction / Military. | FICTION /
    Science Fiction / Adventure.
Classification: LCC PL862.A5343 G5513 2016 | DDC 895.63/5--dc23
LC record available at http://lccn.loc.gov/2015044444

Printed in the U.S.A.
First Printing, November 2017

MAJOR CHARACTERS

GALACTIC EMPIRE

REINHARD VON LOHENGRAMM
Commander in chief of the imperial military. Imperial prime minister. Duke.

PAUL VON OBERSTEIN
Chief of staff of the Imperial Space Armada. Acting secretary-general of Imperial Military Command Headquarters. Senior admiral.

WOLFGANG MITTERMEIER
Fleet commander. Senior admiral. Known as the "Gale Wolf."

OSKAR VON REUENTAHL
Fleet commander. Senior admiral. Has heterochromatic eyes.

FRITZ JOSEF WITTENFELD
Commander of the Schwarz Lanzenreiter fleet. Admiral.

ERNEST MECKLINGER
Deputy manager of Imperial Armed Forces Supreme Command Headquarters. Admiral. Known as the "Artist-Admiral."

ULRICH KESSLER
Commissioner of military police and commander of capital defenses. Admiral.

AUGUST SAMUEL WAHLEN
Fleet commander. Admiral.

KORNELIAS LUTZ
Fleet commander. Admiral.

NEIDHART MÜLLER
Fleet commander. Admiral.

HELMUT LENNENKAMP
Fleet commander. Admiral.

ADALBERT FAHRENHEIT
Fleet commander. Admiral.

ARTHUR VON STREIT
Reinhard's chief aide. Rear admiral.

HILDEGARD VON MARIENDORF
Chief secretary to the imperial prime minister. Often called "Hilda."

HEINRICH VON KÜMMEL
Hilda's cousin. Baron.

ANNEROSE VON GRÜNEWALD
Reinhard's elder sister. Countess von Grünewald.

ERWIN JOSEF II
37th emperor of the Galactic Empire. Dethroned.

KATHARIN KÄTCHEN I
38th sovereign of the Galactic Empire. Empress.

RUDOLF VON GOLDENBAUM
Founder of the Galactic Empire's Goldenbaum Dynasty.

DECEASED

SIEGFRIED KIRCHEIS
Died living up to the faith Annerose placed in him.

FREE PLANETS ALLIANCE

YANG WEN-LI
Commander of Iserlohn Fortress. Commander of Iserlohn Patrol Fleet. Admiral.

JULIAN MINTZ
Yang's ward. Ensign.

FREDERICA GREENHILL
Yang's aide. Lieutenant.

ALEX CASELNES
Administrative director of Iserlohn Fortress. Rear admiral.

WALTER VON SCHÖNKOPF
Commander of fortress defenses at Iserlohn Fortress. Rear admiral.

EDWIN FISCHER
Vice commander of Iserlohn Patrol Fleet. Master of fleet operations.

MURAI
Chief of staff. Rear admiral.

FYODOR PATRICHEV
Deputy chief of staff. Commodore.

DUSTY ATTENBOROUGH
Division commander within the Iserlohn Patrol Fleet. Yang's underclassman. Rear admiral.

OLIVIER POPLIN
Captain of the First Spaceborne Division at Iserlohn Fortress. Lieutenant commander.

ALEXANDOR BUCOCK
Commander in chief of the Alliance Armed Forces Space Armada. Admiral.

LOUIS MACHUNGO
Yang's security guard. Warrant officer.

WALTER ISLANDS
Chairman of the Defense Committee.

CHUNG WU-CHENG
Chief of staff.

JOB TRÜNICHT
Head of state. Chairman of the High Council.

WILIABARD JOACHIM MERKATZ
Secretary of defense of the "legitimate imperial galactic government."

BERNHARD VON SCHNEIDER
Merkatz's aide.

PHEZZAN DOMINION

ADRIAN RUBINSKY
The fifth landesherr. Known as the "Black Fox of Phezzan."

NICOLAS BOLTEC
Imperial resident commissioner. Former aide to Rubinsky.

ALFRED VON LANSBERG
Count who defected to Phezzan.

LEOPOLD SCHUMACHER
Former captain in the Imperial Navy. Defected to Phezzan.

BORIS KONEV
Independent merchant. Old acquaintance of Yang's. Working in the office of the Phezzan commissioner on Heinessen.

MARINESK
Administrative officer on board the *Beryozka*.

DEGSBY
Bishop dispatched from Earth to keep an eye on Rubinsky.

GRAND BISHOP
Ruler in Rubinsky's shadow.

DECEASED

RUPERT KESSELRING
Rubinsky's son. Died in a failed attempt to kill his father.

°Titles and ranks correspond to each character's status at the end of *Stratagem* or their first appearance in *Mobilization*.

TABLE OF CONTENTS

CHAPTER 1:

I

IN THE FIRST MOMENTS OF SE 799, year 490 of the imperial calendar, Duke Reinhard von Lohengramm looked up at the countless constellations dancing wildly against an indigo sky. The ice-blue eyes of the young conqueror, who would be turning twenty-three in the new year, shot frozen arrows through the hard glass ceiling in silent declaration: *All those distant stars exist only so that I might conquer them.* Reinhard swung his luxurious golden hair, his back to the imperial naval commanders gathered in his grand reception hall. Bells pumped in through wall-mounted speakers announced the demise of the old calendar. Reinhard walked over to his table, raising a crystal glass of champagne. The commanders raised theirs in kind, filling the room with waves of reflected light.

"Prosit!"

"Prosit! Here's to the new year!"

"Prosit! Here's to our victory!"

Another cheer peaked above the rest.

"Prosit! Here's to the end of the Free Planets Alliance!"

The speaker held his gaze on Reinhard, raising his glass high. Everything about him screamed pride and arrogance. Reinhard flashed an elegant smile and relifted his glass to renewed cheers and applause, bringing a blush to the speaker's cheeks.

The voice in question belonged to Isaak Fernand Thurneisen, an imperial vice admiral. He was young to be among Reinhard's troops, the same age as his lord. In grade school, he had been in the same honor roll as his class head, Reinhard, and then had made a name for himself at IAF Academy before quitting school midway to join the front lines, racking up medals as both a combat commander and tactical officer. Contrary to Reinhard's other classmates—many of whom had devoted themselves, mind and body, to the Lippstadt League in the civil war of IC 488, to their peril—he had demonstrated sound judgment and veracity by siding with Reinhard and through his great achievements under the late Karl Gustav Kempf. After the war, he'd left Kempf to serve directly under Reinhard, narrowly avoiding Kempf's fate of falling at the hands of Admiral Yang Wen-li. This was enough to convince Thurneisen, and those around him, that a guardian angel had granted him mysterious favor. Obliged to meet the expectations of one so chosen, he excelled in all things. Whether in battlespace or elsewhere, Thurneisen strove to be the brightest star.

Such zeal was by no means unwelcome to Reinhard, but it reminded him even more of a man who had never flaunted his abilities, a man now dead. Siegfried Kircheis, that redheaded friend who had saved Reinhard's life at the expense of his own, would never have tolerated such swagger. Although Reinhard knew better than to compare the two, by force of inner determination he felt compelled to do just that.

More than the splendor of this lavish party, seeing everyone clad in uniform, ready for dispatch at a moment's notice, filled Reinhard with pride. Indeed, some in attendance would be heading into battlespace as soon as the party ended. These were Senior Admiral Wolfgang Mittermeier, commander of the expeditionary force's vanguard, and second division commander Neidhart Müller.

Sandy-haired Müller, the Imperial Navy's youngest admiral, would be twenty-nine this year. His drooping left shoulder was all he had to show for the many wounds he'd suffered over a military career unusually long for his age. Otherwise, he seemed every bit the meek staff officer who held passionately to ideals of virile offense and tenacious defense.

Next to him were Mittermeier, who was known as the "Gale Wolf," and Senior Admiral Oskar von Reuentahl, now tasked with capturing Iserlohn Fortress, who together were known as the "Twin Ramparts" of the Imperial Navy. Mittermeier had the small yet well-proportioned body of a gymnast. He was eight years older than Reinhard and two years older than Müller—by society's standards still a novice in life. None of which prevented Mittermeier from speaking as a man of experience.

"It's encouraging to see so much enthusiasm in the younger generation."

He was the most decorated of the admirals to be passing through the Phezzan Corridor on this occasion, with a record of close calls to show for it. Nevertheless, to him the bravado of younger admirals also revealed an immature subsurface.

"I may be young, too, but I don't have *that* level of energy."

Müller's voice rang with unbefitting cynicism. Among younger soldiers, impatience was sometimes the norm. The most ambitious people preferred change to stability, troubled times to peace, knowing it would accelerate their rise to the top. A living illustration of this phenomenon stood before Mittermeier and Müller's eyes.

Now that Duke Reinhard von Lohengramm's supremacy was nearing fruition, chances for advancement among his men were fading fast. If anything, their narrow vision, restricted by barriers of pretension, effectively slammed the door to fame in their faces. Thus, even as colleagues and mentors alike played each other like rivals, they were becoming equal comrades in life and death. And because Müller had yet to attain the renown of a Mittermeier or a von Reuentahl, he continued to be outspoken about his desires.

"Anyway, I wager the armada's commander in chief will take charge over alliance forces."

"You mean Admiral Alexandor Bucock?"

"He's a real veteran. Even if you combined our military records, along with von Reuentahl and Wittenfeld's, we'd barely scratch the surface of what that old man has accomplished. He's a walking military museum."

Mittermeier gave credit where it was due. Ever since Müller had known this comrade two years his senior, he'd consciously tried to emulate his virtues, though he knew he'd never attain Mittermeier's expressive prowess.

"Quite the lively conversation you're having there."

The two admirals turned in the direction of the voice, then bowed to their young lord, who stood with crystal glass in hand.

After exchanging a few words, Reinhard posed a question to the Gale Wolf.

"There's nothing I can say about a peerless tactician such as yourself, but the Alliance Armed Forces are sure to retaliate once we have them cornered. I'd like to know how you plan on dealing with that."

The empty glass splashed its rainbow refractions across the eyes of the empire's highest commander.

"If the alliance has enough firepower, and they don't mind sustaining some collateral damage, it's safe to assume they'll go head-to-head with us to block entry into the Phezzan Corridor. We'll have no choice but to reciprocate, but it'll cost us heavy losses and, above all, time. In which case, the chances of our rear forces moving into Phezzan would be slim, and without a dedicated core we'd be at a severe disadvantage."

Mittermeier's analysis was accurate, his presentation of it clear. His audience nodded in agreement.

"That being said, I don't see how the alliance has the resources to pull off such a maneuver this time around. They can't afford to lose, as it would leave their capital defenseless. Their first battle would become their last. They'd have to surrender."

Mittermeier took a breath and continued.

"Seeing as they can't sustain a head-on attack, they're more likely to draw us deep into their territory. Once we reach the limits of our mobilization, they'll cut off our supply routes and jam our communications, then isolate and pick off our forces, one by one, in a nearly exact reenactment of the Battle of Amritsar three years ago. Were we to maintain long battle formations for our own vanity, we'd be doing exactly what they expected of us. But there is *one* way we can win."

Mittermeier paused to look at Reinhard. The young lord's smile was an exquisite blend of acumen and elegance in recognition of his subordinate's abilities.

"A double-headed snake, am I right?"

"Precisely."

Mittermeier again expressed admiration for his lord's perspicacity. Reinhard shifted his ice-blue eyes.

"What say you, Admiral Müller?"

The Imperial Navy's youngest admiral gave a curt bow.

"I'm of the same mind as Admiral Mittermeier. Only, I wonder if the alliance will be able to keep its military operations in order."

"There will always be those narrow-minded incompetents who take one look at the enemy and equate pacifism with cowardice," said Reinhard, flashing a derisive smile to an imaginary opponent.

"Which gives us the upper hand. If we can slowly draw them out into a war of attrition without tactical purpose, the goddess of victory will be on our side."

"But where's the fun in that?" Reinhard muttered.

His expression might've seemed arrogant on any other face. But as a genius who'd once vanquished an enemy twice his size in the Astarte Stellar Region and, in the Amritsar Stellar Region, unprecedentedly anni-hilated a Free Planets Alliance Navy force thirty million strong, he was entitled to such an attitude. The only thing Reinhard hated more than an incompetent ally was an incompetent opponent.

"I can only hope our enemies will act with some sense of method."

With this, Reinhard took his leave of the two men and walked over to join another friendly chat.

Reinhard's private secretary, Countess Hildegard von Mariendorf, was sobering up from all the wine with some chilled apple juice. Vice Admiral Thurneisen put down his empty glass and in good humor spoke to the countess, known for her beauty and ingenuity.

"Future historians are sure to envy you, fräulein. Won't you join the party and be a witness to history in the making?"

Vice Admiral Thurneisen, his youthful face brimming with elated conceit, looked at Hilda for approval. Hilda responded affirmatively but could only shrug her shoulders on the inside. She'd never thought of Thurneisen as incompetent, but neither could she suppress her misgivings nor a wry smile over the fact that he was more enamored with Reinhard than was necessary. Reinhard was a genius, to be sure, but geniuses weren't always the most appropriate objects of emulation. If anything, he'd have done better to aspire to the reliability and tenacity of a Müller or a Wahlen, but Thurneisen was too dazzled by Reinhard's inimitable radiance to notice.

Two hours into the new year, Senior Admiral Wolfgang Mittermeier put down his wine glass and, with a rhythm in his step, approached the young lord.

"Well, then, Your Excellency, I shall take my leave," he said, bowing.

Reinhard lifted his hand lightly.

"Here's praying for your good luck in the battlespace. We'll meet again on Planet Heinessen."

The Gale Wolf met Reinhard's fearless smile with one of his own and bowed once more, then left, carrying his black-and-silver-clad body beyond the brilliance of the chandelier. Generals Droisen, Büro, Bayerlein, and Sinzer followed their brave and honorable commander, making their exit in turn. Next, Neidhart Müller bowed before taking his leave of the banquet hall with his own men in tow.

With a third of the attendees gone, the din of conversation quieted like a wind rustling treetops. After making his rounds with the more important admirals, Reinhard sat himself in a far corner of the room and crossed his legs.

For a moment, arid gusts of emotion swept across the plains of his heart. Despite feeling uplifted by the prospect of an epic battle, his insides decompressed, and the scene reflected therein began to fade.

He was uneasy: there was an impossible skip in his heart that he could neither explain nor make others understand. *Once I've captured Phezzan and conquered the Free Planets Alliance to rule the entire universe,* he thought, *how will I ever endure a life without enemies?*

When Reinhard was born into this world, the fires of war had been raging between the empire and the alliance for 130 years. That was 1,140,000 hours. Reinhard had known nothing but war. To him, peace was just a thin slice of ham wedged between the thick bread of strife. But after felling his nemeses and unifying the universe, thereby leading the way to a new dynasty, he'd lose any and all opponents against whom he might wield his intellect and courage.

This golden-haired youth, who from day one had lived to fight, win, and conquer, had to brace himself for the weight of peace and ennui. Then again…

Reinhard smiled wryly. He was getting ahead of himself. Victory wasn't his just yet. Would a sorrowful elegy be played for him instead? How many men of ambition had won battle after battle, only to exit the stage in the final act? But he refused to be like them. He had every intention of spending today without incident while turning his attention toward tomorrow. From this day forward, his life would no longer be his own.

At 4:00 a.m. the party dispersed, and people left for their respective lodgings to prepare for the battle ahead. Senior Admiral Wolfgang Mittermeier's fleet ships were already launching into the dusky heavens from Phezzan's central spaceport. The Gale Wolf's first mission of the new year was to secure the alliance's end of the Phezzan Corridor.

II

Relatively few Free Planets Alliance high officials were lifting their glasses, as most were panicking over a maelstrom of new responsibilities and wanted nothing less than the confirmation of the new year's arrival. Reports of the Imperial Navy's occupation of Phezzan were being kept under wraps, but like a netted beast, that information gnawed a hole through its veil of secrecy and flooded the alliance's media channels. The government's top executives had meanwhile gathered their pale faces in a conference room enclosed by thick walls. But even as they began to discuss going public, on a street corner not one kilometer away from their roundtable, spacefarers who'd returned from Phezzan were broadcasting the dangers to come.

With no effective defense plan in sight, the levees of complacency broke to unleash a muddy stream of mass hysteria. The alliance government's dignity was barely salvaged by the fact that, during the period of informational lockdown, not one high official tried to escape—though rumors insisted this was only because no safe zones had been declared. The alliance government had therefore failed to regain the people's trust, even on a moral level.

Instead, and with no other recourse, good citizens turned to their government authorities as emotional outlets. Between condemning their representatives as "incompetents" and "salary thieves," they demanded decisive action and countermeasures in the same breath.

All the while, the alliance government was under command of the "eloquent sophist" known as High Council Chairman Job Trünicht. As a politician, he belonged to what one might call a younger generation. He was possessed of an outstanding appearance and impeccable career, and was even popular among female voters. A background in the defense industry had guaranteed his access to enormous political funds. Even the Military Congress for the Rescue of the Republic's coup d'état, which might otherwise have destroyed his reputation, hardly left a scratch on him. The people expected nothing less than eloquent persuasion in his speech. And when they couldn't decide whether he was just paying them lip service, he hid himself away from his "beloved people" and issued a statement via the governmental press secretary:

"I fully realize the weight of my responsibility."

Saying only that, and without clarifying his whereabouts, he'd severely deepened the misgivings of his own people. Job Trünicht, they now said, was a pandering demagogue straight out of some classical civilization who ran with his tail between his legs at the first sign of crisis.

Iserlohn Fortress's commander, Admiral Yang Wen-li, who despised Trünicht with every fiber of his being, had a different point of view. His impression of Trünicht was of a man who could wriggle his way out of any situation. Whether Yang's observation was an over- or underestimation, the fact was that Trünicht had wounded his people's short-term expectations. Making matters worse, those same trade journalists who'd once introduced Trünicht has a beacon of hope in the political sphere, and who'd won the public over through their praise of him, now pardoned him by saying, "We must realize it's not the chairman's responsibility alone but the responsibility of all of us." Thus, the press had turned criticism back on its readers, who were "only underscoring the privilege of their government by refusing to go along with its measures."

Walter Islands, chairman of the Defense Committee despite being no more than Trünicht's antebellum henchman, wasn't necessarily seen as being equally untrustworthy. Trünicht had only appointed him as Defense Committee chair in the first place because predecessors of the alliance, fearing dictatorship, had lawfully prohibited adjunct appointments of any council and committee chairman. But as malicious gossip had confirmed, the "moochable" Chairman Islands was nothing more than a point of contact between Trünicht and military authorities. He'd never once shared an independent view or policy and seemed content in being nothing more than a third-rate statesman snatched like so many leftover parts from the conveyor belt that linked Trünicht and alliance munitions corporations.

After the Imperial Navy's invasion of Phezzan, however, his apparently minuscule value had been given a grand amendment.

After manifesting the primary factors behind his future ill repute, Trünicht concealed himself in a private paradise. It took none other than Walter Islands to reprimand his confused colleagues in a flash cabinet meeting, where he adopted political measures to protect against the disintegration of the alliance government. In his midfifties, and now seated as cabinet minister for the first time, he seemed ten years younger despite the difficult situation in which he'd been placed. His posture was upright, his skin luminescent, and his footsteps vigorously paced. The only thing that didn't come springing back to life was the hair he'd lost on his head.

"As far as battle commands are concerned, we'll leave those to the experts. Right now, we need to decide whether to surrender or resist. In other words, to determine the future path of our nation and get all military authorities to go along with it. Shirk this responsibility now, and the effects will trickle down to every soldier on the front line, inviting a chaotic downfall and useless bloodshed. It would mean the veritable suicide of our democratic government," Islands said.

Seeing that no one in attendance expressed an interest in surrender, the Defense Committee chairman changed the subject.

"Should we choose do resist, are we to fight the invading forces until the alliance is razed to the ground and every citizen has perished? Or do we take up arms as a practical measure toward the larger goal of reconciliation and peace? That's the decision we currently face."

The other cabinet ministers sat in silent bewilderment, less over the gravity of the situation than the lucid attack on their prejudice by a Defense Committee chairman who, although until recently a mere nominal official, had grasped the situation with exacting discernment and cognizance, and had now laid before his colleagues the most expedient path toward resolution with dignified speech as his weapon of persuasion.

Islands's existence under peace had been as a parasite on this administration's soiled posterior. But when faced with crisis, his inner spirit arose powerfully, like a democratic phoenix from the ashes of a patronage politician. After half a century of inactivity, his name would at last become engraved in the tablet of posterity.

While it was true that the commander in chief of the Alliance Armed Forces Space Armada, the sharp-tongued Admiral Alexander Bucock, was very much a cynic, such temperament had no effect on his impartiality. The old admiral, now past seventy, was more than willing to cooperate with the Defense Committee chairman, a man he believed was trying his best as both a politician and human being in a compressed timeline. Where before he had vehemently criticized Islands's lassitude and rashness, now he saw a revitalized chairman showing his face at Space Armada Command Headquarters to openly critique his own past behavior. Bucock was half-convinced at first, but as the Defense Committee chairman demanded the cooperation of military authorities in deciding the "terms of reconciliation," he couldn't help but think Islands had finally come into his own.

"It seems the Defense Committee chairman's guardian angel has come out of retirement," muttered the old admiral after Islands had adjourned the conference and exited the room. "Better late than never."

Bucock's aide, lieutenant commander Pfeifer, didn't entirely agree with his superior's quip. He was rather upset that Islands hadn't opened his eyes to reality sooner.

"Maybe I shouldn't say this, but I sometimes wonder if things wouldn't be better if last year's coup d'état by the Military Congress for the Rescue of the Republic had succeeded. It might've been just the shot in the arm our national defenses needed."

"And pit the empire's despotism and the alliance's military dictatorship against one another in a battle for universal hegemony? What hope would there have been in that?"

The old admiral's tone, while far from cynical, was nonetheless acidic. The black beret on the old man's head made his hair appear a shade whiter.

"If there's anything I'm proud of, it's having been a soldier for democratic republicanism. I'd never condone turning the alliance into an undemocratic system as an excuse to oppose the empire's political dictatorship. I'd much rather the alliance perish as a democracy than survive as a dictatorship."

Seeing that he'd made the lieutenant commander uncomfortable, the old admiral smiled impishly.

"I suppose that sounds harsh. But the truth of the matter is, if it can't protect its founding principles and the lives of its citizens, there's no reason for a nation to go on existing as such. If you ask me, it's worth fighting for our founding principles—namely our democratic government and the lives of its citizens."

Admirol Bucock left to pay a visit to Admiral Dawson, director of Joint Operational Headquarters and the only man in uniform he could rightly call his superior. The director was the petty official type whose duties had dulled his complexion and appetite, but who, at Bucock's behest, had restored their headquarters to working order in anticipation of a precise defensive battle.

The top brass of the alliance had consolidated their military forces. Along with the First Fleet under Admiral Paetta's command, a few smaller fleets had been hastily put together since the previous year, consisting mainly of heavy infantry divisions culled from interstellar patrols and guards from every star system, for a meager total of thirty-five thousand ships. Untested and otherwise obsolete ships scheduled for demolition were also included in that number, to be used for communication and as diversions. Bucock divided twenty thousand ships unaffiliated with the First Fleet into the Fourteenth and Fifteenth. Lionel Morton was assigned to the former, Ralph Carlsen to the latter. Upon being debriefed at Joint Operational Headquarters, both were promoted from rear to vice admiral, albeit at the sacrifice of having to wage battle with disorderly, inexperienced troops and inadequate resources against an infinitely stronger Imperial Navy.

Bucock, together with three fleet commanders and the space armada's general chief of staff, drafted plans for counterattacking the imperial forces. General chief of staff Vice Admiral Haussmann, having collapsed from a brain aneurysm, had been relocated to a military hospital. The unfortunate general chief of staff was relieved of duty while still in his sickbed, and vice chief of staff Chung Wu-cheng, a man in his thirties accustomed only to paperwork, walked into the conference room along the carpet of his unexpected promotion. Just three weeks prior, he'd been teaching a graduate course in strategy at the alliance Officers' Academy, a young star among a team of already-gifted professors, but those more experienced in military affairs took to calling him a second-generation baker. Two years ago, during the Military Congress for the Rescue of the Republic's coup d'état, he had managed to meet with Bucock, who was under house arrest for abetting the congress's surveillance. And now, clutching a worn paper bag under the arm of his civilian clothes, he looked curiously around him like some dimwitted country bumpkin.

Chung Wu-cheng bowed to his superiors from his important council seat and mumbled a greeting, a half-eaten ham sandwich peeking out from the chest pocket of his military uniform. Even the tenacious Vice Admiral Carlsen was surprised. The newly appointed general chief of staff nonetheless smiled with an air of composure.

"Oh, this? Don't worry. Even stale bread tastes pretty good when you steam it a little."

Carlsen thought he was completely out of place but saw no use in making a point of it. He turned to Bucock.

His conclusion was to the point. Engaging the invading forces head-on at the end of the Phezzan Corridor was less than ideal. Their only option was to wait for the enemy to exhaust its mobility and supply lines, then force withdrawal by scrambling their command systems, communications, and supplies. For the time being, the alliance didn't have enough military forces to deploy in the Phezzan Corridor.

"What if we called Admiral Yang Wen-li back from Iserlohn Fortress?" proposed the newly appointed general chief of staff, Chung Wu-cheng, the half-eaten sandwich still sticking out of his chest pocket.

The others were taken aback by the disconnect between the seriousness of what he'd just proposed and the leisurely way he'd proposed it. Bucock raised his white eyebrows by way of demanding an explanation.

"Admiral Yang's resourcefulness and the strength of his fleet are extremely valuable to our forces, but if we leave him in Iserlohn as is, it would be like putting freshly baked bread in the refrigerator."

In making use of this simile, the new general chief of staff confirmed his status as a "second-generation baker."

"Once Iserlohn Fortress is hemmed in by military forces on either side of the corridor," he concluded, "you can be sure its strategic value will skyrocket. But if both ends are equally closed off by our enemy, Iserlohn will be as good as sealed. Even if the empire doesn't capture the impregnable fortress through bloodshed, it will have succeeded in rendering the fortress powerless without firing a single shot. Seeing that imperial forces have already passed through the Phezzan Corridor, it would be pointless to waste further resources on protecting Iserlohn."

"You may be right, but Admiral Yang is currently squaring off with a detached force of the Imperial Navy. It's not like we can just move him out of there."

Chung Wu-cheng was unmoved by Paetta's fastidious observation.

"Admiral Yang will figure something out. Without him, we'd be at a great disadvantage from a purely military standpoint."

It was an overly frank opinion but not one they could refute. To the Alliance Armed Forces, the name of Yang Wen-li was becoming synonymous with victory. Paetta, once Yang's superior, had been rescued from certain doom by Yang in the Battle of Astarte.

"Even if we made an overture of peace, the Imperial Navy would demand control of Iserlohn Fortress as part of those conditions. In which case, no amount of resourcefulness on Yang's part would do the alliance any good. With enough strength and time on our hands, perhaps that would be otherwise, but as things stand, we should make him do the dirty work for us."

"You mean we command Yang to abandon Iserlohn."

"No, Your Excellency Commander in Chief, there's no need for anything so specific. It'll be enough to assure Yang that Space Armada Command will take full responsibility and that he should proceed as he sees fit. I gather he won't be too keen on sticking around to protect Iserlohn Fortress."

Thus concluding his audacious proposal, Chung Wu-cheng leisurely plucked the half-eaten sandwich from his pocket and resumed his interrupted lunch.

III

Those suffering greatest censure on Heinessen were a group of refugees who'd once boasted of forming the "legitimate imperial galactic government" not half a year earlier.

Having in their possession Emperor Erwin Josef II, who'd "escaped" from the imperial capital of Odin, and borrowing the Free Planets Alliance's military power, they would overthrow Reinhard von Lohengramm's military dictatorship. According to their pact with the alliance, a shift toward a constitutional system was inevitable, but under that system the old nobility's sovereignty and privilege would be restored, and those who'd been unable to avoid defection would recover many times over all those things they'd lost. The canvas of their self-determination was being torn to shreds before their very eyes.

No longer will those incompetents try to paint a sweet picture of reality by dissolving their paints in sugar water.

Such were the thoughts of Bernhard von Schneider, on whom the so-called legitimate government had bestowed the rank of commander. Being the clever specimen that he was, von Schneider didn't have an ounce of illusion about the exiled nobles' castle in the sky, built entirely on wishful thinking. Although he felt far from hopeless, neither could he act as if he were spectating this farce from a high vantage point. The object of his loyalty, Wiliabard Joachim Merkatz, since defecting from the empire, had been treated as a "guest admiral," but as secretary of defense for the legitimate imperial galactic government he was reluctantly organizing a new regiment. Even as he worked tirelessly as Merkatz's aide, von Schneider was thinking hard about the future.

If the Imperial Navy invaded by way of the Phezzan Corridor, chances of an alliance victory were slim. Even with Yang Wen-li's peerless ingenuity on their side, the scales were balanced at best. The way von Schneider saw it, the worst-case scenario was more than probable.

The most the alliance could hope for was cease-fire and reconciliation. As part of that reconciliation, the higher-ups of the "legitimate government" would need to be punished. Peace would only be a temporary measure. If it was ever going to rebuild its forces, the alliance needed to face its national egotism, which meant the "legitimate government" would become its scapegoat. And the seven-year-old emperor, Erwin Josef, was riding that goat straight to his execution ground.

It pained von Schneider to think of that unfortunate child. The child emperor, whose own will had been ignored in all this, who'd been exploited as a prop for the politics and ambitions of adults, was deserving of sympathy. But no longer could von Schneider afford to consider the emperor's future. He had to throw all his efforts into protecting Merkatz from the political cyclone that was about to hit them. Furthermore, because it went against Merkatz's conscience to protect his own safety at others' expense, von Schneider had to show his concern for Merkatz while feigning emotional detachment. Von Schneider's expression deepened in intensity and shrewdness. The young soldier looked in the mirror, recalling a time in the imperial capital of Odin when he was known as sweet and handsome by the ladies at court. Like a bankrupt man yearning for his former extravagance, he stewed in his discouragement.

Von Schneider nevertheless had a voluntary responsibility and outlook on the future, while most people couldn't even grasp what they were supposed to do to get through today, much less tomorrow. But the legitimate government's acting prime minister, Count Jochen von Remscheid, had been knocked off-balance when the situation had exceeded his expectations, and one could only imagine how many days he'd spent trying to restore his equilibrium. The exiled nobles, lacking in fixed opinions and who under Count von Remscheid's influence had been napping in a garden of optimism, had lost their raison d'être as objects of von Schneider's derisive scrutiny.

Since absconding with Erwin Josef from Odin, Count Alfred von Lansberg had been employed as the legitimate government's military undersecretary. His loyalty to the child emperor and the Goldenbaum Dynasty were unwavering, but as a man who was poetic not only in heart but also in mind, it pained him to have come up with no concrete plan to safeguard the royal family. Former captain Leopold Schumacher, who'd abetted his infiltration of the capital, bore no small sentiment toward the royal Goldenbaum family's betrayal of tradition. Not knowing the well-being of his subordinates back on Phezzan made him quite uneasy. Both men felt powerless, and it was all they could do to keep their emotions from leaping into the abyss.

The legitimate government's first cabinet meeting of the new year was hastily convened, but of the seven cabinet ministers, neither secretary of finance Viscount Schaezler nor secretary of justice Viscount Herder were present. Among the five who were, secretary of the imperial household Baron Hosinger was fuming like a dragon guarding his alcoholic hoard. The bottle of whisky in his hand had been making its way silently around the conference table. Even the Secretary of Defense, Admiral Merkatz, kept heavy silence. This left the debate over the future of the government-in-exile in the hands of three men: prime minister and secretary of state Count von Remscheid, secretary of the interior Baron Radbruch, and chief cabinet secretary Baron Carnap. Like the incubation of an unfertilized egg, the debate was a serious yet futile effort and was interrupted by the secretary of the imperial household's hysterical laughter. Doused in looks of anger and reproach, Hosinger stuck out his bluish-black face in ostentatious display.

"How about telling the truth, my high-minded, loyal gentleman. You're not worried at all about the fate of the Goldenbaum Dynasty. You only care about your own safety, you who carelessly defied Duke von Lohengramm. And when that golden brat steps foot on our soil as victor, where will you hide then?"

"Baron Hosinger, are you sure you want to soil your name in a fit of drunkenness?"

"I don't have a name to soil, Your Excellency Prime Minister. Unlike you." His laugh was loathsome, and his breath reeked of booze.

"I can shout from the rooftops things you'd never say for fear of ruining your precious reputations. Handing over His Majesty the young emperor to Duke von Lohengramm, for example, just to get on his good side."

He waited with bated breath for the reactions of his colleagues, whose pride he'd wounded with an immaterial blade. Even Merkatz was at a momentary loss for words and glanced at the secretary of the imperial household in horror. Secretary of the Interior Radbruch kicked over his chair as he jumped to his feet.

"Shameless drunkard! When did you lose your integrity as an imperial noble? You forget the innumerable graces and honors the empire has given you and think only about *your* own safety, you…"

Unable to come up with the appropriate insult, Radbruch fell short of breath and scowled at Hosinger instead. He scanned the roundtable for support, but not even prime minister and secretary of state Count von Remscheid made any effort to untangle the bramble of this tense silence, if only because he understood that Radbruch's real opponent wasn't Hosinger but the monster of egotism rearing its ugly head from beneath his own shameful conscience.

This confrontation was no small thing. Apart from Merkatz, their participation in the government-in-exile was indeed the result of self-interest, and when that self-interest failed them, another would inevitably take its place on the stages of their hearts. The idea that they'd handed over the child emperor to Duke Reinhard von Lohengramm to save their own skins, while a tempting leap of intuition to make, was enough to plunge them into a self-loathing so deep that alcohol was their only defense against it.

Further complicating the mood of the exile government leaders was the fact that the object of their loyalty, the child emperor Erwin Josef, couldn't have cared less about their sympathy. Having never learned to suppress his ego, and unaware that he expressed it only by lashing out, this emotionally unstable seven-year-old, in the eyes of his weary subjects, was also a manifestation of their innermost demons. Their loyalty was nothing more than narcissism reflected in the fun-house mirror that was Erwin Josef. Naturally, however, none of this was the responsibility of a seven-year-old child who'd been snatched from his unwitting throne as quickly as he'd assumed it. Of the adults who admired and respected him with formulaic affection, not one made had ever taken responsibility for his character development.

Erwin Josef was no longer fit to be called emperor. More than ten thousand light-years away, in the imperial capital of Odin, a change in the master of the throne was already under way. After Erwin Josef's departure, on the gold and jade throne sat an infant whose teeth had yet to come in: "Empress" Katharin Kätchen I. She was the youngest sovereign in the history of the Galactic Empire and would also be the last ruler of the Goldenbaum Dynasty founded by Rudolf the Great five centuries ago. Erwin Josef was already listed in public record as a "dethroned emperor."

When the politico-military flow of events between Lohengramm's despotic empire and the Free Planets Alliance went from swift stream to raging waterfall, the exiled nobles' state of mind was inevitably shaken. Self-interest reigned supreme—enough, as Hosinger had so carelessly remarked, to blind them to the fact that they'd handed over the "dethroned emperor" to their bitter enemy Lohengramm to protect themselves. Try as they might to deny it, they'd overcome their shame and delivered the emperor into enemy hands, and without guarantee that Duke von Lohengramm would pardon them. If anything, he was likely to persecute and punish them severely for their treason and foul play.

Running away from the invading forces in the belief that one day the Goldenbaum Dynasty would be restored meant a life of flight and vagrancy. While romantic in theory, in practice such a life would be far from easy. Without either the political protection of the Free Planets Alliance or the economic clout and organizational capacity of the Phezzan Land Dominion, in addition to lacking even inchoate military power, it was unlikely they could manage a life on the run in enemy territory. However much these nobles might have lacked in foresight, they couldn't have been quite *that* oblivious.

In the end, there was no exit in sight. Knowing it was pointless, von Remscheid felt sorry for Hosinger and adjourned the meeting, having reached the limits of his fatigue.

Another serious yet unproductive assembly of exiled nobles was held the following day. But Jochen von Remscheid, serving as its chair, was met with five empty seats and Secretary of Defense Merkatz sitting alone in silence. Von Remscheid had been left high and dry.

IV

Amid passive upheaval, the people feared what might become of them. Even if they were too proud to resign themselves to unilateral victimhood, events on a macro level were overwhelming their willpower and discretion at the micro level. It was like running in the opposite direction across the deck of a ship: no matter how fast one ran, one could never reach land.

Boris Konev felt that helplessness in his veins. Since being posted in the Phezzan high commissioner's office on Heinessen, he'd been working as secretary. Despite having no desire to be a government official, he'd taken the position by order of Phezzan's highest administrative official, Landesherr Adrian Rubinsky. Boris Konev was an independent merchant whose tendency to follow his own convictions was strong even for a Phezzanese. His father and his father's father had sailed merchant ships all around the universe, overcoming political and military powers and living out their lives based on their own will and wit alone. It was a family tradition that Boris still hoped to continue, and so being stuck in a rut of government service was enough to wound his self-importance.

Not a single day went by that he didn't think of slapping down his resignation letter and becoming an ordinary citizen again, forsaking rank and title. Now that his birthplace of Phezzan was occupied by the Imperial Navy and Landesherr Rubinsky had gone incognito, he had a mind to abandon his post and go incognito himself. And yet he stayed put. Irrational as it was, it was beneath him to abandon a sinking ship.

He feared for his merchant ship, *Beryozka*, which he'd left back home along with a twenty-man crew. But communications with Phezzan were, like the routes that could've taken him there, under strict alliance suspension, making a return next to impossible. Something dramatic, such as the Imperial Navy withdrawing from Phezzan or defeating the Alliance Armed Forces, would need to occur before he could even think of reuniting with his beloved ship and crew. In Boris's eyes, the latter possibility was far more likely. He prayed to a god he didn't believe in for just that, keeping up appearances at the commissioner's office, where his work had already been reduced to nothing.

That year, SE 799, IC 490, would go down in history as the Galactic Imperial Navy's longest march. At the end of the previous year, after occupying Phezzan as a rear base, the empire had brought all inhabited worlds in the Phezzan Corridor under its control. Understanding the relevance of government, Phezzan's order was stable for the time being. But if the imperial occupation dragged on at the expense of their material resources, the Phezzanese, independent by nature, would quickly tire of their subservience.

For now, Wolfgang Mittermeier's duty and concerns were not behind but ahead of him. Three days after placing his brave Vice Admiral Bayerlein at the vanguard in hopes of detecting alliance activity, he received word from Bayerlein.

"No signs of the enemy at the end of the Phezzan Corridor."

Upon receiving this report, Mittermeier looked warily back at his chief of staff, Vice Admiral Dickel.

"Well, they've let us into the foyer. Now the question is whether we'll make it to the dining hall. And even then, when I sit down at the table, the food brought out to me might very well be poisoned."

On January 8, SE 799, the First Imperial Fleet passed through the Phezzan Corridor as uninvited guests of the alliance, sailing forth into a giant ocean of fixed stars and planets they'd never seen before.

CHAPTER 2:
ADMIRAL YANG'S ARK FLEET

I

AT ISERLOHN FORTRESS, on the other side of the Free Planets
Alliance, the new year was also rearing its impartial head. Had its soldiers,
besieged as they were by the Galactic Empire's grand fleet under command
of Senior Admiral Oskar von Reuentahl, even wanted to toast the new
year, they were in no mood to get comfortably drunk.

The only thing preventing them from lapsing into absolute despair
was the firm faith they had in Admiral Yang Wen-li, their "Miracle Yang,"
who held dual commandership over Iserlohn Fortress and its fleet.
The young, black-haired, dark-eyed commander would be thirty-two
this year. Since graduating from Officers' Academy, he'd accumulated
medal after medal in wars both abroad and at home, catching the
eyes of even the enemy Galactic Imperial Navy's admirals as the alliance's most resourceful general. To all outward appearances, he was
a budding scholar and nothing like a soldier obsessing over order
and rank.

"No matter what I try to do in this world, it always fails. I might as
well drink and go to bed."

With these quiet self-admonishments, Yang welcomed the new year, caught between danger and distress. But even as he gazed at the distant hatching of gunfire and light beams on-screen, a directive from the capital bypassed the Imperial Navy's communications block to reach him.

"Space Armada Command assumes full responsibility. You will take whatever course of action you feel is necessary. Commander in Chief of the Alliance Armed Forces Space Armada, Alexandor Bucock."

As Yang read over the message a few times, the muscles in his face resolved into a delicate smile, as if he might burst into song at any moment. He very much approved.

"Everyone should be so lucky to have such an understanding boss."

After saying as much, he unconsciously knitted his eyebrows. With all the pieces now in place, it was time to get cracking. Had this been a simple and unenlightened order to "protect Iserlohn to the death," Yang would've used every tactical trick at his disposal against siege commander Oskar von Reuentahl. But now that he'd been given free rein, it would only be in the Free Planets Alliance's best interests that Yang should respond to Bucock's good graces by considering the war at the meta level, far beyond the confines of the battlespace before him. Anyone meeting him for the first time wouldn't have believed it, but Yang was highest in command after admirals Dawson and Bucock.

"That shrewd old man," Yang grumbled. "He expects me to work beyond the terms of my salary."

He consigned the admiration he'd expressed just a moment ago to oblivion, adding:

"How much per enemy ship will I increase my pension?"

Lieutenant Frederica Greenhill, ever by his side, was within earshot. Yang had only spoken this way to his ward, Julian Mintz, and so most future historians would know nothing of that fact. What they would know is that Yang stood up from his commander's seat and, through his aide, convened a meeting of executive leaders. Then, to those leaders gathered in his conference room, spoke freely once the lunch menu was decided:

"We're abandoning Iserlohn Fortress."

Iserlohn's leaders shouldn't have been all that surprised. Fortress administrative director Rear Admiral Alex Caselnes, chief of staff Rear Admiral Murai, vice commander of Iserlohn Patrol Fleet Rear Admiral Fischer, commander of fortress defenses Rear Admiral Walter von Schönkopf, deputy chief of staff Commodore Fyodor Patrichev, and division commander within the Iserlohn Patrol Fleet Rear Admiral Dusty Attenborough were all living witnesses to Yang Wen-li's ingenuity. Nevertheless, they returned their coffee cups to their saucers in a clinking symphony of misgiving.

"What did you just say, Your Excellency?" said Rear Admiral Murai, who thought of common tactical wisdom as a fur coat in a cold spell, in his low voice.

Rear admirals Caselnes and von Schönkopf exchanged quick glances as the ingeniousness of Yang's stratagem sank in.

"We're abandoning Iserlohn Fortress," repeated Yang robotically.

Steam rising from coffee cups tickled the chins of staff officers still trying to process this statement. Yang was used to having a teacup in front of him, but since Julian Mintz had gone, and with him the best black tea in the universe, Yang had given in to coffee as much as he could stand.

"Not that I wish to oppose you, but could you at least give us an explanation?"

Yang nodded to Rear Admiral Murai's question, which was equal parts faith and suspicion.

Although Iserlohn Fortress was situated at the heart of a long corridor, it had strategic significance only insofar as military powers could cap off either end of that same corridor. Caught between a rock and a hard place, Iserlohn had no way of relinquishing its isolation. The fortress, as well as the fleet stationed there, were powerless if they didn't fight. And so, while Iserlohn was strategically impregnable, Reinhard von Lohengramm's ploy had ingeniously rendered it insignificant. Not only was it unnecessary for the Alliance Armed Forces to stick it out on Iserlohn, it was also foolish.

At the very least, even if only by means of their stationed fleet, they had to act practically in the event of an imperial attack.

"Couldn't we hold firm, using the fruits of our military gains to broker some sort of peace treaty with the empire?"

"But wouldn't they demand relinquishment of Iserlohn Fortress anyway, as part of that treaty? And then where would we be? Either way, Iserlohn is as good as lost. It behooves us to leave now."

Although Yang spoke in generous terms, his chiefs of staff knew better than to think he was handing over the fortress as a present to the empire.

"But how can we stand by and watch as something we fought to win for ourselves falls back into enemy hands?"

Deputy chief of staff Commodore Patrichev looked around the table, leaning his hulking body forward.

"How much more regretful for the Imperial Navy, who at great pains expended so much in the way of resources and labor to make the fortress, only to have it snatched away in the first place," answered Yang nonchalantly.

Three years ago, he'd dispossessed the Imperial Navy of Iserlohn, much to the continued chagrin of the commanders under Reinhard von Lohengramm's dictatorship. Yang Wen-li was in no position to criticize from the standpoint of a philanthropist. The reason Rear Admiral Walter von Schönkopf laughed so cynically was because at that time he had fulfilled an important role in Yang's military operations, having been the one who thrust his blaster muzzle at the Imperial Navy's fortress commander, Admiral von Stockhausen.

"But, Commander, even if we do abandon Iserlohn, I doubt the Imperial Navy will look on passively. How are we to stave off an attack?"

"Perhaps we should try making an earnest request to Admiral von Reuentahl of the Imperial Navy? Since we're giving up the fortress, we might ask him to turn a blind eye to the women and children."

No one laughed at this ill-conceived joke. Then again, even a good one might not have been enough to pierce their shells of tension and impending doom. Even as they spoke, a large fleet of Imperial Navy ships was unfolding before their very fortress under Admiral von Reuentahl's exquisite tactical command, setting their nerves on edge. The blade of von Schönkopf's ambush had swung close to von Reuentahl, but the honorable heterochromatic admiral wasn't about to let that happen a second time. In spite of von Reuentahl's renowned hand-to-hand combat skills and heroism, von Schönkopf kept beating himself up over letting the big fish get away.

Rear Admiral Murai held his ground.

"Still, one cannot deny the psychological ramifications. If Admiral Yang is chased off Iserlohn Fortress by the Imperial Navy, the citizens of the alliance will be greatly disturbed. Tormented by a sense of defeat, they'll lose their morale before we've even fought. Which means a rematch will be out of the question. I would advise you to consider that possibility."

Yang recognized some truth in Murai's remarks but in all honesty didn't see the public's reaction as his responsibility. Fighting against the enormous Imperial Navy using only the single fleet with which he'd been entrusted would require him to use up every ounce of his tactical reserve if he was going to prevail.

Von Schönkopf was the first to chime in.

"I agree with the chief of staff's opinion. We'd do better to let those big shots go red in the face demanding we leave Iserlohn before we bend over backward for them. Only then will those ingrates realize just how much Your Excellency's existence means to them."

"By then, it would be too late. We'd lose our chance at victory."

"Wait a minute. By 'chance at victory,' do you mean to suggest we could still win?!"

Outside of Iserlohn Fortress, such a remark would have been inappropriate. But Yang was open-minded when it came to his subordinates' viewpoints, and he was sometimes criticized by superiors of his generation and later historians alike for being too forbearing in that respect.

"I know what you want to say, Rear Admiral von Schönkopf. Militarily speaking, we are in an exceedingly disadvantageous position, and our training tells us that a tactical victory cannot trump a strategic one. But here we have one chance, and one chance only, to turn the tables in our favor."

"And that is…?"

Even the discerning von Schönkopf had difficulty grasping his answer. Miracle Yang smiled coolly.

"Lohengramm is unmarried. That's his weak point."

II

The meeting adjourned, Yang called for his aide.

"Lieutenant Greenhill, take whatever measures are necessary for a full civilian evacuation. We'd better just follow the manual procedure for this type of situation...assuming there is one."

"Right, I'll wait for Your Excellency's command, then," answered Frederica Greenhill in a voice that was clear and filled with conviction. "Does this mean you have some grand scheme already in mind, Your Excellency?"

"Yeah, well, I do need to live up to expectations as much as I can, right?"

Yang wasn't one to brag. He held extreme contempt for delusions of "certain victory" and "huge military gains." Such ideals had never helped Yang win a single battle.

Frederica had her own reasons for trusting her superior. When she was fourteen, still living with her mother on the planet of El Facil, she had experienced the Imperial Navy's terrifying power firsthand. Still a girl at the time, Frederica had handled it better than her mother, who was prone to hysterics. And the person responsible for getting the people safely off the planet was none other than Yang Wen-li, who had recently been promoted to sublieutenant. Frederica made sandwiches and brought coffee for the twenty-one-year-old sublieutenant, who'd just reluctantly cut his hair. Timidly, she probed him about the possibility of a strategic success, but the sublieutenant had his head in the clouds and responded with noncommittal phrases like "Well..." or "Somehow..." that only increased the people's uneasiness and distrust.

"I'm doing the best I can. Anyone doing less than that is in no position to find fault with me."

Frederica, who always defended him, had been Yang's only ally. But after he had succeeded in formulating a miraculous escape strategy and had become revered as a hero, such was not the case.

"We've believed in his genius since the time he was anonymous," chorused the masses.

At this, Frederica cast a sidelong glance before returning to the capital, where she reunited with her father, Dwight, nursing her mother while endeavoring for the Officers' Academy entrance exam. Her father had long thought of his daughter's military ambitions as the consummation of his influence.

While the Frederica of the past had helped Yang, it had only been with the little things. Now her abilities and position were considerably strengthened, and without her Yang's inability to deal with paperwork would've drained him completely. The amplification of her own value was, to Frederica, no small joy—but an exceedingly private one about which Yang's aide, who embodied beauty and brains in equal measure, kept silent.

Walter von Schönkopf came back. It seemed that the commander of fortress defenses, known for his boldness and sharp tongue, hadn't yet finished speaking his piece. Stroking his tapered jaw, von Schönkopf faced Yang without shame.

"I was just thinking, you see. What will those bigwigs do once they know they're no longer safe on Heinessen? And then it hit me: won't they just abandon their citizens and escape from Heinessen with their loved ones to the impregnable Iserlohn?"

Yang said nothing. Because he couldn't or because he didn't want to, he couldn't say for sure. Yang was upset over high officials abusing their political power in the Free Planets Alliance. Not because they disavowed the alliance's political system, but because they looked down on the spirit of democracy itself. Either way, he was in no position to voice such opinions.

"Those who have an obligation to protect their people yet instead protect only themselves should be punished accordingly. It might be good to round them up where they've fled and turn them over to von Lohengramm in one neat package. Or maybe we could just execute them for treason. That would put you at the summit. A republic of Iserlohn isn't such a bad idea."

Although it was difficult to tell just how serious von Schönkopf was being, he clearly had his heart set on Yang's authority. If Yang agreed, he'd likely command his own Rosen Ritter regiment and set out to arrest those high officials himself. Yang gave his reply but avoided a direct answer.

"If you ask me, political power is like a sewer system. Without one, society can't function. But the stench from it clings to everything it touches. No one wants to get near it."

"There are those who can't approach it no matter how much they want to," parried von Schönkopf, "and those who are the rare opposite. It's odd for me to be pointing this out now, but you didn't become a military man because you liked it."

"I don't think it logically follows that all dictators start out as military men," said Yang. "But if it does, then I'd like to wash my hands of this worthless business sooner rather than later."

"If the people are the ones who support the dictator, then it's also up to them to resist and demand their emancipation. It's been thirty years since I was exiled to this country, but there's one question I still can't answer: How does one reconcile the paradox of a majority that desires dictatorship over democracy?"

Von Schönkopf noticed an unusual dexterity in the young commander as Yang involuntarily shrugged his shoulders, shaking his head at the same time.

"I doubt anyone could answer that question." Yang paused, deep in thought. "It's been a million years since humans discovered fire, and not even two millennia since modern democracy was established. I think it's too soon to tell."

Everyone knew Yang aspired to be a historian, but such reasoning was more befitting of an anthropologist, thought von Schönkopf.

"More importantly," said Yang by way of changing the subject, "we have some urgent business ahead of us, so let's attend to that first. Here we are arguing over tomorrow's breakfast when we haven't even prepared tonight's dinner."

"Granted, but you're being too generous by giving the ingredients back to those who provided them."

"We just borrowed them as we needed them. And now that we don't, we're simply giving them back."

"And what happens when we need them again?"

"We borrow them once more. Until then, we'll let the empire look after them. I only wish we could collect interest."

"You can't borrow a fortress—or another man's wife, for that matter—so easily."

Von Schönkopf's suggestive metaphor prompted a wry smile from the young, black-haired commander.

"If you ask to borrow it, naturally you'll get turned down."

"What you're saying is that we can only trap them."

"Our opponent is von Reuentahl. One of the Twin Ramparts of the Galactic Empire. He's not one to be trapped."

Despite Yang's attempts at derision, from where von Schönkopf stood, his commander's expression, more than that of a resourceful general working out a grand strategy, was of a student playing a practical joke on an infamous teacher.

III

The Galactic Imperial Navy's senior admiral and commander of its Iserlohn-bound fleet, Oskar von Reuentahl, welcomed the new year on the bridge of his flagship *Tristan*. On the main screen, the silver orb of Iserlohn Fortress, separated by eight hundred thousand kilometers of empty space, hung like a disembodied eyeball.

Von Reuentahl was a handsome man with dark-brown hair, but nothing gave so deep an impression as his differently colored eyes. The heterochromia that left his right eye black and his left eye blue had no small influence over his life. The fact that his mother had tried to scoop out one of his eyes before killing herself, that his father had drowned himself in alcohol to the brink of self-sufficiency—these were all deformed chicks hatched from the intangible eggs laid by his condition.

His father, since confined to the second level of their spacious mansion, who'd abandoned the diligence and honesty of his bachelorhood to share a perpetual bed with Bacchus, would sometimes stamp his way down to the first floor. Standing in front of his son, now free from the control of his steward and wet nurse, the elder von Reuentahl would glare with his bloodshot eyes and say things like "No one ever wanted you" and "I wish you had never been born."

The latter had become the refrain of Oskar von Reuentahl's discontent. Over time, he'd come to believe that indeed he *shouldn't* have been born. But at some point—when, he couldn't say—he'd gone from a death wish to making the best of things.

At present, he had two fleet commanders awaiting his orders: admirals Kornelias Lutz and Helmut Lennenkamp. By way of contrast to Lutz, Lennenkamp had caught von Reuentahl's attention for his uncooperative attitude toward a younger supreme commander and continued to press for an all-out attack against Iserlohn in the strongest terms possible.

Von Reuentahl didn't think of Lennenkamp as incompetent. Reinhard von Lohengramm would never have permitted incompetence among his ranks. Lennenkamp had sufficient tactical and command abilities. His purview was mostly limited to the battlespace at hand. He placed the highest value on tactical victories and couldn't see the forest for the trees when it came to war's grander purposes.

Von Reuentahl pegged him as a "one-track fighter."

Indeed, von Reuentahl didn't even put so high a valuation on himself. Winning or losing, superiority or inferiority—these were all relative and subjective.

"An all-out attack would be futile," said von Reuentahl to Lennenkamp in the hope of persuading him. "And if it *could* be taken by force, Iserlohn Fortress would've changed hands five or six times by now. The only one to have accomplished this is that impostor who oversees Iserlohn as we speak."

For this reason alone, von Reuentahl held the black-haired enemy general in high esteem.

Lennenkamp, too, had a foundation for his assertion. Reports of Mittermeier and the others on Phezzan were already reaching them. As things stood, a fruitless standoff against Yang Wen-li in the Iserlohn Corridor would only serve Phezzan and its allies. At least they wouldn't have the honor of recapturing Iserlohn Fortress. With the overwhelming military power of three fleets at their disposal, shouldn't they strategize more violent attacks to crush the enemy—mind, body, and soul?

"An interesting opinion, but the more intensely one refuses, the quicker one exhausts oneself."

Sensing malice in von Reuentahl's tone, Lennenkamp glared at his supreme commander with a wounded expression.

"I cannot abide by your position, Admiral. If Yang Wen-li abandons the fortress, he'll be accused of acting for the enemy's benefit. And in any case, a real military man defends his post to the last."

"What would be the point of that? The Imperial Navy is already attempting to invade alliance territory from the Phezzan Corridor. Back when the Iserlohn Corridor was the only target of military action, the fortress's existence had meaning. But times have changed. Clinging to the fortress for the sheer sake of it does nothing whatsoever to move the war along."

Not only that, but if they couldn't get the fleet stationed on the fortress mobilized, the Alliance Armed Forces would have nothing to show for itself militarily. As it was, chances of an alliance success were negligible at best, and the possibility of this reserve force, which had yet to see combat, inflicting a fatal blow was nonexistent. Their only logical recourse was to withdraw from Iserlohn.

"Yang knows this," said von Reuentahl. "There's a slight gap in the angle of the foul line between Yang Wen-li's good sense and yours."

Lennenkamp countered with an obvious question: "And if the alliance is destroyed and Iserlohn remains impregnable, won't Yang's reputation remain untarnished?"

"Yes, Yang might think that way were he you."

Unable to hide his scorn, it took von Reuentahl all his strength to keep calm. The "one-track fighter" was incorrigible, unable as he was to imagine the grander significance of the battle ahead.

On a strategic level, Reinhard had rendered powerless the tactically impregnable Iserlohn Fortress via his passage through the Phezzan Corridor, which meant that Reinhard was no simple military man. But

Lennenkamp, for whom victory was solely a tactical outcome, couldn't quite grasp the revolutionary change of circumstance.

Von Reuentahl nodded cynically to himself. *I see, so this is why that blond brat can take over the universe.* The battlespaces were filled with brave men, but strategic masterminds orchestrating the wars taking place within those battlespaces were few and far between.

"Admiral Lennenkamp, if it were possible, I would also like to launch a mass offensive against the fortress, but our supreme commander says it's a no-go. We can only follow orders."

Kornelias Lutz had to step in to intervene. Von Reuentahl wiped the expression from his mismatched eyes and bowed slightly to both admirals.

"It seems I've crossed the line. Forgive my impudence. But sooner or later the ripe fruit will fall. Right now, I don't think we need to over-extend ourselves."

"Then we just stop attacking Iserlohn and surround them?"

"No, Admiral Lutz. That won't work, either. It would buy the enemy precious time. If they're planning something, that doesn't mean we allow them undivided attention to their preparations."

"You mean we subject the enemy to harassing fire?"

"That's putting it too bluntly. Let's just say we're laying every possible gambit."

As for von Reuentahl, who erred on the side of political forethought, he didn't harbor the same fighting spirit that animated a man like Lutz. He was only fit to be commander of one fleet, as the subordinates under his command were aware.

The full-scale attack instigated by von Reuentahl disturbed Yang Wen-li to the core.

Even as he was dealing with von Reuentahl's fierce offensive, Yang had to prepare for evacuation. He'd entrusted Caselnes with the practicali-ties involved, but for the sake of allaying the outrage and discontent of civilians being snatched from their homes, direct persuasion was necessary. A public appearance, he thought, might be enough to assuage their fears.

"Things are getting hectic around here fast. I wasn't built for overtime."

The captain of the First Spaceborne Division at Iserlohn Fortress, Lieutenant Commander Olivier Poplin, had earned both immense hatred and respect from the opposing side's fighter pilots. The number of imperial pilots who'd fallen like so much space dust through his fingers was enough to constitute an entire fleet in and of itself. Those pierced by the fangs of the dogfighting squadrons under his command numbered ten times more. His ability to band three single-seat spartanian fighter craft together as a single unit was something instilled in him by military drill command as a desperate measure, but in the world of dogfighting, where individual skill was paramount, bringing team strategy to the table was groundbreaking. In the future, he would go down in history as an ace pilot, a topflight innovator of dogfighting techniques, and a libertine extraordinaire, but only he would know which honor was highest.

After repeated sorties, at last he had a brief respite. In the officers' mess, he griped like an early advocate of socialism.

"When I get back to Heinessen, I'm going to form a labor union for pilots. I'll dedicate my life to getting rid of overwork. You just wait and see."

"I thought you were going to dedicate your life to women?" quipped Lieutenant Commander Ivan Konev, leader of the second airborne fleet.

Despite being an ace of comparable ability and deeds of arms, Konev was an upright man chiseled out of basalt who steered clear of Poplin's debauchery. While Poplin was making merry with women and wine, Konev made companions of crossword puzzle books so thick one would almost have mistaken them for dictionaries. These two contrary personalities made for a surprisingly complementary pair.

IV

By the next day, the Imperial Navy had been pummeling the fortress without rest, and commander of fortress defenses Rear Admiral von Schönkopf was being hotly pursued in retaliation. Employing as many gunners as he could spare, he dispatched his corps of engineers to assess all damage points and answered every shot that fired upon the fortress in kind. The operators were feeding constant updates, messages, and instructions. One collapsed from overwork, another found his vocal cords paralyzed, and both were quickly substituted. Rear Admiral Caselnes was likewise going on no sleep in preparing for mass evacuation, but a delegation of civilians had managed to push their way through and surround Yang's quarters in protest.

"Please, good citizens, calm down."

Yang's expression was seemingly nonchalant, but it was all he could do to conceal the trepidation in his heart. His plan involved making sure that all fleet stations on Iserlohn were relatively unharmed and unobstructed. With a tactical expert like von Reuentahl as his enemy, Yang felt the battle had become meaningful again, and the possibility of being forced into a war of attrition was furthest from his mind. Add to that a populace teetering on the edge of mass hysteria, and it was a wonder he wasn't teetering along with them.

"Don't worry—everything will be okay. Rest assured, we'll get you all to a safe star zone unharmed."

Offering this token promise to an uneasy delegation, he could only hope that someone might guarantee that very success. More than an atheist, he was an unbeliever, and so he wasn't in the least bit inclined to entrust the fate of himself and others to a god he'd never met. In the same way that, from time immemorial, there existed no righteousness where human anger was unnecessary, neither was there success where human ability was unnecessary. Even so, bearing the burden of five million military and civilian lives was too much for Yang to handle alone.

Surely an intelligent man like von Reuentahl had already distilled the essence of the situation. Yang had only two paths to choose from: stay on Iserlohn or abandon it. When the time came, whether by hindering Yang's escape or weakening his military power, any intensification of attacks would be no skin off von Reuentahl's back. This realization only added fuel to Yang's hatred.

Even as the middle commanders of Yang's fleet were busy managing frustrations between themselves and their subordinates, they were forced into a difficult position. Commander Yang Wen-li granted a single sortie but strictly prohibited going outside the range of the fortress's main battery.

Rear Admiral Dusty Attenborough, who gave the order, continued to sustain severe fire in close combat, but with help from the fortress's bombardment, he succeeded in driving back imperial forces. It was, however, a half-planned retreat on the Imperial Navy's part. Attenborough barely managed to keep his men from continuing their pursuit. Pressured by their constant griping, he begged Yang back on base to go after them again.

"Out of the question."

"There's no need to put it like that. I'm not some kid asking for his allowance. This is about the morale of our troops. Please, I implore you. Let us go out on another run."

"Not on your life." Yang refused him like a miser being asked for a loan. Realizing the futility of negotiation, Attenborough could only withdraw into his dejection.

Yang was indeed in a miserly state of mind. Maintaining a woundless fleet and preserving firepower had exhausted the lion's share of his mental energy, and so he couldn't help but be frugal about endangering his crew. This self-awareness put him in a considerably sour mood.

Nicknames like "Miracle Yang" weighed heavily upon him. They harbored an unavoidable danger not only of faith but also of overestimation. Soldiers and civilians alike seemed to believe that Admiral Yang would come through somehow, but what about the one in whom they believed? What did *he* have to rely on? If Yang wasn't almighty, neither was he omnipotent. In truth, he was nothing more than diligent. Among the alliance's frontline commanders, no one had used up as many paid vacation days as him, and he would be the first to admit that his strategies and tactics were nothing more than armchair victories. As Yang had once been told, culture emerged from humanity's innate desire to produce much by doing little, and only barbarians considered it right to exploit mind and body in search of justification.

"And if I took full responsibility? Would you let me go then? Please, just get me out there."

Yang had little patience for begging. Despite being a young and highly decorated military man himself, Yang despised all militant value systems, ways of thinking, and expressions. Such thinking would earn him the designation of "walking contradiction" in the future.

His ever-present aide Lieutenant Frederica Greenhill picked up on this. A discreet cough on her part alerted Attenborough to his commander's discomfort. He immediately changed tactics.

"I've come up with a fairly easy way to beat our enemy. Would you allow me to put it to the test?"

Yang eyed Attenborough, then Frederica. He shook his head with a bitter smile. Frederica demanded details. Chipping away at the imperial forces as much as possible was, in the long run, not such a bad idea.

When, after a few amendments, Yang gave Attenborough permission to proceed with his plan, the young division commander left Yang's office with an overt spring in his step. Yang heaved a sigh and aired his discontent to his beautiful golden-brown-haired aide.

"Don't be so shrewd, Lieutenant. We have enough troubles as it is."

"Yes, I went too far. My apologies."

Frederica held back a smile, and so Yang didn't complain any further. Had Rear Admiral Caselnes heard Yang's complaint, he would've smiled himself. Because, for his professed "troubles," Frederica handled almost all the paperwork.

∴

Approximately four hundred transports departed from Iserlohn Fortress for Free Planets Alliance territory, escorted by five times as many warships.

In response to reports from his enemy scouting team, von Reuentahl frowned and looked over a shoulder at his nearby comrade.

"What do you think, Bergengrün?"

The young heterochromatic commander's chief of staff answered tactfully.

"On the surface, it would seem that Iserlohn's VIPs or civilians are attempting an escape. Considering the position they're in, it's not unthinkable."

"But you're not buying it. Your reason?"

"This is Yang Wen-li we're talking about. You never know what kind of trap he might be setting."

Von Reuentahl smiled.

"Yang Wen-li's a big deal, a veteran hero who makes us tremble in our boots."

"Your Excellency!"

"Don't be upset. Even *I* am afraid of his tricks. I'm not exactly thrilled to take von Stockhausen's place after he had Iserlohn taken from him."

Von Reuentahl didn't need to bluff to protect his honor. Accomplishments, ability, and confidence: these three fulcrums stabilized his judgment of a formidable enemy. Signs of a trap lit a signal in his brain. Then again, maybe Yang was trying to convince him of just that and coax him into a deadly pursuit. It wasn't so easy for one first-class general to perfectly divine the tactics of another.

After receiving word that Lennenkamp had mobilized his fleet in pursuit of Iserlohn's evacuees, von Reuentahl flashed a deviant smile.

"Splendid. I'll leave it to him."

"But what if Admiral Lennenkamp catches the big fish? Are you really going to give up the honor of that accomplishment?"

Bergengrün's remarks were 80 percent warning, 20 percent suspicion that his commander was too trusting. Von Reuentahl held his tongue for a few moments to take stock of this questionable cocktail.

"If Lennenkamp should succeed, it would mean the well of Yang Wen-li's ingenuity has run dry. I don't know whose misfortune it'll be, but I don't think he's finished quite yet. Let's just observe Lennenkamp's tactics and hope he doesn't disappoint, shall we?"

Bergengrün nodded in silence, watching as von Reuentahl turned his tall figure in fluid exeunt. Bergengrün had once served under the command of the late Siegfried Kircheis and had since been reassigned to von Reuentahl. He began to wonder just how different these two admirals were in temperament.

To be sure, Lennenkamp was a skilled commander. Forgoing something so simple as a linear pursuit, he divided his forces in half in a pincer attack, sending one out in a gentle arc before the enemy to cut off their escape route, while the other attempted to close off the rear. The brilliant encirclement looked complete, and so von Reuentahl, closely watching his screen, clicked his tongue in simultaneous astonishment. But only for a moment.

The Alliance Armed Forces, following their own clever plan, had anticipated the movements of Lennenkamp's fleet and had lured the Imperial Navy within range of Iserlohn Fortress's anti-ship turrets. This strategy, which in the past had dealt a hard blow to Neidhart Müller, shouldn't have worked a second time, but Lennenkamp became a repeat example. A terrible spectacle ensued as, hit by a shower of light, his fleet exploded in fireballs of obliteration. Von Reuentahl found out moments later.

"We can't just stand by and watch them die. Help them!"

This time, tens of thousands of imperial light beams showered Iserlohn Fortress. Enormous amounts of energy silently impacted the fortress's outer wall. Without making so much as a dent, the bombardment shrouded the enormous man-made globe, sixty kilometers in diameter, in a rainbow-colored mist. Storms of energy swirled along the outer wall, gun turrets and emplacements crumbling from the heat. Fragments thereof battered the outer hull with white-hot hail. The alliance's firepower was severely diminished, and Lennenkamp's fleet, writhing like a snake bitten on the belly, managed to restore order.

But that didn't mean the Imperial Navy's bitter symphony—composed by Attenborough, orchestrated by Yang—had disclosed every movement.

Of the Lennenkamp fleet, one forward division was still unharmed. Enraged by a desire for revenge, it stormed the enemy fleet. But even as it did so, the Imperial Navy was already showing signs of disintegration, and after a shoddy counteroffensive, the enemy commenced their retreat like sediment diffusing in a lake.

"Even with such a thoroughly disciplined commander, it seems those cursed Alliance Armed Forces don't feel any shame in running away."

Lennenkamp was by nature a man who underestimated his own enemies, but this time he was keeping a close eye on general commander von Reuentahl. Lennenkamp wanted, at all costs, to avoid being ridiculed by von Reuentahl for recovering points lost in the first half.

Oskar von Reuentahl, insofar as his talents as a tactician and abilities as a commander were concerned, was never deserving of criticism. His subordinates had abundant confidence in him, but as a philanderer susceptible to scorn, he earned occasional animosity from his colleagues. That this animosity wasn't deeply rooted made Chief of Staff Paul von Oberstein hate him more conspicuously than anyone. It was enough that his commendations caught the attention of so many colleagues. Moreover, when the death of Siegfried Kircheis plunged Reinhard into a stupor of grief, von Reuentahl was among the first to calm turmoil among the admirals and take advantage of threats to Reinhard's stability to establish his dictatorial regime. Kempf, too, who'd fought and lost against Yang the year before, had a competitive streak that led him to chase too hard after success. As did Lennenkamp, of course.

He handed down a stern command, closing in on the sluggish transports before giving the signal.

"Stop those ships. If they refuse, open fire upon them."

At that moment, a flash of light bleached their entire field of vision as all five hundred transports exploded. Those who had been glaring at their screens felt like their eyes were going to burst. The flash became a rapidly swelling ball that swallowed the imperial forces whole.

The imperial fleet lost to inertia's perfect control, and as it decelerated was plunged into the muddy stream of its own energy. Any ships that came to a full stop were hit from behind by those that couldn't, and together they danced into an entanglement of light and heat, all the while stretching their collision avoidance systems to their limits. Within the larger explosion, chains of smaller ones appeared, destroying everything, living and nonliving alike.

"Of all the underhanded tricks!"

Lennenkamp was foaming at the mouth. As the one on whom this trick was being played, he was completely deflated. His flagship had barely escaped the energy corona. Most of his ships hadn't been so lucky.

Not missing the chance, Attenborough ordered a rolling attack. Yang's Officers' Academy underclassman was a tactical prodigy in his own right. His command exceedingly and efficiently unleashed his subordinates' zeal for combat.

Admiral Lutz acted quickly and, in the short time it took to pull off a cross-strike, had broken through and pulverized the imperial forces. Of all the battles that had taken place between Yang and von Reuentahl, none had ever been decided with such a unilateral outcome.

The Imperial Navy was defeated, losing more than two thousand warships and sustaining a hundred times as many casualties.

Lennenkamp returned to base utterly dejected. Von Reuentahl only looked at him as if to say, "Serves you right." But he didn't say it, and instead acknowledged his services and had him dismissed. Von Reuentahl didn't see any reason to mark this as a deficit, so to speak, in their ledger. Although on a tactical level they'd conceded a step, the Alliance Armed Forces making such light of their plan ensured the Imperial Navy would be discouraged from going after them when the time came to evacuate in earnest. Had they desired a simple tactical victory, there'd have been no need for all the theatrics.

"Does that mean we should prepare to pursue them?" asked Bergengrün.

"Pursue them?"

Von Reuentahl's mismatched eyes glinted cynically.

"Why should we have to pursue them? If we allow them to escape, we can take Iserlohn Fortress for our own without having to lift a finger. Don't you think that alone is enough of a victory for us, Bergengrün?"

Were they to go after them on impulse, the probability of falling prey to another clever counterattack was high. Yang had been driven into battle with the Imperial Navy's main forces. Shouldn't they just let him go where he wanted to go?

"But if we allow Yang Wen-li to go free, somewhere down the line he might come back to haunt us, like a disease."

Von Reuentahl curled his lips slightly.

"In that case, we'd better work together on this. Our fleet shouldn't be the only one to run the risk of infection."

"But, Your Excellency…"

"I wonder if you know the maxim, Bergengrün: 'Without prey, there'd be no need for hunters. That's why they don't just kill everything that moves.'"

The chief of staff looked back at his commander, his green eyes quivering with the brilliance of understanding and anxiety. He spoke in a low voice.

"Your Excellency, don't say such rash things, which might invite useless misunderstandings. No, more than misunderstandings—they might be taken for slander. Please restrain yourself. As one of the Imperial Navy's most renowned generals, any mistake Your Excellency makes will have a major impact on others."

"Your advice is sound. I'll try to be a little more careful with my words."

Von Reuentahl spoke frankly and expressed gratitude for his chief of staff's advice. Von Reuentahl knew such a man was hard to come by.

"I'm glad you take my advice to heart. Even if we're not going after them, we should prepare to occupy Iserlohn Fortress."

"Yes, get right on it."

And with that, von Reuentahl set in motion a bloodless recapture of Iserlohn.

⋱ ⋰

As Yang Wen-li had once said to his ward, Julian Mintz:

"When it comes to both strategy and tactics, it's best to lay a trap while giving the enemy what it wants."

He'd also said:

"There's nothing better than waking up after a sound sleep to find that the seeds you've sown have produced a towering beanstalk."

And now, Yang was trying to put those very stratagems into effect. His escape from Iserlohn Fortress—what Lieutenant Commander Poplin called a "night flight"—had hardly been clever, but rather a necessary measure by which to capitalize on the strength of his garrisoned fleet. Otherwise, he'd have been wasting the power at his disposal, not to mention the many lives depending on it. When it came to protecting the safety of Iserlohn's civilian population, abandoning Iserlohn Fortress like so much hardware was like taking off a heavy coat in springtime: a mere change of season.

Because Rear Admiral Caselnes, administratively in charge of evacuating five million people, had never been one for creativity, Yang felt his heart sink when he gave the operation the code name "Project Ark." Although he didn't think it was enough to blow wind into their sails, rather than worry themselves over such trifling things, said Caselnes, he thought they should be concerned about the fact of having wasted five hundred already-decrepit transport ships in Yang's scuffle with Attenborough.

It was safe to say the effect on the capacity of their transport ships and hospital ships had been detrimental, and so a fair number of civilians were distributed aboard ships normally reserved for combat.

Six hundred newborns and their mothers, along with doctors and nurses, were placed aboard the battleship *Ulysses*. The *Ulysses* had a flawless track record, having survived numerous battles unscathed, and was therefore considered the most secure means of transporting infants, whose safety was of the utmost priority. A growing cynicism on board, however, left the crewmen feeling ill prepared for such a task. Even the captain, Commander Nilson, was disheartened by the prospect of seeing thousands of diapers hanging out to dry on his ship's bridge. Although chief navigations officer Sublieutenant Fields tried his best to boost morale by insisting that women were at their most alluring after giving birth and that three companies of them would be coming along for the ride, his men's imaginations were stimulated less by the thought of legions of beautiful Madonnas than by a choir of wailing babies, and so the sublieutenant's encouragement fell on deaf ears.

Accommodating a grand total of five million people—5,068,224, to be exact, a mixture of soldiers and civilians, men and women—was no small feat. Caselnes saw that the situation wasn't being handled with enough empathy. Even his own family—a wife and two daughters—was upset over leaving Iserlohn. The work proceeded swiftly.

The corps of engineers under Engineering Captain Links's command had set extremely low-frequency bombs everywhere in the fortress, including in its hydrogen-powered reactors and control centers. Those ranking higher than field officers were aware of this, but only a select few knew the duties being carried out by Lieutenant Frederica Greenhill on Yang's strictly secret orders. Yang was laying the groundwork for Iserlohn's future recapture. When briefed on the details, Frederica held back her surprise and excitement.

"Ideally, we have to make sure the enemy discovers our explosives, but not without some effort. Otherwise, they'll see through to the real trap. Do I have that right?"

"That's it exactly. In other words, Lieutenant, I've set up a diversion to lure the eyes of the Imperial Navy away from the real trap."

The trap in question was ridiculously simple, and therein lay its effectiveness. Yang explained it to Frederica again.

"If the fortress and its operation systems are left as is, our subterfuge has no value whatsoever. We'll just have to throw them off before they notice."

Frederica turned the contents of the order over in her mind and couldn't help but admire their simplicity and the grandiosity of their outcome.

"It's nothing ingenious or first-rate. Cunning is all it is, although I'm sure they'll be livid once it's over," answered Yang by way of deflecting her compliments. "Besides, we don't know whether it will even have the desired effect. It's possible we'll no longer need Iserlohn."

For a moment, Frederica gazed at the young commander's profile with her hazel eyes as if he were receiving divine revelation or spouting prophecy, although such was not at all the case.

"I suspect it'll come of use someday. Iserlohn Fortress is our home… the home of the entire Yang fleet. We'll be back. And when that happens, Your Excellency's plan will bear its fruit for all to see."

Yang stroked his face with one hand, as was his habit when he didn't know how to express himself. As he lowered his arm, the young, dark-haired commander spoke like a boy of little experience.

"In any case, Lieutenant, best of luck as we move forward."

It was just the kind of thing Frederica expected Yang to say.

VI

Reports of ships commencing their departure en masse from Iserlohn Fortress converged on von Reuentahl from multiple sources. Half of them expected an order to retaliate. The heterochromatic fleet commander strictly prohibited the opening of hostilities without his express order. He'd been too quick to pull the trigger last time, and his tendency toward action was known throughout the navy.

"It's useless going after them," assured von Reuentahl. "It's not like the alliance can take Iserlohn Fortress with them. Total occupation of the fortress is our top priority."

Soon thereafter, Admiral Lennenkamp inquired directly about the advisability of an attack, but the commander's answer was a definite no.

"It would only incur another counterattack. Let them go for now. I'd rather not go down in history as someone who brought harm to fleeing civilians."

Lennenkamp obediently withdrew, his belligerence dampened by the other day's defeat. Von Reuentahl gave a curt nod of satisfaction. *Good, now things will go more smoothly, one way or another.*

"Bergengrün, you're to go after Yang Wen-li—but only after you've secured the fortress. It won't be necessary to catch up with him or engage him in combat. We'll save that for another day," he said to his chief of staff. "Just keep on his tail. Admiral Yang will lead the way. Shall we make fall at Iserlohn, which they've so diligently prepared for our arrival?"

On the matter of who should go first, Kornelias Lutz offered his thorough opinion. Although Yang Wen-li had evacuated Iserlohn Fortress, they had to watch out for any "parting gifts" the alliance might've left behind. As far as Lutz was concerned, it wasn't paranoid to assume the alliance had planted bombs in the fortress's power centers to massacre imperial forces at a single stroke when they came to occupy. Given the speed at which the alliance fleets were hastening away, the degree of risk in approaching the fortress was extremely high. The best thing for them to do now was to dispatch bomb experts to investigate and, once that was done, occupy only after the all clear had been given.

"Admiral Lutz has a point that's not to be taken lightly."

Von Reuentahl ordered all fleets to retreat from the vicinity while a group of experts led by Engineering Captain Schmude was escorted to the fortress.

Having received this unexpected honor, Captain Schmude was in high spirits but nervous as he entered the former enemy camp. Lutz's suspicions were confirmed when a careful sweep revealed a series of low-frequency bombs. These were successfully dismantled.

"We got there in the nick of time. The bombs were quite cleverly hidden. Five minutes later, and Iserlohn Fortress would've gone up in a ball of flame, inflicting considerable damage on our forces."

Captain Schmude couldn't suppress his excitement as he delivered his report. Oskar von Reuentahl nodded, a waterwheel of consideration turning in the current behind his mismatched eyes. Was it possible that Yang had arranged this for his own benefit? Then again, the fortress's explosion would've forced a counterattack he might not have been able to sustain. All the same, were they supposed to be satisfied with their success? And were these the only parting gifts that Yang Wen-li had left behind? The heterochromatic admiral was gripped by doubt. He wondered whether Yang hadn't hidden something more sinister.

"He's a cunning man. I wonder what he's planning now..."

Meanwhile, Yang Wen-li, riding the success of his night flight, was on the bridge of his fleet battleship, *Hyperion*, unable to tear his anxious gaze away from the orb of Iserlohn Fortress hanging in the center of his main screen. He didn't think it would happen in a million years, but on the infinitesimal chance that the Imperial Navy failed to detect the bombs, not only would Yang have destroyed the fortress, but he would also have uselessly compromised many human lives. The appointed time of the explosion passed, and once he confirmed that no cracks had appeared in Iserlohn's beautiful surface, he breathed a sigh of relief.

"Thank goodness, it looks like they found them."

Yang put a hand to his chest in relief, tearing himself away from the screen, and left the bridge to take a nap in his private room, bowing to the silver-white globe as he did so. It was, for him, a way of showing gratitude where it was due.

"Farewell, Iserlohn. Don't cheat on me while I'm gone. You truly are the queen of space. No woman comes close to you," said Lieutenant Commander Olivier Poplin, bidding his reluctant farewell with characteristic chivalry.

Next to him, Rear Admiral von Schönkopf silently raised a pocket flask of whisky to eye level. Murai stood upright and performed a salute. Frederica and Rear Admiral Caselnes followed suit. They each had their own thoughts as they said their goodbyes to the space fortress where they'd spent the last two years. Several among them would step foot once more on Iserlohn's artificial surface.

* * *

Back at Iserlohn Fortress, now reoccupied by the Imperial Navy, a modest interlude was under way. It was discovered that a long-serving managing officer had misappropriated some of the alliance's abandoned supplies without noting them in the public record. When the military police investigated the matter, it was revealed he'd done this many times in the past. Von Reuentahl had no tolerance for this kind of insubordination. In compliance with martial law, he sentenced the man to death at a summary hearing and carried out the act himself. The officer screamed hysterically up until the moment he was dragged to the execution ground, where he sobbed for mercy. But upon finally realizing it was futile, he resorted to outright accusations.

"The world is unfair. It doesn't matter if you destroy cities or kill tens of thousands of people in the name of war. So long as you win, you admirals and commanders are given fancy titles and medals. And yet you treat me as a criminal just for stealing a negligible amount of material resources."

"What's the point of crying foul now? Just listening to you hurts my ears."

"This goes beyond reason. You may call Duke von Lohengramm a hero or a genius, but at the end of the day, is he not a villain trying to conquer the galaxy? My crimes are nothing compared to his."

"Then why don't *you* try taking over the galaxy?"

Von Reuentahl's shapely eyebrows quivered slightly as he pulled the trigger and sent the officer's brains flying. His comrades held solemn silence.

After von Reuentahl had installed himself in Yang Wen-li's executive office, the engineering officer came to deliver his written report. Until the Imperial Navy's own software could be installed, mountains of written reports would accumulate on his desk. According to this one, all data in the tactical computer had been wiped, meaning the Imperial Navy would need to input its own from scratch. This was to be expected. All practical matters following the fortress's recapture were outside the scope of von Reuentahl's duties, as his concerns would be purely strategic from now on.

The future was beyond deliberation. Regardless of whatever strange tactical trick Yang Wen-li had used to force Iserlohn Fortress's recapture, as long as he, Oskar von Reuentahl, managed to avoid being the comic relief in all of this, he would be content in his position. Von Reuentahl saw it all. First and foremost, Yang Wen-li had essentially handed Iserlohn Fortress to them on a platter. Which meant the likelihood was high of something brewing further beyond his reach than he could possibly imagine.

The fortress is ours in any case. I'll take whatever is offered to me in good faith, he thought, and sent word through his communications officer.

"Contact Odin. Tell them I've captured Iserlohn Fortress."

And so, on January 9, Iserlohn Fortress was returned to the hands of the Imperial Navy for the first time in almost two years.

CHAPTER 3:
IN SEARCH OF A FREE UNIVERSE

I

THIS YEAR, SE 799, Julian Mintz would be seventeen, and for the second time he welcomed the new year not without worry.

The first time had been when he'd become Yang Wen-li's ward under Travers's Law. Yang, then a captain, had become an admiral, and Julian himself had gone from being a civilian in military employ to a full-fledged soldier, advancing to ensign. His compensation came in the form of reassignment to Phezzan as Yang's resident officer, but his itinerary had detoured him from Iserlohn Fortress to the capital, Heinessen, and only then to Phezzan, nearly ten thousand light-years away.

It hadn't even been six months since he'd bid farewell to those he loved and begun a busy new life on Phezzanese soil. What kept Julian's heart in check was the fact that here it was as if he didn't exist at all.

"Be sure to find yourself a beautiful girl and bring her back."

Lieutenant Commander Poplin had spurred him on with this kind of talk, but Julian couldn't have taken on a lover even if he wanted to. Had he even 10 percent of Poplin's passion, he might've at least entertained the notion, but...

"And so, our hero dies alone and in obscurity," Julian muttered to himself.

On his way to seventeen, Julian's height had reached 176 centimeters, at last approaching that of his guardian, Yang. *But only in physical stature*, thought Julian. The flaxen-haired boy was very much aware that in all other respects, he could barely keep a foot in Yang's shadow. He still had much to learn and had yet to step out from under Admiral Yang's wing. Until he could strike out on his own path using the strategies, tactics, and histories he'd learned, he would always be less than Admiral Yang.

In his hideout nestled in a back alley of imperial-occupied Phezzan, Julian brushed away the flaxen hair stubbornly falling across his forehead. The features this gesture revealed, graceful yet vivacious, were almost feminine. Not that he cared. His only point of pride, at present, was how much he'd leveled up since gaining tactical knowledge from Yang, marksmanship and hand-to-hand combat skills from Water von Schönkopf, and air-combat techniques from Olivier Poplin.

"Are we still grounded?" Julian asked Marinesk, who'd come to the hideout at his invitation.

Marinesk, who by his good offices had arranged a spaceship and astrogator, was the administrative officer for *Beryozka*, an independent merchant ship. Marinesk was also a trusted friend of Boris Konev, who was getting anxious about his compulsory idleness on the alliance capital of Heinessen. Although still in his thirties, his hair was thin and his body slack. Only his eyes were abundant in youthful vitality.

"Not just yet. Please, don't get impatient. Oh, I said the same thing yesterday, didn't I?"

Marinesk's smile was devoid of cynicism or sarcasm, but Julian, cognizant of his own impatience and unease, couldn't help but blush. For the moment, the Imperial Navy wasn't admitting civilian ships through the Phezzan Corridor. No matter how well-planned their escape from Phezzan was, they'd surely be captured if they left now. The Imperial Navy was likely to allow passage of civilian ships once military activities had died down, if only to appease the Phezzanese public. And when that happened, spontaneous inspections of every single ship would be impossible. This, assured Marinesk, would make their escape much easier.

Although his predictions and conclusions persuaded Julian, it was all he could do to endure the nervous wingbeats of his heart, which compelled the boy with all the power of a homing instinct.

"Be that as it may, how long must we wait?"

These words, thick with discontent, tumbled out of Commissioner Henslow's mouth. Henslow, owner of a certain large company, had been abandoned by high executives for his lack of business acumen and talent, after which he had been given an honorary position in the alliance government and discreetly exiled to a foreign planet. Had the alliance been sincere about the importance of diplomacy, a man of his position would never have been sent to Phezzan, a modest symbol for a broken democracy.

"How long? Until we can depart safely, obviously."

Marinesk gave respect to Julian where it was due but to Henslow showed not the least bit of deference.

"We've already paid for a ship."

Henslow didn't go so far as to say that the money had come from his pocket, but maybe that was because his peculiar standards wouldn't allow it.

"And that's *all* we've done. So I'd prefer it if you didn't act so high and mighty about it. The guest cabin is under Julian Mintz's name. You're just extra baggage."

"But I'm the one who paid for it!"

In a flash, Henslow's character had been jarred from its reserve, but it left no dent on Marinesk.

"As far as I'm concerned, it was Ensign Mintz who paid. You may have loaned him the money, but that's between you and him and not for me to know."

More than Henslow himself, it was the one sitting next to him—Warrant Officer Louis Machungo—who sensed that Marinesk was toying with him. The magnificently proportioned black man, whose physique recalled that of a bull, nonchalantly stepped in to neutralize the rising tension.

"Marinesk, when you came in, I sensed you had some kind of present for us. I wonder if I was wrong."

His consideration was rewarded with sympathy. Marinesk aborted his pointless exchange with the commissioner and turned to the face the dark-skinned giant.

"You've quite the eye, Warrant Officer. In fact, I came here to give you these."

Beryozka's administrative officer pulled out three authorized passports from his inner pocket.

II

Julian Mintz was walking down the street holding a large paper bag from the bakery. He made an effort to leave his hideout once a day to familiarize himself with the city. At present, he had yet to incite the suspicions of roving imperial soldiers. Julian, for different reasons than Yang, didn't seem at all like a military man. He was attracting the interest of girls his age, and even that minor issue threatened to compromise his low profile.

Julian froze in his tracks as a sudden shock seized his ankles. The curious gaze of his dark-brown eyes darted around nervously. He saw nothing out of the ordinary. And then he understood.

The cause of his shock wasn't physical but aural. A single proper noun had leapt out from the pedestrian conversations around him and assaulted his consciousness with an overbearing energy: Lohengramm. Duke Reinhard von Lohengramm was going to pass by, soon, along this very street! The imperial prime minister, the Galactic Imperial Navy's highest commander, imperial marshal—Duke Reinhard von Lohengramm was coming this way!

A bitter sense of regret obliquely penetrated Julian's chest. On the off chance of an imperial inspection, he'd left his blaster back at the hideout. Had it been on his person, he might've taken the fate of that blond-haired youth who'd brought certain calamity to the Free Planets Alliance into his own hands. Had he been able to go back in time, he would've holstered his blaster against the wishes of Warrant Officer Machungo.

Julian closed his eyes and took a deep breath, at the same time ejecting a violent fury from the pilot's seat of his composure. He barely managed to pull himself away from the abyss of foolishness in which he had yielded mind and body to this useless fantasy. No amount of wishing would materialize that blaster in his hand. Besides, hadn't Admiral Yang once told him something? "Neither terrorism nor mysticism have ever moved history in constructive directions." Julian had thought about becoming a military man since he was a little boy, but had never once considered becoming a terrorist. Taking down that blond-haired tyrant, Duke Reinhard von Lohengramm, should not be through an act of terrorism, he thought, but rather through a fair fight. It was all for the best that he was unarmed.

This was an opportunity for something other than terrorism: the chance to see Reinhard von Lohengramm with his own eyes. He knew von Lohengramm's elegance only as rendered in holograms or in the media. Not even Admiral Yang had seen him in person. And now, that same tyrant would be here, in the flesh, at any moment. Having returned to his senses, and now driven by an even more intense desire, Julian swam through a small ocean of people.

Barriers had been set up along the roadway and sidewalks. Rows of hulking guards, armed and in uniform, gently forced back waves of people in the front and rear. Considering the position and authority of the one they were guarding, it was a rather underwhelming level of protection. Julian made his way to the front and, as he casually brushed back the hair from his forehead, waited for his glimpse of the young dictator.

A procession of land vehicles came trundling down the roadway. The first was an automatic armored vehicle, followed by a luxury car, which on its own wouldn't have caught anyone's eye. Julian had always heard that, as a rule, Duke von Lohengramm wasn't fond of excess extravagance, and the rumors were proving true. On that point alone, Julian already had a favorable impression of Reinhard.

The landcar bearing a high official passed in front of the crowd. Julian strained his eyes, but what caught them was a pale, angular face with streaked hair. The light emanating from his eyes had an inorganic quality to it, and his expression was thoroughly heartless. Julian guided that impression through the library of his memory and stopped in front of the shelf marked "Chief of staff of the Imperial Space Armada, Senior Admiral von Oberstein." But there was no time to ponder that name because the next landcar had entered Julian's vision. The moment he recognized that luxurious golden-blond hair in the back seat, Julian's heart did a vigorous tap dance.

Was that Duke von Lohengramm? Julian gathered the entirety of his visual memory to etch the young dictator's elegant face into his retinas, only to realize that such efforts were unnecessary for a face so impossible to forget. Not only because of its rare features, but also because of the type and volume of mental vitality behind it. Julian heard the sigh escaping from his lips as if from a distance and slightly shifted his line of sight.

The person sitting next to Reinhard at first appeared to be a beautiful boy the same age as Julian. But the short-cropped dull-blond hair and dignified expression revealed a young woman's face. This had to be Duke von Lohengramm's private secretary, whose name Julian couldn't remember.

From inside the landcar, Reinhard scanned the crowd. His gaze flowed horizontally, passing over the flaxen-haired boy.

For the briefest of moments, his and Julian's gazes intersected. It was a far more meaningful moment for Julian. For the other, it was but a small wave in a sea of many. If Reinhard, like Yang Wen-li or Julian, wasn't superhuman, then neither was he an apostle chosen by some higher power. Although his disposition far surpassed the average person in the scope of its proportion, it was still within the limits of what any human being could possess. Others who had surpassed the enormity of his military genius, the magnificence of his political ambition, his fair elegance, and the intensity with which he carried himself had existed in the past. Only those who possessed each of these qualities in equal measure were rare, as was the sheer number of fixed stars and planets he was attempting to bring under his rule. In any event, he couldn't perfectly foresee the future, and years from now he wouldn't even remember the events of this day.

When Reinhard's landcar had sped away and the crowd had dispersed, Julian drifted away as well. He, for one, wouldn't forget this day for as long as he lived. Just then, he felt a light tap on his arm. In his surprised eyes was reflected the smiling face of *Beryozka*'s administrative officer.

"Marinesk…"

"Sorry, didn't mean to startle you. So, how do you feel now that you've seen Duke von Lohengramm for real?"

"I'm no match for him."

Those words slipped meekly out of Julian's mouth. In both Reinhard's expression and physical appearance, Julian recognized only the shining brilliance that so overwhelmed everyone around him. Now Julian understood why Admiral Yang admired the blond-haired dictator he'd made an enemy of.

Hearing out the boy's brief yet heavy thoughts on the matter, Marinesk lightly raised his eyebrows.

"I see. He might seem like a young noble now, but it's not like he was born that way. The family name of Lohengramm, until he received the title of duke, was just the name of a poor man who happened to be nobility. His father sold his own daughter to guarantee a better future for his son."

"Sold his daughter...?"

"Had her locked up in the emperor's rear palace. Not that he officially sold her, but he might as well have."

To a low-class noble of the empire, a daughter was a precious commodity, a golden key opening the door to a veritable banquet hall of wealth and power. Reinhard and his sister Annerose's father wasn't the only one to make practical use of it. Nevertheless, had the younger brother of the emperor's favorite mistress been incompetent, he might've dispelled any animosity, but Reinhard's unparalleled ability put a stopper in the exhaust port of a person's jealousy until it exploded. Naturally, Reinhard had never granted the slightest favor to anyone who clung to outmoded values. In Reinhard's worldview, they existed only to be dominated. Even his own father was no exception. Reinhard had never forgiven him in the ugliness of his old age for selling away Annerose. Before his sudden death, Reinhard's father had used up what little vitality he had left on debauchery and extravagance, and Reinhard had vehemently refused to make amends. The only reason he'd attended his father's funeral at all had been so as not to upset his sister.

Julian had known something of Reinhard's past, but, hearing about it again now, couldn't bring himself to hate the enemy of the alliance. If anything, he felt somewhat embarrassed. The figure of a boy who, despite his violent disposition, was thinking only of his elder sister erased the power-hungry portrait he'd built up in his mind.

"Given these circumstances, it's been said that Reinhard owes his success to his sister's influence. Honestly, without her, he's nothing."

"But wasn't he already a highly decorated, first-rate military man when he was my age?"

"You've been decorated yourself, Ensign. And if you don't mind my saying so, our very own Miracle Yang was just a mediocre student at the Officers' Academy at your age. Compared to him, you're a step or two ahead."

A cloud of deep thought passed over Julian's eyes.

"Marinesk, by exploiting only the most convenient points about Admiral Yang and Duke von Lohengramm, one might think you were trying to provoke me, but it's a lost cause. Had you compared me to someone of a lower level, I might be willing to go along with a little flattery. But when you compare me to the likes of Admiral Yang and Duke von Lohengramm, any self-confidence I have vanishes. It's having the opposite effect. Makes me feel even more inadequate."

Julian tried to control his tone but without success.

"Oh, so you take it to mean I was trying to provoke you?" said Marinesk without a trace of timidity, caressing his thin hair. "My sincerest apologies if it came across that way. I was only trying to point out that no one is born a hero or a great commander, but I guess I went too far."

"No, I'm the one who went too far."

"Let's let the matter drop then, shall we? Anyway, I've wasted enough of your time. I'm actually on my way to see a customer."

"A customer?"

"Truth be told, I wouldn't be able to make a profit just transporting you and your party. I aim to round up as many customers as I can. It'll help dispel some of the danger around you as well."

Julian could understand where he was coming from. The more targets there were, the less rigorous surveillance and inspection would be. Even so, Julian couldn't help but think this was how the Phezzanese liked to do things. Weren't there people who'd lost money trusting their logic at face value? Then again, the Phezzanese in question probably believed in the correctness of their own logic as more than mere rhetoric.

Julian asked who the customer was, if only to keep the conversation going, having little interest in the answer. Julian was worried about his own background attracting the attention of other customers, who'd probably hide theirs if it bothered them for him to know.

"A priest of the Church of Terra," said Marinesk offhandedly. "Come to think of it, someone more important than that. A bishop, maybe? In any case, he doesn't work and puts food on the table by giving sermons."

Marinesk saw no reason to hide his narrow prejudice toward people of such status.

"But I can't very well deny the needs of a clergyman. Make an ally of one, and I can make a hundred of his believers into the same. That'll get me access to a wealth of information. Even so…"

Marinesk added with displeasure that he could never understand the contradiction of how all these emperors, nobles, and clergymen—people who'd never survive without followers working for their cause—were so often worshipped. His opinion, as an industrious and profitable Phezzanese, was shared by many.

"But he's an important customer, right?"

"No, but he was once an important man."

Marinesk knew this not by his own gathering. Like some jewel with a sinister legend, the information had passed through many merchants' hands before landing in his. This former priest had once prospered under the landesherr's patronage, coming and going as he pleased. Knowing this was enough to incite the caution of conservative wealthy merchants. So long as Landesherr Adrian Rubinsky was in good health, he would try to win his favor, but Rubinsky had gone incognito immediately following the imperial occupation. Although neither hide nor hair of him had been seen in public since, the bishop's loyalty was unshaken.

Marinesk was seldom prone to speculation, but if pushed he could grab Captain Boris Konev, a man who rarely set foot on land, by the neck and pull him down. As quietly as possible, of course. But now that he'd already decided to brave the danger of ferrying Julian Mintz into Free Planets Alliance territory, *Beryozka*'s administrative director didn't see the danger as a problem. A proverb of Phezzan corroborated his thinking on this matter: *If the poison is lethal enough, the result is the same no matter the dose.*

"So, Ensign, care to stretch your legs a little and come meet your fellow passenger?"

Marinesk scrutinized Julian's expression, gently spreading out his hands in mimicry of his smile.

"To be honest, I've yet to meet this priest or bishop or whatever he is, and I'm a little uncomfortable about the whole thing. I won't be able to manage him on my own if he turns out to be a nut. I'd feel better having you there."

Marinesk was impossible to hate. Moreover, Julian saw no harm in doing him a small favor, considering all he'd done. If Marinesk had wanted to lay a trap, he'd had multiple occasions to do so already.

Julian agreed and, still clutching his bakery bag, walked a step behind Marinesk into a long-abandoned building that was on the verge of crumbling. The stagnant air was like a sludge turned into vapor. The two of them walked to the second floor with the accompaniment of rats chorusing their threat to these intruders. Marinesk opened a door.

"Bishop Degsby, of the Church of Terra, I presume?" he intoned courteously into the dim room.

Having never seen this man before, Marinesk had chosen to call this person, of whom he thought so unkindly, by that higher form of address. A blanket shifted sluggishly, and a pair of hazy eyes regarded the visitors.

III

A report detailing Senior Admiral von Reuentahl's recapture of Iserlohn Fortress was waiting for Reinhard when he stepped into his makeshift prime minister's office.

"Congratulations. With this, Your Excellency has control of both corridors."

Von Streit spoke courteously, but somehow as if he were reading from a script. Admiral Lutz also offered his congratulations, but the poetic contrast of his words intrigued Hilda.

"May events continue to be in your favor."

It was good news, and Reinhard had no reason to be in bad spirits, but the swelling balloon of his mood was one needle away from popping. The last time Reinhard had taken Iserlohn Fortress, the statesmen of the Free Planets Alliance had been convinced their rule was manifest. He saw no reason to celebrate this small win.

"I take it Yang Wen-li is safe and sound," muttered Reinhard from behind his desk, his nimble fingers flipping through the pages of the report. Nowhere did von Reuentahl's report glorify his own achievement. It was thoroughly objective in its perfect reconstruction of events.

Von Streit looked at his young master.

"Your Excellency, I hear that Yang Wen-li has abandoned and evacuated the fortress, but won't those actions incite the anger of the alliance government and spell certain execution for him?"

Reinhard looked up from the report. Most times, he welcomed questions from subordinates. With enough merit, they served as moderate stimuli for his thinking.

"And if they executed him, who would command Admiral Yang's fleet? Even if he does nothing but sanction documents as commander in some safe place, his soldiers will never be able to handle themselves. And if he ignores that…"

…*then the alliance government's highest commanders are even more feeble-minded than the high nobles of the empire*, Reinhard thought derisively to himself.

"As you wish, but if he could secure the Iserlohn Corridor, then he could also keep our imperial aggressions in the Phezzan Corridor at bay. Why wouldn't he take such precautions?"

"It wouldn't be very safe. Still, emancipating his soldiers is the only way for the alliance to gain victory."

"How so…?"

"You don't get it? By killing me in battle."

Reinhard's expression and voice were indifferent. Only Hilda gave a momentary indication of a response. She saw that his eyes, for all like azure jewels abandoned in an ice floe, were starting to flicker with renewed brilliance.

After Admirals von Streit and Lutz took their leave, Reinhard called his orderly and had coffee prepared for him and Hilda. The boy, chosen from among the students of the military prep school, had been with him throughout this expedition. Coffee and cream were brought in, and the pleasing aroma of their admixture tickled their nostrils.

"You've seen through Admiral Yang's plan, and yet you still intend to lead the navy yourself?"

"Of course. Fräulein von Mariendorf, I intend on being supreme ruler, and if I'm ever going to realize that goal, I must insist on following my own law. Standing at the front lines is what separates me from every incompetent noble I've ever fought and defeated. It's also why my soldiers support me."

Reinhard lowered his gaze, comparing the black of the coffee with the white of its porcelain vessel. Hilda offered her opinion all the same.

"I daresay, Your Excellency, you mustn't waste your time with another useless battle. Return to Odin. If you leave the Phezzan Corridor to Admiral Mittermeier and the Iserlohn Corridor to Admiral von Reuentahl, they will surely win. I'd rather you sit back and savor the fruits of their victories."

Although Reinhard wasn't angry, neither did Hilda's words change his mind, because as she herself knew, her suggestion was eminently ordinary.

"Fräulein, I want to fight."

Reinhard's tone alone told the tale. More than that of an ambitious person craving power, it suggested a boy who wanted nothing more than to claim the traces of some forgotten dream. To Reinhard, fighting could never be so simple. For a moment, Hilda thought of herself as a strict and unsympathetic teacher trying to deprive a child of his curio box. No doubt this was a delusion, but practically speaking she was correct. Leaders, rather than racking up medals themselves, were supposed to let subordinates rack up medals in their stead. But depriving Reinhard of battle was to force a proud, wild bird of prey into a birdcage like some common parakeet. Such confinement would surely dampen the keen glint in his eyes, along with the gloss and power of his wings.

Reinhard had unraveled a life for himself from the entrails of the many enemies he'd fought. During the first ten years of his life, his only friend was his sister, Annerose, five years his senior. As his one unconditional ally, Annerose was a source of light and, before she was held captive by an aging ruler, had given him his second friend.

The redheaded boy, Siegfried Kircheis, taller despite being of the same class and age, was constantly by Reinhard's side and had felled many enemies in his name. Whenever they returned triumphantly home after dispersing any number of bullies, Annerose never praised them but did make hot chocolate for the little heroes. Those cheap cups and the cheap hot chocolate that filled them appeased the boys well enough with their warmth. No matter how tough boyhood got, such moments were reward enough. Compared to the joy and satisfaction of those days, any reward he might offer his sister in return was trivial at best.

He'd granted her a high position but had yet to dull the labors of his heart to the point of imagining she was happy with that. But it was the only way he knew how to show the world just how much he treasured her existence. Her title of countess (sans count), and the estate and money that went along with it, barely expressed the full magnitude of Reinhard's feelings for his elder sister.

On the laundry list that Reinhard had drawn up for her, the item of "husband" was conspicuously absent. Whether consciously or not, he refused to accept a partner for his sister. Seeing him like this, Hilda couldn't help but feel anxious. So long as his incomparable elder sister was around, Reinhard would never love like a commoner. To be sure, it was a needless anxiety. It was simply that a woman he might fall in love with had yet to cross his path…

Reinhard averted his eyes from his expensive white porcelain coffee cup.

"We leave Phezzan," he declared. "Tomorrow, as planned."

With that, Hilda's heart, swimming in space, was yanked back to reality by gravitational pull. She answered in the affirmative.

"Fräulein, if I'm to hold the universe, I'd much rather do so not through gloves, but with my bare hands."

Hilda assented to Reinhard's sentiments with her body and soul, even as a shadow clouded her heart. A stitch in the massive curtain of time was coming undone, and the weak light before daybreak momentarily illuminated his future profile. Maybe it was just the crude neutral colors woven of a hallucination, but to Hilda, Reinhard's words hinted not only at how he lived but also at how he would die. That was still a long way off, and right now Reinhard was a veritable flame of life. The vitality of his body and soul shone through his every limb, down to the fingertips.

IV

On the same day that Duke Reinhard von Lohengramm left Phezzan and steeled himself for fresh conquest, both admirals Wittenfeld and Fahrenheit took fleets from the empire to Phezzan. Five days later, they planned to join Reinhard on his expeditionary operation. The soldiers were given a final day off in their respective hometowns.

Phezzan's citizens had mixed feelings about the fact that Nicolas Boltec was aboard an imperial warship just one step behind Fahrenheit and Wittenfeld. Having held successive jobs as Landesherr Adrian Rubinsky's aide and imperial resident commissioner, at least no one could call him incompetent. Although he hadn't warned them of an imperial invasion, being given the title of "Phezzan's acting governor-general" by Duke von Lohengramm at the spaceport just before his departure made it clear enough that he'd known of the invasion beforehand. Clearly, the one once known as the landesherr's right-hand man had sold off Phezzan's freedom and independence, taking the acting governor-general position as payment for his treason.

"Whether it's your country or your parents," went one Phezzanese joke, "don't hesitate to sell them. But only to the highest bidder."

Now that the Phezzanese were the ones being sold, however, they didn't have much reason to laugh. Indeed, some believed that recent events had been designed for the sole purpose of advancing the Imperial Navy's immediate domination. The more assertive citizens preached a change of tide and, seeing that the arrival of the grand empire's total rule of human society was taking shape before their very eyes, desired a path on which Phezzan would flourish under the new system. They had arbitrarily decided it was foolish to be so fixated over a mere token of political status.

Both sides of the debate had a valid point, but the human brain had a difficult time sorting through emotions, and the people kept a close eye on Boltec as he settled into the acting governor-general's office and began dealing with its administration.

A common ideal of the Phezzanese people asserted that one should stand and walk on one's own two feet. It was therefore difficult to blindly praise Boltec as he went by, enshrined in the empire's perambulator.

People concealed their voices in bars and behind the closed doors of their own homes.

"Where could Rubinsky, the Black Fox of Phezzan, have disappeared to? Where is he watching from, doing nothing while Boltec carries on as usual?"

In any age, in any political system, authority figures will always have secret hideaways unknown to the public. To any child who turned their attic into a castle of dreams, it was familiar only in shape, as it had unique reasons for existing. For those with power, it was their fear of abasement and the egotism of self-protection.

Adrian Rubinsky's secret shelter wasn't something he'd created, but something he'd capitalized on through a predecessor's inheritance. Wisely, if also cunningly, placed at a level below an underground shelter for high officials and known only to a select few in the autonomous government, this vast system of energy and water supplies, of ventilation, drainage, and waste, required an even siphoning from public facilities so that the possibility of being discovered was minimal.

Concealed with no more than ten close associates in a nameless underground palace, Adrian Rubinsky was enjoying the repose offered to him by his self-imposed house arrest. No expense was spared in making his shelter feel as luxurious as possible, outfitted as it was with high ceilings and more than enough space for his needs. The menu was so extensive that one could eat a different meal every day for a year and still not exhaust its abundance of options. Rubinsky's mistress, Dominique Saint-Pierre, was the only woman present, and she spent most of her time with the landesherr. And while the conversations between these two lovers may have been prosaic, their devotion was unimaginable to even his closest associates. One quarrel between them went as follows:

"It seems that Degsby, that crafty Church of Terra bishop you helped get off Phezzan, has been picked up by a new god," said Rubinsky. "So that's good."

"What the hell are you talking about?"

"You were always talented as a singer and dancer, but never as an actress."

Rubinsky's tone was like that of a teacher sighing over an unworthy student. Dominique set a whisky glass in front of her lover with a louder clink than usual.

"Is that so? That beloved son of yours, Rupert Kesselring, believed I was on his side up until the moment you killed him."

"He wasn't the most attentive audience in that regard. Never the type to observe actors' performances so much as to intoxicate himself by projecting his own self-delusions onto them."

When Dominique expressly named the young man who'd tried to kill his father yet had been killed by him instead, the murderer deprived her of the pleasure of a reaction. The surface tension of the whisky glass in his hand didn't tremble in the slightest. Such composure, or the ability to feign it, set Dominique's nerves on edge. She gave up on feigning ignorance and launched her counterattack.

"You might think about getting some insurance, assuming you care even a little about the one who controls your fate."

Dominique had kept silent about the fact that the late Rupert Kesselring had ordered Bishop Degsby's escape in full knowledge of the relationship between Rubinsky and the Church of Terra.

"You force me to spell it out for you, but don't go thinking I willingly abetted your son's murder. I can't even tell you what a bad taste that leaves in my mouth."

"I always thought you wanted to help me."

Rubinsky stared, oddly expressionless, at the light reflecting off the ice in his drink before returning his gaze to Dominique.

"Does that mean you chose me over Rupert out of sheer instinct? And now that your instinct has proved correct, there's no use in crying over spilled milk? Am I right?"

"The spilled milk, in this case, was exactly like the cow it came from, who claims to be the clever one."

"You're right—in that respect he was too much like me in the worst ways. If only he'd learned to control his ambition a little more, he wouldn't have died so young. Then again…"

"It's a father's responsibility to educate his son."

"When it comes to life in general, yes. In any event, I'm the last person he should've emulated. No matter how talentless he might've been, had he aspired to become a scholar or artist, I would've offered whatever support he needed."

Dominique cast a probing glance, unable to grasp Rubinsky's true meaning.

"In the end, you prioritized self-preservation. So surely you understand my position."

"I do, as does anyone who's had to stoop to the level of someone beneath them," responded Rubinsky scornfully, as he refilled his glass. "I have every intention of cutting ties with the Church of Terra anyway. What you did for me was basically in line with my objective. And so, I acquiesced."

The power held by the Church of Terra was, for the most part, founded on the secrecy of its existence. And when the shutters of that secret were broken and the sunlight of truth came flooding in, the evil spirits lurking in that unopened room for eight centuries were as good as vanquished.

Rubinsky arranged in his head the many people and schemes he'd have to employ in the future. Until that complex blueprint was finished, these days spent in hiding would be an ideal breeding ground for the budding of spring.

U

The independent merchant ship *Beryozka*, ferrying eighty undocumented passengers, left Phezzan on January 24. In the wake of Reinhard's departure and Phezzan's return to democracy, at last civilian routes were reopened and *Beryozka* was among the first to leave the planet. Only those routes between Phezzan and the empire were green-lit. Anything in the direction of the alliance was still closed off. Marinesk had, of course, falsified their destination, and would have no choice but to surrender in the event they were captured by the Imperial Navy.

Prior to departure, Marinesk insisted on further safety measures, one of which was to lodge a complaint with the acting governor-general's office, claiming the existence of a group that planned on flying through the path toward the alliance.

"They'll never think that the one reporting it is also the mastermind behind the whole operation," explained Marinesk to Julian, who saw no need to throw a firecracker into a snake den.

Warrant Officer Machungo, as an aide, entrusted things to Marinesk, a self-professed expert in such things. To understand human nature, one had to respect the achievements and pride of one's opponents. As for Julian, the top of whose head barely reached Machungo's face, he was ready. Considering how many places were beyond his reach, what was the point in worrying about all of them? Hadn't Yang Wen-li always said as much? "Even if you do your best, there will always be things you're bad at. And no matter how much you worry about those places beyond your reach, you're better off leaving them to those who can reach them." In light of this, Julian knew he was just making excuses for himself.

Their pilot, Kahle Wilock, had had a favorable impression of Julian since they'd first met. In fact, he'd already decided to like Julian before then. He praised Julian for being bolder than he looked in attempting passage to alliance territory beneath imperial detection and vowed to do everything in his ability to ensure a successful flight. Although Julian thought him to be a man worth relying on, Wilock also had an aggressive streak. He said that if the remaining alliance forces joined up with Phezzan's wealth, taking down the Imperial Navy wasn't impossible, and proceeded to list concrete methods by which to do just that. He abandoned all technical explanations and, with a sardonic laugh, fervently proposed the formation of a united front against von Lohengramm. It was unthinkable for Julian to hear of the alliance being spoken of as if it had already been defeated and destroyed. With Yang Wen-li still in good health, he believed the alliance forces would never give up so easily. More than a belief, it was a creed, as Yang himself had averred. In Julian's mind, Yang Wen-li, democracy, and the Free Planets Alliance were still an indivisible trinity.

Among their fellow passengers—most of whom had been hit with a dart thrown by the goddess of chance with her back turned—Julian was primarily interested in this man known as Degsby, bishop of the Church of Terra. In a short period of time, he'd gone from fanatical puritan to blasphemous libertine, and it was impossible to fathom the spiritual conduit that had led him there. Julian's interest was first piqued when visiting Degsby in his dank hideout with Marinesk. He was also intrigued by the church's political clout, the origins of which still confused him.

And so, Julian left Phezzan as a passenger aboard *Beryozka*. This was half a month before the imperial and alliance forces would clash in the Rantemario Stellar Region, when he would be riding a ship of a different name, as several history books would record it, and touch down on the alliance capital of Heinessen.

CHAPTER 4:

I

MITTERMEIER'S IMPERIAL FLEET continued its charge without attack 2,800 light-years away from Phezzan. While waiting for companion forces in the Porewit Stellar Region, his ships assumed a spherical formation, arranging battleships around a core of transports, ready to receive enemies from all directions.

Porewit had been named after a mythical god of war with five faces because, in addition to a mature sun, the star system boasted four gas giants. Mittermeier knew this from Phezzan's navigation data.

Until they arrived at the Porewit Stellar Region, the alliance bases they'd intended on using for communications, supplies, and combat, despite numbering more than sixty, were considerably insufficient when compared to those near Iserlohn. Most had already been abandoned on orders from the capital, and the Mittermeier fleet passed through various remote stellar regions with the force of a fire burning in an arid desert, holding its breath all the while.

Meanwhile, a side story in the Alliance Armed Forces unknown to Mittermeier involving the JL77 communications base in the Špála star system was unfolding. Even as other bases were being summarily evacuated,

JL77 had become a functional hub. It continued to gather and transmit information about the imperial invasion until just before it happened, by which time its soldiers found it impossible to escape.

JL77 had only two thousand battle personnel. Its firepower was insubstantial, its mobility nonexistent. It hadn't a single battleship to its name. A mere touch of the imperial pinkie would've been enough to squash it like an ant under an elephant's foot. While JL77 bore a huge responsibility as Free Planets Alliance Military Joint Operational Headquarters, to neglect it in the face of adversity would've made those who worked there feel guilty beyond measure. Thirty thousand battle personnel and three hundred battleships were to be dispatched to support them. Nevertheless, when acting base commander Captain Bretzeli received word of these reinforcements, he wasn't exactly jumping with joy.

"I appreciate the gesture," he said with enough courtesy, and rejected the reinforcements outright.

Perhaps anyone but him would've been horrified.

"Does this mean we are to accept our defeat with honor? Surely we can't just pass up this offer?" asked his subordinate, with a pathetic expression on his face.

Bretzeli shook his head.

"It's not so simple. My refusal will ensure our very survival. As it stands now, our existence poses no threat to the empire. The Imperial Navy knows this from all the data they got on Phezzan. The moment we mobilize thousands of battle personnel and three hundred battleships, the empire will be very much aware of our approach. In which case, an enemy who once resolved to let us go will be forced to change its mind. If they want to spare us, I see no point in spoiling their offer."

Bretzeli's foresight was on point. With no apparent need to attack and destroy the defenseless JL77 base, Mittermeier had calmly passed it by. Mittermeier was, of course, no sucker, and wouldn't hesitate to obliterate JL77 at the slightest hint of retaliation.

As Bretzeli put it to his wife the next day:

"To tell you the truth, I don't know whether the enemy let us go or not. But if they'd attacked, thousands would be dead. I'd like to think they chose to spare us. I doubt that kind of charity will ever come our way again."

On January 30, an imperial expeditionary force under Reinhard gathered in the Porewit Stellar Region. Leaving half of their ground forces back on Phezzan, they joined up with the Wittenfeld and Fahrenheit fleets deep in the heart of alliance territory. All told, these forces reached a grand total of 112,700 battleships; 41,900 support ships for supplies, transport, and med bays; and 16,600,000 officers. It was the first time for Reinhard to have such an extensive command in actual combat. Even when he had confronted the alliance, over thirty million strong, at the Battle of Amritsar, his forces had been less than half that number.

As Reinhard and his admirals assembled on the bridge of the imperial flagship *Brünhild*, Mittermeier stood up to deliver his report.

"It's likely the Alliance Armed Forces regards this sector of space as our naval threshold, and it would seem they're preparing for a counterattack or an all-out offensive."

As Mittermeier spoke, the superior intel they'd gathered on Phezzan was put up on several screens. One of the most significant strategic successes of their occupation of Phezzan was the wealth of cartographic information they'd confiscated regarding the alliance's vast territory. With this in their possession, the fruits of total victory were all but guaranteed.

"From the Porewit Stellar Region all the way to Rantemario, we detect no inhabited planets. To avoid bringing harm to its citizens, the alliance will have no choice but to wage battle in this sector. I say this with absolute confidence."

When the Gale Wolf was finished, Reinhard rose to his feet in one flowing motion.

Those who saw him in his uniform couldn't help but imagine that the fashion house originally entrusted to outfit the Imperial Navy had designed this black-and-silver uniform somehow knowing that, in the distant future, a young man would appear whom it would fit so perfectly.

"I think your observations are correct. The alliance forces have managed to hold out this far, but any day now they'll have to go to war to put their people at ease. Rest assured, we'll answer their salutation in kind with a two-headed snake formation."

In response to Reinhard's triumphant declaration, a hot wind of excitement whipped around the admirals.

The two-headed snake was a traditional battle formation often employed by armies in surface combat and now utilized in outer space.

Imagine a giant snake, with a head on either end of its long body. If someone goes in for the kill by attacking one of its heads, the other comes around and bites the aggressor. And if the body is attacked anywhere in the middle, both heads simultaneously strike.

A victory gained by means of this formation would burn a most magnificent and dynamic display of commanding genius into the eyes of the regretful losers.

The catch to using this formation was that it required having numerically superior forces. If one part of the formation were subject to concentrated attack, it had to withstand that attack long enough for the heads to come around. Otherwise, the enemy might breach the entire formation and prevail.

And because flexibility and adaptability were essential, maintaining the snake's functionality was of the utmost importance, especially when it came to communication and maneuvers. If these networks were compromised, soldiers would be forced to look on as their comrades were attacked in the distance.

For this reason, the Imperial Navy's communications network was outfitted with an anti-jamming system. In the unlikely event that this failed, two thousand shuttles with short-distance warping capabilities were readied for backup. Commander in chief Reinhard's leadership was impeccable, and so long as transmission of his commands and the mobility to answer them were possible, victory was sure to be swift. Once that point was settled, the topic of discussion shifted to reassignments.

"It goes without saying that the first division—the first head, if you please—will be commanded by Mittermeier."

At least that's what the admirals had expected him to say, but they doubted their own ears when he commanded otherwise.

"Are you suggesting that *you'll* be commanding the front?" Neidhart Müller rose halfway from his seat. "It's a big risk. The alliance forces may be weakening, but that just increases the likelihood of them fighting like berserkers. I think you should stick to the rear and let us fight."

"In this battle formation, there is no rear, Müller. There's only the second head," Reinhard pointed out coolly.

Müller went silent, and the young dictator untangled his luxurious golden hair with supple white fingers.

"Mittermeier, you command the body. That's where the alliance is sure to attack if it plans on breaking us apart. You will, obviously, be the actual front line."

"But…"

"I came here to win, Mittermeier. To do that, we must fight, and I'm not about to curl up in a corner for my own protection."

After allocating all other assignments, Reinhard motioned for a one-hour recess and walked off as his admirals stood and saluted behind him.

"A warrior to the end."

Mittermeier felt this sentiment more strongly than ever.

"He finds meaning in the victory of battle. No born ruler would be so obsessed with *how* we get there."

As Reinhard walked toward his private room, his elegant cadence was interrupted by a reserved yet determined voice coming from a corner of the hallway. Reinhard swung his piercing gaze to see a boy soldier of thirteen or fourteen with reddish-brown hair standing against the wall. The boy's flushed cheeks and nervous posture gave him an impression of innocence. From his uniform, Reinhard pegged the boy as a cadet in training.

"May I help you?"

"Your Excellency, please forgive my rudeness, but I wanted to ask something of you if I could. Please win, and unite the universe…"

Thoughts of pure, intense admiration and aspiration made the boy's voice tremble passionately. Seeing in the boy a living mirror of himself in the distant past, Reinhard's ice-blue eyes softened. From that same mouth that rebuked grand space armadas came a gentle voice.

"May I know your name?"

"Yes, it's Emil von Selle."

"A fine name. So you want me to win, do you?"

"Yes…I do!"

"Very well. Then you'll understand if I don't leave any enemies behind for you to defeat in the future?"

The young dictator smiled at the boy, who was at a loss to answer. The grace of that smile was something the boy would never forget until he felt the cold hand of death closing his eyes.

"Emil, I will win because you wish for me to win. So that you can go back home alive and tell your family, 'I'm the one who inspired Reinhard von Lohengramm to victory at Rantemario.'"

II

The alliance, which should've held a welcome banquet for the invaders, had no room on its menu for a full-course meal of such high uniformity and integrity as the empire's. That they'd chosen the Rantemario Stellar Region as their decisive battlespace was, of course, the result of a process of elimination.

"The Imperial Navy has gathered the entirety of its forces in the Porewit Stellar Region, and while they're reorganizing, I suspect they'll advance on the capital of Heinessen."

The last information to be sent from the JL77 base, despite the empire's jamming signal, arrived during a joint session between Space Armada Command and Joint Operational Headquarters on the first day of February. Sleep-deprived and impatient, the faces of the high-ranking officers assembled in an underground conference room were pale and streaked with worry lines.

"Assuming they proceed straightaway to Heinessen, they'll pass through the Rantemario, Jamshid, and Kerim stellar regions along the way."

"Do you really think the Imperial Navy would take such a direct route? It's too obvious."

"At this point, the empire has no reason to do otherwise. They're sure to take the shortest route to Heinessen."

"All the planets between Jamshid and here are inhabited. Rantemario, no longer worthy of being called a frontier, is our last line of defense against the enemy."

"That goes for timing, as well."

The timing of which they spoke wasn't purely military. It was also political.

The alliance government had only managed to defend the capital of Heinessen, and fears that they'd forsaken citizens elsewhere were piling in through invisible channels from every stellar region. To make the best of their minimal resources, the plan was to shield Heinessen with their remaining forces and court a decisive battle with an enemy who'd made the long march to get there.

But since a walled city had been built somewhere on the planet's surface, suspicions arose that those in power, hiding behind their precious just cause, were only hogging military power to protect themselves when they should've been safeguarding their citizens. As those suspicions grew and fears intensified, and the alliance government showed no signs of wanting to protect its territories, there was a very real danger of frontier star system governments declaring neutrality in secession from the alliance. One cry of foul might be enough to trigger a chain reaction among the masses, from the mouth of the Phezzan Corridor all the way to the sparsely populated Bharat star system. Neutrality would therefore be something of a misnomer, as each nation hid itself under the empire's coercive umbrella. The alliance had no choice but to secure loyalty by fighting and winning. Such circumstances were difficult for the government to accept, but it was true that they had no excuse if their inability to guarantee the safety of those star systems was thrown back in their faces. Three years earlier, diehards of both the government and military authorities had conspired together to carry out an impulsive invasion of imperial territory, losing the greater part of their military forces at Amritsar, and now they were feeling the pinch of that folly.

Drafting strategies at Joint Operational Headquarters was no longer an option. They'd been forced into a woefully disadvantageous position, swaying on a narrow bridge over a chasm between panic and nihilistic defeatism. And so they'd taken over Space Armada Command instead.

Director of Joint Operational Headquarters, Admiral Dawson, revealed that, through a connection with a government VIP, he'd been given highest military clearance. While he wasn't openly overwhelmed by this, it drained him of his assertiveness and independence, and without orders from the National Defense Committee chairman or counsel from his subordinates, he played things safe. By only approving the documents submitted to him and handling everyday administration, he'd holed himself away in a monomaniacal cell of self-isolation, continuously averting his eyes from impending catastrophe.

The Alliance Armed Forces had inspired everyone to give it their all. No one had asked what might happen if they lost.

.·.   .   •
:   •
.   .   •

After being ordered to carry out a full-frontal attack, proximate in time and distance, the entire military, apart from Dawson, was buzzing with activity. Their narrow tactical objective was easy enough for career soldiers to have real feelings about. Only Yang Wen-li hadn't battled with the empire head-on in the past two years, and everyone found inspiration in their inborn will to fight.

Taking Chung Wu-cheng's advice to delay the battle, Yang Wen-li abandoned Iserlohn and headed for Heinessen to protect his citizens. Chung Wu-cheng had been insistent on the value of Yang's soldiers from the beginning.

Yang relinquished Iserlohn on January 18. He hadn't gone far, but if somewhere along the way he found refuge for his citizens on a suitable planet and hurried toward Rantemario? Chung Wu-cheng had entertained this very possibility and found it difficult to abandon. Assuming all went well, the Yang fleet would reach the Rantemario Stellar Region on February 15. And if they postponed an outbreak of war until then, they could rapidly fortify their forces and oppose the empire. Then again, there was a distinct possibility that imperial forces could pour into the Bharat star system ahead of Yang's arrival, to say nothing of the grand detached imperial force closing in from behind, which meant that while Yang was battling in the Rantemario area, he might end up sacrificing the Bharat star system to an imperial detachment. These risks rendered the plan dead on arrival.

Now at least, the Defense Committee—that is, the alliance government under a different name, and fueled by a fervent leadership unthinkable half a year ago—evacuated the planet Heinessen's urban population into the mountains and forests for their protection and launched its space armada, all while preparing to receive Iserlohn's refugees. The committee also sent out edicts to every star system in support of any planets wishing to surrender to the empire to avoid conflict.

On February 4, the Alliance Armed Forces Space Armada left Heinessen and the Bharat star system. Under Alexandor Bucock's direct command was a core first fleet of 32,900 ships and 5,206,000 soldiers.

The old admiral, who this year would turn 73, received word from the government just prior to launch that he was being promoted to marshal.

"Is this their way of telling me not to come back alive?"

"No, it's probably just out of desperation," came the deadpan reply of chief of staff Chung Wu-cheng, himself newly promoted to full admiral, as he brushed bread crumbs from his chest.

Yang Wen-li, for reasons of his own, didn't look the part of a military man. When he assumed the role of an academy instructor and appeared for inspection in civilian clothes, he was escorted to the rear door of the mess hall by a student who mistook Yang for a food vendor. It was a well-known legend, but because the name of that student was never given, people doubted its authenticity. Either way, a man for whom such a story wasn't surprising was an unlikely candidate for admiral in such times of fading peace.

As the alliance forces approached the decisive battlespace of the Rantemario Stellar Region, their collective nervousness intensified. Those employed in the enemy search and reconnaissance divisions were acutely aware of their enormous responsibility. This awareness alone fueled their stress. Their faces pale and stern, operators betrayed their anxiety by wringing their hands out of sight, under the control panels at their stations.

"It's a shame to see this," said Bucock's new aide.

Said aide was the butt of constant ridicule on the part of his comrades and subordinates, and by no fault of his own. His appearance and demeanor were quite ordinary, but he could accomplish any given task. The reason behind this mistreatment could be traced back to a distant relative, from whom he'd inherited a meager plot of land and with it a uniquely odd surname: Soulzzcuaritter.

His self-identification as such was inevitably followed by a question on how to spell it. And anyone who saw it in writing, without exception, would furrow their brow, wondering how to pronounce it. Moreover, his given name was "Soon," and when he was honored as the head of his class in middle school, every syllable of it was like a knife in his chest.

"Graduating class representative: Soon Soulzzcuaritter!"

That voice still rang in his head, as did the laughter that erupted throughout the hallowed graduation-ceremony hall. Even the principal, who had power to put a stop to it, joined in.

When Soulzzcuaritter entered Officers' Academy, he dreaded the embarrassment of becoming head of his incoming class. This proved to be a needless fear, however, when he became aware of another class representative by the name of Fork. From then on, his career as an alliance military man began in earnest, and in the same way he cursed his ancestors, he himself would come to be cursed by future historians. Not even the most brazenly lazy scholar would disavow that name in the Battle of Rantemario.

The day before the fleet launch, Lieutenant Commander Soulzzcuaritter was appointed as Marshal Bucock's aide because his former aide, Lieutenant Commander Pfeifer, had fallen into in a deep coma after a heart attack and was being kept under observation at a military hospital. The young officer with the strange name who'd frequently helped Pfeifer with military affairs was known for being outspoken, but because of his tireless emergency first aid he grew close to the old admiral. In succession with the alliance's chief of staff, the division's central personnel were exempted from battle and switched out.

The old admiral easily dispensed with the question of the aide's unusual and difficult name and decided on calling him by the first four letters of his fifteen-letter surname. Thus, he was nicknamed "Lieutenant Commander Soul." Much to his delight, this eventually became his official surname. Although it meant profaning his heritage, he was more than happy to avoid the usual insult: "The truth is, he's got three potential fathers, and since no one knows which is the real one, they mashed all three names together to make his last name." As long as he was Lieutenant Commander Soon Soulzzcuaritter, he would never be free from such harassment.

The new aide conveyed his trepidation to the old admiral at 1240 on February 7, after the officers had finished eating their lunch. Bucock, along with chief of staff Chung Wu-cheng and Commander Emerson, captain of the flagship *Rio Grande*, were in the high-ranking officers' mess hall. The chief of staff was clumsy and careless when it came to eating, and so his napkin was ten times as stained as everyone else's. Once, at a party, Yang Wen-li had whispered to Julian Mintz, "He makes even me look refined."

To which Julian had said, "Don't set the bar so low for yourself."

An urgent message from the first reconnaissance ship alerted them to the location of the Imperial Navy, followed by a flood of similar reports. All twelve screens on the ship's bridge were alive with tactical data being relayed to headquarters.

"The empire has assumed the two-headed snake formation? In which case, they'll want us to attack the middle. It's too risky, if you ask me."

Bucock nodded deeply in response to the young aide's advice.

"Perhaps. Well, scratch that—I'm sure you're right. But we have no other strategy to fall back on. We must exploit the enemy's formation to destroy the middle, one fleet at a time."

As he said this, the old admiral sighed at the disparity between their determination to fight and their preparedness to do so. The Imperial Navy was purported to have at least one million ships at its disposal.

"Be that as it may, Duke von Lohengramm didn't earn his reputation as a genius by letting down his guard. He's always been a step ahead of us."

"Which is why Yang Wen-li and all the rest praise his tactical abilities so highly. I wonder if you know what Yang Wen-li said, Lieutenant Commander Soul. I heard it from the man himself: 'Had I been born in the empire, I would've proudly hoisted his flag.'"

"That's a pretty dangerous thing to say, isn't it?"

"How so? I'd do the same. Not that Reinhard would have much use for me, feeble and unskilled as I am," said the old admiral indifferently.

The young aide was perplexed for a moment, then smiled with understanding.

The next day, on February 8, at 1300 hours, the distance between imperial and alliance forces was reduced to 5.9 light-seconds. From the vantage point of the battlespace's zenith, clusters of luminous points indicated the vertical approach of the Alliance Armed Forces toward the midsection of a long, horizontal stretch of imperial vessels curving slightly inward: an arrow aimed straight at the body of a giant serpent.

On approach, however, Bucock reconsidered attacking the middle. The body of the imperial formation was especially well fortified, and even if he could make quick work of breaking through it, Bucock risked being flanked on both sides. Wasn't it easier to let the enemy make the first move, lure them out while fending off their attacks and then destroy each head as it came around?

By 1340, he'd put a new plan into effect. After narrowing the gap between them to 5.1 light-seconds, the first shot was fired five minutes later.

III

The artillery battle was over in thirty minutes. Energy beams and missiles crossed and collided in a mesh of light, spreading out soundlessly in infernal yet beautiful shapes.

Mittermeier's fleet—the snake's body—made the first move. An FTL message ordered a simultaneous advance. All fleets did as they were told, firing continuously. Not to bring about a swift victory, but to demonstrate their firepower and test the enemy's response. Hence Mittermeier's ordinary method of approach. But the sight of grand forces drawing near in countless points of light held a strangely abstract fascination for the alliance's frontline commanders, whose throats constricted with fear. Despite the veteran Bucock's careful insistence that everyone remain on standby, one of his divisions accidentally returned fire. Although oriented toward the imperial forces, most of their shots fell short or fired in random directions. It was enough to incite chaos.

As the alliance pounded away indiscriminately with high-density energy beams and missiles, it didn't seem like it would be enough to breach the massive imperial wall, much to the surprise of both sides. But then, as the imperial defenses reached their threshold, a temporary crack opened. Against all better judgment, the alliance's vanguard scrambled forward, and with bared fangs tore its way through. The imperial forces had been compromised.

Mittermeier stared at the flagship screen and clicked his tongue faintly. Kicking at the polished bridge floor with the heel of his military shoes, he turned to his aide, Lieutenant Commander Amsdorf.

"I'd personally like to ask the devil whether he's making room for the alliance or for us."

Observing the progress of the war on the screen of his flagship *Brünhild*, Reinhard held firm. His secondary aide, Lieutenant von Rücke, broke the silence with a voice of meek admiration.

"I'm surprised that Admiral Mittermeier is being forced back. The alliance has its fair share of courageous fighters, does it not?"

"The alliance is more maniacal than it is courageous," said Reinhard by way of cool correction. "Mittermeier is a matador. It might look like he's being pushed around by the bull when in fact he's conserving his strength and looking for a chance to win. But…"

Reinhard lightly and gracefully inclined his head, muttering to himself through a strained laugh.

"Perhaps he really has been stumped by this attack. Shall I make my move now…?"

Reinhard's observation had hit the mark on both points. Mittermeier was indeed drawing away the alliance forces while fending off their attacks in order to scatter them, but he was amazed by their spiritedness.

He was a fierce tiger being snapped at by, and shrinking back from, a pack of savage hounds that had never known fear. The Imperial Navy might have the upper hand when it came to its commanders' abilities, and in the quality and quantity of its soldiers, but an alliance tendency toward erratic vigor often compromised imperial plans and calculations.

Doubtless, the alliance's attack wasn't just erratic. As they opened all gunports, loosing arrows of light from multiple directions, they barreled at high speed through uninhabited space. Some warships disabled their own anticollision systems, slicing enemy destroyers in two with their hulls. Cruisers volleyed their main artillery into those enemies directly ahead of them, engulfing their own ships in balls of explosive light. This mad rush broke all reasonable rules of self-defense, spreading out a banquet of destruction. Bucock exhausted every medium available to him before seizing control of the main ship's communication channel.

"Fall back! Retreat and rejoin the formation! Haven't you tasted enough blood for one day?"

Drunk with carnage, the alliance fighters at last came to their senses and ceased their rampage, rearranged their ships, and attempted to pull back the war front.

But the imperial forces weren't about to let the alliance quit while they were ahead. Mittermeier's most valiant generals—Bayerlein, Büro, and

Droisen—launched a counterattack with seemingly predetermined precision, their stomachs churning with the scorching lava of revenge. At that
very moment, the large snake, consisting of 150,000 ships, formed a sickle
shape and swooped down on the alliance. The entirety of the imperial
force, five times the size of the alliance's, let out a soundless tremor, like
a dragon waking up atop its pile of gold.

In a grim reversal of fortune, the alliance went from perpetrators of a
slaughter to its victims. They were assaulted from the fore by a glittering
firestorm. From the left, the division under Reinhard's direct control spit
out hundreds of thousands of flaming tongues of pure energy, and from
the right, Müller, Fahrenheit, and Wahlen hurled unrelenting spears of
the same.

The explosions were so bright it was as if the universe was burning to
its ends, and the alliance, now the target of concentrated fire, was being
cremated alive. Even if the outer walls of a ship could withstand the heat
of such an attack, the men inside them couldn't. They were thrown into
walls and onto floors, as well as into the embrace of death by the rapidly
mounting temperatures inside their ships.

Those who died instantly were rather fortunate. For those who suffered
their fatal wounds over the course of minutes until the doors of final
mercy opened to them, their bodies convulsed from the agony of boiling
internal organs in the sludge of their own thrown-up blood, which then
evaporated into white smoke. Melting floors incinerated the bodies of the
living and the dead alike, and a pure-white light bleached out this hor-
rible spectacle as ships were torn asunder in balls of flame. A tremendous
waste of life, materials, and energy spread across the battlespace like a
great wave of futility.

On this day, from 1600 hours to 1900 hours, fighting on both sides
reached peak intensity. The alliance's Dieudonné division, consisting of 840
ships, was reduced to 130 in a mere three hours. Wahlen's fleet attempted
to finish off the Dieudonné division. As Wahlen advanced, cutting in on
the alliance's port side with unceasing fire, he tried to drive a wedge into
its formation. Against Admiral Morton's counterattack, Wahlen held port
and brought about alliance bloodshed through repeated, systematic attacks.

Fahrenheit circumvented the Wahlen fleet and, in a bold maneuver, tried to sneak around to the alliance's rear, but this brought his ships dangerously close to the fixed star of Rantemario, the magnetism and heat of which made their instruments go haywire, and they reluctantly retreated. The alliance, thanks to Bucock's levelheaded commands, escaped an hour-long predicament with its front intact.

"Victory won't come so easily," said Reinhard to himself. "This old man is unyielding. Just like Merkatz."

Reinhard called for his chief aide, Rear Admiral von Streit. Seeing that the battle was deadlocked, he withdrew his forces to avoid unnecessary damage and ordered all officers to take a rest to replenish themselves.

Since the battle had commenced, the soldiers had been repeatedly downing high-calorie biscuits fortified with calcium and vitamins, along with ionized drinks. A presence or absence of appetite revealed a striking dissimilarity between rookies and veterans. The latter made a show of their surplus, blaming the blandness of the food, while the younger officers in their first campaign, out of sheer fatigue, wanted to vomit at the very thought of putting solids in their mouths, and they tolerated the ionized drinks as best they could. Even so, they'd pulled through so far, even as many of their comrades were missing out on their chance to become experienced soldiers.

On February 9, an overwhelming difference between these two military factions emerged. The imperial forces pushed their front lines forward, condensing into a half-encircling ring to overcome the alliance's resistance. The hole in the imperial formation was closed as quickly as it was opened, whereas the one opened in the alliance stayed that way.

Cornered, the alliance abandoned its offensive tactics, going instead on the defensive. Cut by hailing swords of light, discharging energy instead of blood and penetrating armored planks instead of flesh, the alliance forces persevered with all their might. From behind the floating debris of destroyed ships, they rained fire down on their enemies. What particularly made the empire marvel at the alliance's ingenuity was how it used single-seat spartanian fighter craft to lure enemy ships within firing range. While the empire was busy chasing after an enemy they thought was trying to escape in confusion, lethal blows pummeled their engines from behind and above.

Overall, the empire's superiority showed no signs of wavering, but the alliance, strengthening the unity and coordination of its chain of command, needed just one strong blow to turn the tide of the battle into a scenario of mutually assured destruction. A tactician as seasoned as Bucock was determined to win, and not even Mittermeier knew how to read one so focused.

"I guess we have no choice."

Reinhard stared at the screen with his arms crossed, at last summoning his communications officer and, turning his ice-blue eyes on him, giving his command.

"Signal Wittenfeld. Tell him, 'It's your turn now. Hoist the alliance commander's beret on the end of the Schwarz Lanzenreiter's spear and bring it to me.'"

IV

It was 1100 hours on February 9 when the Schwarz Lanzenreiter, boasting incomparable firepower, moved out on the orders of the high commander. Having not received the order to fire the day before, Admiral Wittenfeld wanted nothing less than to watch from the sidelines, but now, letting out an ecstatic whistle, he threw up an arm high before the communications screen and swung it downward.

"The Schwarz Lanzenreiter are on the move."

In response to Vice Admiral Bayerlein's report, Mittermeier vigorously rustled his honey-colored hair with one hand.

"The final hour is close at hand. It appears that Wittenfeld, their best performer, will make an appearance after all."

"What would you have our fleet do?"

"We move to strike. We can't let the Schwarz Lanzenreiter hog all the best meat of our prey."

"You read my mind."

With a broad smile, Bayerlein gave the order to his fleet, encouraging his men to keep pace with the Schwarz Lanzenreiter.

Upon receiving Wittenfeld's dispatch, the Müller, Wahlen, and Fahrenheit fleets grew excited. The imperial troops felt deeply and unanimously that victory was theirs.

An enormous river of excess energy, guided by a constant flow of solar winds and planetary movements, stood in Wittenfeld's way. Wreckage of ships stripped of their mobility and scores of human bodies rendered inorganic floated along its soundless, surging current into the edge of darkness beyond the gravitational pull of the sun. Perhaps in due course it would send that wreckage and those bodies back to where they came from.

This formidable river was nothing Wittenfeld could easily circumvent, but neither was he about to compromise his reputation for bravery. He ordered all ships to advance.

This group of jet-black warships drove boldly into the ferocious current, which disrupted their orderly formation more quickly than he expected.

Seeing this, the alliance's chief of staff, Chung Wu-cheng, shouted at the flagship's operators.

"Figure out the velocity of the imperial fleet's charge and that of the energy current! With the right calculations, we should be able to determine their exit point."

After quickly crunching some numbers, the operators had their answer. The commander in chief's orders flew again, and the alliance prepared to fire upon the Wittenfeld navy's "river crossing."

At 1120, the alliance opened all gunports.

At last, the Schwarz Lanzenreiter ships were spat out on the opposite shore of the rapid energy current, only to be met with a storm rush of beams and missiles. Nuclear fusion explosions went off in succession, and broken warships were thrown into the river of energy from which they'd just surfaced, to be carried downstream.

But the admirals of the Schwarz Lanzenreiter weren't pacifists who embraced the ethos of total nonresistance. They held their own, unsheathing blades of energy and fiercely slashing at the alliance. Beam crossed beam, sending blinding spirals of light streaking across the black sky.

Carbide-steel bullets fired from rail cannons pierced composite armor, and fired photon bullets battered the fleet in haphazard array. Energy beams rushing down at acute angles hit hydrogen-power reactors, sending gun turrets flying and consigning crew members to deadly cyclones of hot wind and radiation.

Using up all their strength at last, the weakening alliance was mowed down like grass by the merciless Schwarz Lanzenreiter. Nuclear fusion detonations overlapped into a giant wall of white-hot light. Within that wall, the alliance's ships exploded into pieces, went up in flames, or sank into spiraling beams of light, only to be erased by the afterglow, crews and all.

"We've taken great damage! Our ship is immobilized."

"Human and material losses are overwhelming. We cannot maintain the front. Requesting permission to retreat."

"Mayday! Requesting immediate assistance!"

These cries for help clogged the alliance's communication channels, but to no avail. Before long, the screams lapsed into silence. Death had prevailed.

"I guess that's that. And so the sun sets, and a general ascends to fame on the bodies of thousands of soldiers."

Marshal Alexandor Bucock stared blankly at the screen. Nearly all of his fleet, along with the bevy of officers under his leadership, had been reduced to atoms as unilateral targets of destruction and carnage. With every blossoming of light, casualties were mass-produced, as were the orphans and widows left by their destruction. Bucock didn't have a single ship or soldier to spare for rescue. Around the flagship *Rio Grande*, thirty cruisers and destroyers at his front and rear were all that was left; the faces of the few survivors were pale with fear.

"I need some time to be alone," murmured the old admiral before leaving the bridge.

Confined in his private room, he removed a blaster and a writing imple-
ment from a desk drawer. Just then, the door, which should've been wire
locked, opened with great force to reveal his chief of staff.

"You mustn't take your own life, Your Excellency Commander. Even
Admiral Merkatz persevered after his loss, did he not?"

Seeing the small unlocking device in Chung Wu-cheng's hand, the old
admiral slowly shook his head. In that gesture was the shadow of his
accumulated fatigue.

"What's the point of a commander living on when his fleet has been
destroyed?"

Chung Wu-cheng closed the device and softened his expression.

"Our forces haven't been completely destroyed. Yang Wen-li's fleet is
still going strong. Even with one last ship to his name, it's a commander's
duty to carry on."

"Are you saying there's a way for me to take responsibility for this defeat
outside of dying?"

The old admiral looked yearningly at the blaster on his desk. Since
they'd suffered proper defeat at the hands of an enemy five times their
size, and with no miracle in sight, there was only one thing left to do, or
so every fiber of his old body told him. But his aide purposefully ignored
the old man's silent speech.

"In committing suicide, you'd only be taking responsibility for your
allies. But I'm talking about the enemy—yes, responsibility to the ones
who gain victory over us."

Those words were unexpectedly clear to Bucock. The old admiral's
gaze broke away from the desk at last and turned toward his forthcom-
ing intruder.

"What I'm about to say may sound inhumane," said Chung Wu-cheng
by way of prefacing his explanation. "If you don't like it, then feel free to
turn that gun on me."

Even if the Free Planets Alliance went down in flames, its national
organization would be allowed to flourish. When things went from
cease-fire to reconciliation by grace of Yang Wen-li's ingenuity, the empire
would hold a trial for war criminals. But if, when that time came, their

highest commander was already dead in action or by his own hand, then those who worked under him would become his scapegoats in the defendant's chair.

At this point, understanding dawned in the old admiral's eyes, and a rather bright expression overtook his aged face.

"Yes, you're right. I'll need this old body to face my enemy's muzzle."

The commander in chief bowed politely, and with reverence.

"Myself and Marshal Dawson included. A military courtroom needs at least three men in uniform to stand trial. Let's not make things harder than they need to be. For the future of the alliance, Yang Wen-li and the others must survive."

Even as they talked about their responsibility and behavior following defeat, the battle was bounding up the final step toward its conclusion.

But behind the imperial forces, which were trying desperately to sustain an all-out attack, a modest yet unusual situation was brewing.

V

The first to notice it were the operators of the cruiser ship *Oberhausen*, attached to the Müller fleet. Having lost more than half of its gun turrets in the heat of a fierce battle, and because the captain had been knocked unconscious by a serious injury, the ship had withdrawn from the front line on the first officer's orders and docked with a repair ship in a safer area of the battlespace. Nevertheless, more ships were spotted approaching from the opposite direction of where the battle raged on.

"Which side are they on?"

It was cruel for the first officer to ask in such a manner that betrayed his lack of concern, especially when victory was almost upon them. But when he sent out a formal identification signal, they were met with energy arrows in return. Because they were far away, they lacked intensity and accuracy and didn't cause much in the way of damage, but it was enough to trick the cruiser into a panic. The tables had suddenly turned.

"Are those fresh troops sent by the alliance?!"

The attack emboldened the empire. The alliance's military power was larger than they'd anticipated. There was plenty of leeway for one division to attack the imperial forces from the fore while another detoured farther afield to cut off the empire's path of retreat.

The very thought of this gave even the empire's leaders, peerless in valor, momentary goose bumps. They'd invaded their way 2,800 light-years deep into enemy territory. The exaltation of conquest and victory had put to sleep the termite of homesickness in their soldiers' mental infrastructures. Once awakened, the house of their success was destined to fall tragically.

"They're cutting us off! Reorganize into battle formation and prepare yourself for the enemy at the rear."

This tense command shot through the empire's command system by whatever media they could mobilize. But what pulled the curtain on their victory was the equal difficulty of reducing their flight speed. The empire's ships were out of formation. Knowing this, the alliance had taken advantage of an ideal opportunity to return fire while falling back, and so they opened all gunports, plotted a new course, and concentrated every beam and missile on the flustered imperial forces.

"Our path to Phezzan is blocked! Now we'll never get back to the empire."

It took Reinhard's rebuke to silence these cries of panic.

"What are you so afraid of?! Who cares if more alliance forces have appeared? We crush them, one by one. Don't lose faith in yourselves! You will retreat in an orderly fashion."

His coolness and courage under fire made for an exquisite blend.

"In the unlikely event that the path toward Phezzan *is* closed off, we just press on to the Bharat star system and put an end to the alliance once and for all. After that, we pass through the Iserlohn Corridor and make our triumphant return to the empire. Does that not put you at ease?"

As Reinhard said this, his firm voice seemed to lift the fog of panic. The soldiers looked up at their sun—that young, undefeated conqueror—and quickly their faith was restored. So long as they had this young man, his hair golden like a lion's mane, they would persevere without ever knowing defeat.

On his comm screen, Mittermeier expressed gratitude for keeping the situation under control.

"I behaved disgracefully. My apologies. We let winning get the best of us and got sloppy. I guess we've gotten so used to victory that we're rusty when it comes to dealing with sudden turnabouts."

Reinhard didn't rebuke him.

"It's understandable. Even I never expected the enemy to have the reserves to pull off such a maneuver. At any rate, this could all just be a diversion, so we'll proceed with caution."

"Roger that. Either way, do you think this is Yang Wen-li's doing?"

Reinhard curled his elegant lips slightly, but enough to reflect his beauty.

"If anyone can pull off something so underhanded, it's that trickster."

Meanwhile, the black-haired commander known as a "trickster" in both Reinhard and von Reuentahl's parlance was assessing the battlespace, by now a giant sea of residual energy, from the bridge of his flagship *Hyperion*.

Were Yang to take on the empire in earnest under present circumstances, he had no chance of success. Waging a futile battle alone was one thing, but to do so as a commander with subordinates under him was the lowest corruption. Yang's goal was to confuse the empire with a large-scale diversion and to prevent total annihilation of the alliance. On that point, Reinhard had correctly discerned his plan.

From Iserlohn, Admiral Yang accelerated, shedding the citizens' transport ship under Caselnes's command along the way. He made a stopover in the Bharat star system and, without wasting time on orders, arrived faster than even Reinhard had anticipated.

"But we're half a day late. I guess I'm losing my touch."

Yang was dipping his feet up to the ankles in a pond of self-admonition. And while the possibility of Reinhard von Lohengramm successfully carrying out an invasion from the Phezzan Corridor hadn't escaped him, his formulation of countermeasures had again been forestalled.

The Imperial Navy had been led to believe that the alliance had a secret naval force lying in wait, that it meant to cut off the empire's path to Phezzan, and that this had been done to disperse the imperial forces via dis- and misinformation. Duke von Lohengramm, genius that he was, had seen through their plan, which nevertheless had bought them some time. And yet, why hadn't he informed Commander in Chief Bucock or Chief of Staff Chung Wu-cheng beforehand? Had he done so, they might've fought differently…

Yang shrugged his shoulders.

"It was too close to call," he muttered.

Wasn't convincing himself that his presence could have changed things a case of overestimating his abilities? Yang had to tell himself that he'd done his best this time. Even in the worst-case scenario, with Bucock and the rest annihilated, he might still waltz into the battlespace, crushing every target in his path. And now that he'd saved the alliance from certain doom and the empire was retreating, he had to restore his forces, return to the Bharat star system, and protect the defenseless capital from being consumed by von Reuentahl's forces.

"All ships, set course for the capital at once!" ordered Yang, feeling overworked.

He, too, had been frustrated by Reinhard and couldn't afford to yield himself to simple pleasures.

At last, the remaining divisions of a stubbornly overwhelmed alliance consolidated themselves around the Yang fleet. Communications were carried out without delay. Yang inquired about the old admiral Bucock's safety and was relieved to see a familiar white-haired figure on his comm screen.

"I made it, but not without sacrificing my subordinates in vain."

"What are you saying? You must move on and take command for our battle of revenge."

Yang entrusted the last defenses to Admiral Fischer and made haste to the capital of Heinessen. Then, as Fischer began his retreat while pretending to change course in pursuit of the imperial forces, an approaching imperial destroyer was detected on their radar. The Fischer fleet nervously sent out a signal—"Stop your ship. If you don't, we will open fire"—but the answer was most unexpected.

"This is Julian Mintz of the Free Planets Alliance, Phezzan detachment. We commandeered this imperial ship. We stand against the empire. Requesting permission to be escorted to the alliance capital of Heinessen."

Hardly believing their ears, the communications officers quickly apprised Admiral Fischer of the situation.

"This is unexpected. Julian Mintz? Then he's safe?"

Fischer's voice was filled with wonderment, but, ever the skillful commander, he exercised caution in welcoming the oncoming destroyer. He considered the possibility of subterfuge—that Julian Mintz was unknowingly abetting the enemy. While the warship kept its main battery locked on the destroyer, the sixty men under Lieutenant Piazzi, armed to the teeth, confirmed that the communication from Julian was genuine. The report flew to the capital over the FTL hotline.

Olivier Poplin muttered to himself when he saw it.

"So, he commandeered an enemy destroyer? That bastard sure is quick."

⁘　　•

"Seems there really is such a thing as a natural enemy."

Reinhard was talking to himself while, on his screen, the imperial forces were halfway restored to order. The aura of something more than anger wavered across his white face.

Reinhard thought back to when he had vanquished an enemy twice the size of his fleet in the Astarte Stellar Region, and again an alliance thirty million strong at Amritsar. In both instances, the one who'd warded off total victory at the last possible second was Yang Wen-li. Just after the Battle of Amritsar, Reinhard had reprimanded Admiral Wittenfeld in front of everyone for misjudging the timing of their attack, thus attesting to Yang's renown in the process. He'd tried to have Wittenfeld punished, but it took his late redheaded friend Siegfried Kircheis to nip his rage in the bud. Kircheis spoke plainly, saying that Reinhard was only angry with himself and that Wittenfeld had become the unfortunate object of his self-projection. He demanded that Reinhard reflect on his actions.

"Kircheis, if only you were here, we wouldn't let Yang Wen-li strut his stuff out in the open."

Again, Reinhard found himself speaking to a dead man. The elegant dictator told himself he couldn't afford to lament the dead, but the sentiment blew through the void in his chest, and nothing remotely constructive came forth in return. When he lost his thoughts of Kircheis, Reinhard knew he would lose the most temperate and clearest days of his past. This fear outweighed all reason and self-interest.

The imperial forces left the battlespace, traveling 2.4 light-years to the Gandharva star system, where they made planetfall on Urvashi. Gandharva's second planet had a meager population of approximately 100,000, undeveloped land, and vital water resources. At one time, a planetary-development corporation had acquired enormous land shares, which they'd quickly lost in a race for monopolistic development, and for a long time the land had been left as is. Reinhard planned to put it to good use by building a semipermanent military base on it. In the future, when all alliance territory had fallen into his hands, this anonymous planet would serve as a significant base of operations for suppressing military insurrection and piracy.

CHAPTER 5:

I

EXTANT RECORDS PERTAINING TO THE DAYS of February, SE 799, are extremely shoddy. Memories of that time are jumbled, the data inconsistent. Every account tells a different story:

"The people, trying to avert their eyes from an impending catastrophe, were flooding the pleasure quarters, and cases of alcohol poisoning and injuries from drunken brawls were rampant. The streets were cloaked in a fog of hysteria."

"Even in the normally tumultuous pleasure quarters, for those few days it was quiet as an old elephant lying down near water to die. The silence was broken by a trumpet signaling their destruction."

"Despair was suffocating the people. The air was so heavy as to be almost solid."

"Political and military adversity didn't necessarily have an influence on people's everyday lives. Music and other entertainments were, if anything, more vibrant than ever."

Ultimately, vast regional and personal differences, along with lack of resolution, were cause for great confusion and inconsistency.

The people tried their best to enjoy a nice tall drink of optimism, but there were too many unknowns floating in their glasses. In any case, their best-fortified space fleets had suffered crushing defeat, and the capital of Heinessen was about to fall into enemy hands. Other star systems were barren, abandoned to the enemy.

Crouched at the bottom of a valley of pessimism and indulging in tears of self-pity, the people still had one ray of hope to cling to. Miracle Yang and his fleet were still going strong, now fortified five times over. In addition, reports that Yang's adopted charge, Julian Mintz, had commandeered an imperial destroyer and repatriated from Phezzan fanned the flames of the people's naive hero worship.

"Only a protégé of Marshal Yang could've done such a thing. Whatever devilry he used, he's as cunning as his mentor."

Two hours after setting foot on Heinessen, Yang had been awarded a promotion to marshal. Only to Yang, who wasn't without misgivings about being criticized for abandoning Iserlohn Fortress, was it unexpected. Chief of Staff Chung Wu-cheng was of the same mind, thinking that the opportunity to treat human rights as a plaything was something one made best of only out of desperation.

Either way, at age thirty-two, Yang had become the youngest fleet marshal to ever represent the alliance. The previous record had been set by Admiral Bruce Ashby at age thirty-six, and because his was posthumous, once again Yang had rewritten history, although he was, of course, never one to be innocently happy.

"I'm not so modest that I would turn down this honor, but I'm not exactly thrilled to receive it, either. I suppose I'll share it with Admiral Bucock."

Under the auspices of his new title, Yang rode in a landcar sent for him by the chairman of the Defense Committee and headed for the committee's headquarters. Not even a year ago, he'd ridden in an official committee vehicle just like this as a defendant and been treated almost like a prisoner, but now he was a guest of honor. He was joined by two fellow passengers: "Vice Admiral" Walter von Schönkopf and "Lieutenant Commander" Frederica Greenhill. By including even "Vice Admiral" Alex Caselnes as a placeholder, the Defense Committee was clearly trying to make up for its stagnation of human resources in one go.

The three of them entered the Defense Committee building. Showered with gazes of anticipation, they were welcomed into the chairman's office. Despite being already aware of Chairman Islands's transformation—considerably revitalized as he was in mind and body under pressure of an enormous crisis—they couldn't help but be impressed, even if they harbored cynical misgivings about just how long this would last. After offering the three of them a seat, Islands caught Yang with a gaze that put him at ease.

"Admiral, I love my homeland in my own way," he said.

Yang knew this already. Nevertheless, he couldn't bring himself to respect it unconditionally. His face twitched slightly, prompting a devilish smile from von Schönkopf.

As far as the human spirit and history were concerned, Yang didn't think patriotism held any supreme value. The people of the alliance felt patriotic for the alliance, while those of the empire felt patriotic for the empire. In the end, patriotism justified only the uniqueness of the flag to which one saluted. It was used to validate slaughter, was sometimes coercive, and was in most cases incompatible with reason. When the elite weaponized it, the extent of its harm was unimaginable. When Islands spoke of love for his country as Trünicht's henchman, Yang wanted to be anywhere else but there listening to it.

"If you love this nation as much as I do, Marshal, then I hope you'll be willing to collaborate with us."

It was the type of reasoning that Yang detested the most, but he couldn't avoid being entangled in the threads of this situation, and so he only expressed meek affirmation. At least Islands, who until now had been nothing but an insubstantial political contractor since awakening to consciousness as a patriotic public servant, saw no need to throw water on these helplessly rising flames.

"I'll certainly do my best to protect the fruits of our democracy."

Yang had been careful to say nothing about his "nation." As it was, he barely struck a balance between formality and sincerity. The chairman nodded.

"And I—no, the government—will reward your efforts. If there's anything we can do, don't hesitate to ask."

"For the time being, I'd only like you to consider what happens if we lose. If we win, we'll be able to rest on our laurels for quite some time. After that, we'll carry out peaceful diplomacy and replenish our forces. Such things are within the purview of politicians and are not for a military man to meddle with."

"Would it be foolish to ask you to promise that you'll win?" Islands asked.

"If I could promise my way to victory, I'd promise anything, but…" Yang tried not to sound heartless, despite the heartlessness of his remark. But Yang spoke the truth. Lacking the ability to shape the world through words, he couldn't very well make promises about a future unregulated by his opinions alone.

"Indeed. How foolish of me. I'd be grateful if you would just put what I said out of mind. I would never presume to restrict you in any way."

Upon being shown such deference, Yang sensed this man was trying to milk hope for all it was worth.

"If we're ever going to make up for our strategic inferiority by means of a tactical victory, I can see only one way."

Yang stopped here for a moment. Not for dramatic effect, but because he needed a drink to lubricate his throat. The glass of iced tea placed in front of him when he came in was empty. Yang felt awkward asking for a refill, but an untouched glass was slid across the table to him as Frederica gently pushed hers over to Yang. Yang opened the curtains of hesitation and gratefully accepted her goodwill.

"Namely, to kill Duke Reinhard von Lohengramm in battle."

As Yang spoke, glass in hand, a momentary confusion contorted the chairman's face. It seemed it was too obvious a thing to have said. Before that confusion could rewrite "despair" on its name tag, Yang geared the conversation toward the crux of his argument.

"Duke Reinhard von Lohengramm is a bachelor. I aim to exploit that."

This time Chairman Islands stared back at the marshal, as if being shown the path of reason. Even a guardian angel awakened to its task had not the discernment to extract the true intentions behind this surprising statement. Naturally, Yang had every intention of spelling it out for him.

"In other words, if in death Duke von Lohengramm were to leave behind a wife and children, especially a male heir, his subordinates would simply groom that heir to further the Lohengramm Dynasty. But he has no children. If he dies, the Lohengramm order dies with him. The loyalty and unity of his subordinates will inevitably lose cohesive power and dissolve into thin air. They will return to the empire at a loss as to whom they might fight for and will argue violently about a successor," Yang said.

Islands's eyes—those eyes which had for so long been focused on factional infighting, office seeking, and concessions—shone with the light of understanding and admiration. Driven by a comfortable stimulation, he nodded repeatedly.

"Of course, you're right, Marshal! The planets cannot live without their sun. With his death, the empire will fall apart and the alliance will be saved."

Never had Islands in his lifetime so fervently and truly wished for the death of another human being. Yang went on:

"If we can somehow break imperial forces apart and destroy them one at a time, then Duke von Lohengramm, being a man of great courage and ambition, will come for me directly. That's the opportunity we need to create. It's our only chance at winning."

"If his subordinates are taken out one by one, then he'll have no choice but to show himself. Yes, it makes sense."

"Well, it's more a matter of psychology than tactics."

Yang solemnly crossed his arms. Reinhard von Lohengramm wasn't holing himself up contentedly within his palace, but standing at the head of a military force in want of danger and hardship. Had this luxuriously golden-haired young man merely been a soldier, he would only be looking for a fight. And if he were merely a ruler, then he would only desire victory. Reinhard valued both fighting *and* winning, and more than anything else. And wasn't this, thought Yang, one reason why he was the supreme ruler of supreme rulers?

Yang was confident that Reinhard would show himself but couldn't say for sure until it happened. He might corner Reinhard into a compromising position for five minutes and, if he was lucky, face that brilliant war genius head-on. Moreover, he would first have to fight and defeat Reinhard's veteran generals in succession. On a tactical level, he had no doubts about the uncommon difficulties ahead. The heterochromatic von Reuentahl and "Gale Wolf" Mittermeier: the involvement of these two alone made Yang feel weary.

We'll try our best to avoid Mittermeier and von Reuentahl at all costs. We mustn't compromise our performance by wasting too much mental energy on them, thought Yang.

Chemical elements of masochism and narcissism existed only below the waterline of his spirit, and so he wasn't poisoned by the notion that "playing against stronger opponents only makes you stronger," which confused combat with sports. If Yang had to fight, then he might as well do it efficiently—which was to say, with as little effort as possible. If forced into battle against Mittermeier and von Reuentahl, winning would come at a great expense of energy and time.

Cold light cast a faint shadow at Yang's feet. As he left the room, glancing sullenly at the movements of that shadow, a voice of grave doubt reverberated in his brain. Narrow-mindedness and false patriotism aside, hating someone just because they looked up to a different flag was about as foolish as believing in one's own. But did that justify Yang's position? Was it possible for people to throw themselves and others into the crater of war without madness? And Yang had an even graver doubt, which was...

Suddenly, a figure appeared before the three of them. Yang was deep in thought when he noticed that von Schönkopf had drawn his blaster and rushed in front of Yang. There stood a man who identified himself in a metallic voice as a reporter on assignment. His request was clearly rehearsed.

"Admiral Yang, please promise all of the citizens of the alliance—right here, right now—that you'll save our country and our people from the bloodied hands of those fiendish invaders, that justice will prevail over evil when Armageddon comes, that you'll answer our citizens' hopes with victory. Please promise us. Or can't you?"

Although the door to Yang's emotions was secured with a lock of endurance, by now it was ready to pop off. He turned to face the intruder and was on the verge of giving him a piece of his mind when a much calmer voice came to his aid.

"His Excellency the Marshal is tired, and we're not at liberty to discuss anything remotely related to classified military information. If you want us to win, then I ask that you please understand this and leave us be."

Something in Frederica's hazel eyes made the man stand back. Von Schönkopf pushed the reporter aside. If not for her quick wits…

II

No one objected when Julian Mintz was promoted to sublieutenant. Defending his superior, Phezzan's resident commissioner Henslow, he'd managed to escape from enemy territory and take an imperial destroyer by force. If one achievement was worth a rise in rank, then no one would've been surprised to see him promoted two steps up to full lieutenant, but as an apparent formality, this was substituted with a "Freedom Fighter" medal.

In any case, the emergence of a hero too young for his own good was all the rage among a certain journalistic sector. One e-paper wrote, "Marshal Yang recognized Sublieutenant Mintz's prodigy from an early age and took him on as an adopted son," but such words were quintessentially exaggerated. The young hero in question wasn't very sociable with those praising him.

"I believe that I—or, more accurately, the tactic I employed—will be extremely effective when the alliance battles future invaders. Therefore, please understand that disclosing any details before our decisive battle with the enemy would only offer them an advantage."

With that one page torn from Frederica Greenhill's book of reasoning, Julian shored up a broken levee of one-sided, irresponsible news coverage. When he was at last released from the press, Julian hoped he might reunite with those he'd left behind on Iserlohn, but all he knew was that Vice Admiral Caselnes was in a three-legged race trying to process all refugees. Julian was riding the beltway, thinking he might have to go back to the official residence on Silverbridge Street if he was going to meet Yang, when a woman's voice called out his name. His heart skipped a beat when he turned to see Frederica Greenhill's golden-brown hair. A few pedestrians were clearly annoyed at her for blocking a fast lane.

"Welcome back, Julian. Seems you've grown into quite the hero."

"Thank you. But even though the admiral will be glad I'm back, I don't think he'll be so happy about me being put on such a high pedestal."

"Are you saying he might be jealous, Julian?"

In contrast to Frederica's shapely lips, her hazel eyes didn't seem to be smiling. Julian stared back at her, unable to answer right away, and his heart and lungs went all out of order.

"Not a chance. The thought never crossed my mind."

"Good. If it had, I would've given you a good slap, like this," she said, miming it. "I was known for my quick hands when I was little."

Yet again, Frederica had succeeded in surprising the alliance's boyish hero. Frederica smiled at Julian's face, which betrayed his disbelief.

"Since entering the military, I've had to be more ladylike. It hasn't been easy."

"I wouldn't know it to look at you."

"Why, thank you."

Brushing back her golden-brown hair, Frederica told him that it had been arranged for Yang to stay at the Hotel Capricorn, near the Defense Committee building. And so, on February 13, Julian was at last able to reunite with Yang at a dreary hotel reserved for military personnel. When Julian opened the door, Yang's nostalgic voice welcomed him.

"Hey, Julian. Take a look. It's like my heart, and the ways of our age."

Yang was pointing at a table piled indiscriminately, and without regard for aesthetics, with sausage, eggs, fried fish, mashed potatoes, and meat-balls. Julian reverted to his old stern criticisms.

"You won't find many marshals eating such crude meals at any point in history."

"I agree. Now that I'm a marshal, my pension will be higher, so let's go out to eat in celebration of our reunion, shall we?"

"I'd be delighted. All things considered, you're as particular as ever about your finances."

"Naturally. I won't get paid anything if the alliance government ceases to exist. I fight the empire to guarantee a stable retirement. I'm nothing if not consistent."

"At any rate, congratulations on your promotion."

"Your promotion to sublieutenant is far more impressive than mine to marshal," Yang said.

Yang grabbed a topcoat sprawled across the large sofa and looked at the flaxen-haired boy with warm, dark eyes.

"I'm glad you got back safely. You've really done well for yourself. Even sprouted a few centimeters to show for it. You're coming into your own."

"No way, I'm barely half a man," answered Julian, meaning every word. "I still have a lot to learn from you."

"I don't think there's anything left for me to teach."

Yang threw on his coat and headed out the door. Julian followed close behind, rushing down the dimly lit hallway.

"If anything, I want *you* to teach *me*. What kind of sorcery did you use to commandeer an imperial destroyer?" Yang asked. "I know it's classified, but you *will* tell me, won't you?"

The pleasantness of Yang's tone indicated he'd seen the solivision report. Because he was also fed up with impudent journalists, dealing with Julian gave him hope again, but Julian only blushed.

They made their way to an old standby, the March Rabbit. It was packed when they arrived. The old waiter grinned as Yang congratulated the restaurant on its continued success.

"Thanks to you. Despite these uncertain times, a society without restaurants and hotels is no society at all. Skillful chefs are always in demand. Maybe it's imprudent for me to say so, but I can't be bothered to worry about the war and our ruined nation."

"Here, here," said Julian.

Yang, who had never aspired to become a military man, nodded enthusiastically and ordered roast beef for his main dish. He'd wanted to make a display of originality, but the deterioration of interstellar distribution meant there weren't enough ingredients to make a variety of dishes.

"Now then, Sublieutenant Mintz, I'd like to hear all about your heroic deeds over dinner."

"Please don't make fun of me. I just put to practical use the same method you did to take over Iserlohn Fortress."

"Hmm, put to practical use, did you? I should've copyrighted it. A pension plus royalties…"

Thinking this didn't sound like a joke at all, Julian began his tale.

When planning his escape from Phezzan, most vexing for Julian was the Imperial Navy's erratic behavior. He had no idea when they might show the true nature of their military rule by cracking down on civilian ship traffic.

Marinesk had confidently assured them that they were okay on that front. At the time, the empire had yet to bring all civilian routes under control. The reason for this was twofold. First, from a political standpoint, they'd failed to gain the popular sympathy of military-occupied Phezzan. For this reason, they abolished direct rule and groomed former landesherr aide Nicolas Boltec to be governor-general of a sham democracy. With stricter management in place, they prevented a rebellion among the merchants.

"I see. And the other reason?" asked Julian.

Marinesk winked.

"Because it's physically impossible."

However extensive the imperial forces were, they paled in comparison to the scope of Phezzan's population and economic activity. There was no way to control it all, and if done carelessly, circulation of money and goods would stagnate, resulting in a Phezzanese uprising.

It was in this climate that Julian and the others made their escape, although when their ship left the planet, Julian was prepared for the worst. Because he wasn't involved in a peaceful business in a peaceful time, he had no reason to feel 100 percent confident about their safety. They only acted by a combination of the resourcefulness of Marinesk, the pilot Wilock, Warrant Officer Machungo, and himself, along with a little fate for good measure. Or maybe fate had played a bigger role than all their planning combined.

Indeed, even a man attentive to every little detail like Marinesk had overlooked one thing: the existence of a traitor in his midst. Acting governor-general Boltec felt it necessary to demonstrate his loyalty to the empire first, sending his own subordinates in imperial patrol ships to police those routes under imperial surveillance and making them participate in imperial raids. As he saw it, determining Landesherr Rubinsky's whereabouts would serve the empire's needs and increase the stability of his position. He was beyond enthusiastic. Historically, collaborators of occupied nations were always more capable than the soldiers occupying them in the lowly work of surveilling and unmasking civilians. Before Julian and the others made their escape, Boltec had discovered more than two hundred stowaways from thirty ships and had them all detained. Among them, as Julian subsequently learned from data on board the imperial destroyer, was the alliance's military attaché, Captain Viola.

"It seems I underestimated things."

When Marinesk said this, examining the classified information from other ships, a week had passed since leaving Phezzan behind. There was no turning back now. They continued to avoid the empire's surveillance network. Considering all the Phezzanese collaborators lurking about, even forged passports wouldn't serve them. But before they could decide on a backup plan, the operators announced the approach of an imperial destroyer. Marinesk looked at Julian with dejection.

"I wish I could've been more reliable. Forgive me, but I guess this is where it ends."

"Not so fast. There's still a chance we might get away with this."

When Yang had occupied Iserlohn Fortress without spilling a single drop of his comrades' blood, Julian was still fourteen and not even a legitimate military man, but he had learned two lessons from Yang's exemplary success: First, when your enemy cannot be captured from the outside, you do it from the inside. Second, your enemy will always hold hostage the most important member of your crew. Julian's train of thought ran at full speed. Within five minutes he had a plan, and for the next three he explained it to a group of fellow passengers.

"Well then, let's give it our best shot," he added at the end, consciously adopting a Yang-like air of composure.

There was no guarantee his proposal would work, but it was their only hope, and so it was accepted.

When the imperial destroyer *Hamelin IV* ordered the suspicious civilian ship to stop, its captain was informed that stowaways on board had tried to take over the ship and that the only reason they'd changed course was to make contact with *Hamelin IV*. *Beryozka*'s administrative officer, Marinesk, implored them to take these dangerous elements—regular and noncommissioned alliance officers alike—off their hands as soon as possible. Cautiously, the destroyer's captain confirmed the information that came up on his comm screen and, during docking, had the "dangerous elements" brought aboard his ship.

"Which one of you is the alliance officer who planned the hijacking?"

As Julian was pulled forward, his flaxen hair disheveled, his face dirty, and his clothes torn, the captain lifted his eyebrows in an affected manner.

"Well, this is surprising. You're still a kid. Looks like the alliance is scraping the bottom of its human resources barrel."

The captain let out a scornful laugh that would never reach its coda. The boy's wrists, which appeared securely shackled in electromagnetic handcuffs, shot up, pushing him from under the chin. Moments later, the captain's body had fallen to the floor. While he was pinned down by the boy, three of his bodyguards were thrown against the wall by Machungo's pillar-like arms. A fourth leapt back from Machungo's whirling attack, readying his gun, but a beam shot from the side caught his right calf. He let out a scream and fell to floor, writhing in pain. The shot came from the gun that captain Wilock had once had trained on Julian.

Thus, the destroyer *Hamelin IV* was taken over by an unlawful gang.

But the victors weren't ready to celebrate just yet. They still had to be careful of other imperial forces and take precautions accordingly. Julian and the others transferred over to the destroyer and left *Beryozka* empty. Marinesk was sad, but it was an unavoidable consequence of their success: *Beryozka* would have to be sacrificed.

They set the ship on autopilot, and after giving out three warning signals, Julian apologized in his heart, blowing *Beryozka* to atoms. After making a convincing show of it for the eyes of the Imperial Navy, the moment he entered alliance territory, Julian evicted the destroyer's crew and put them on a rescue shuttle, inside of which sat the Phezzanese collaborator. At first, looking at the image on the comm screen, he confirmed the faces of Marinesk and the others. Wilock and friends had every intention of killing this man who'd become a hunting dog for the empire, but Julian was hesitant to take the life of an unarmed man. Julian provided them with food and water and had set a time-release lock to open communications after forty-eight hours. Otherwise, the evicted crew might never have been able to contact the Imperial Navy for pickup. Such was the meticulousness of Julian's technique. After that, his only aim was to link up with the alliance.

Everything was far from over. Marinesk kept stressing that the destroyer now belonged to the *Beryozka* crew and readied himself for a lawsuit with the alliance…

III

As Julian narrated these events, the meal progressed to a dessert of cranberry pie and black tea.

"We should compensate Marinesk somehow. For his cooperation above and beyond."

Yang was generous enough to think he should be the one to provide that compensation. And on that front, Yang had succeeded in the most daring way. Now it was Julian's turn to ask questions.

"So, you handed Iserlohn Fortress back to the empire? I'm sure you had some ulterior motive for doing so, but can you tell me what that was?"

"It was nothing, really. I just set a trap is all."

Yang wasn't being particularly modest. The explosives were a diversion, and when Yang told him his plans, Julian shrugged his shoulders.

"That's underhanded, even for you. If it works, the empire will no doubt kick itself. You're a wicked man."

"Fine with me. I'll take that as the highest compliment."

Yang's expression changed slightly.

"The only ones who know about this are von Schönkopf, Lieutenant Commander Greenhill, and now you. Maybe it'll amount to nothing, but remember it just in case."

Julian was glad to know it, but when he was asked about the rest of his journey, he remembered something important.

"I got to know two, and only two, remarkable people. One directly, the other indirectly, and who's now on Heinessen. An old acquaintance of yours, apparently."

"Oh, is she pretty?"

Yang's comment was only slightly serious.

"It's a he: Boris Konev. Do you know him?"

"Boris Konev…?"

He held his knife in midair, digging through the mines of his memory, but nowhere in the ore he came up with was that name carved. Yang discovered it, at last, deep down the tunnel when Julian mentioned he was a childhood friend.

"Ah, *that* Boris. Now I remember him."

"I hear that senility starts with not being able to remember people's names."

"Who are you calling senile? I'm only thirty-one," said Yang, unabashedly shaving off a year, and thrusting a fork into his cranberry pie. "It's only because you called him by his full name, Boris Konev, that I couldn't remember. If you'd called him 'Boris the troublemaker,' then I'd have known who you were talking about."

"He was that bad?"

"Sure was. He made everyone cry. His parents, his friends, you name it. He was a first-rate hooligan, a real nuisance. He always got in my way."

"Really?" said Julian sarcastically. "According to Marinesk, Boris was able to pull off his numerous pranks only because of his excellent partner in crime."

"I'm sure I'll run into Konev one of these days. Now, who was the second person?"

Yang's attempts at glossing over his complicity weren't exactly convincing, but Julian didn't pursue the matter.

"The other was a man by the name of Degsby, a bishop of the Church of Terra. He claimed that he was no longer a clergyman, that he was an apostate, but…"

"There must've been a reason for his self-abasement."

Julian told Yang what Degsby had told him. Yang learned for the first time of the conflict between Landesherr Rubinsky of Phezzan and his son and aide Kesselring.

I see, thought Yang. *So that's why they were playing out their secret feud behind the scenes.* Even so, for a son to try killing his father, only to have the tables turned on him, was like something out of a medieval court tragedy. None of which explained, however, why it was possible for a bishop to have such insider knowledge of Phezzan's elite. It seemed the Church of Terra's relationship with alliance leaders ran deep, but perhaps its relationship with Phezzan ran deeper still. Did the rhizome of the Church of Terra branch out that far?

"Yes, there was. Degsby left me with something before he died. He said that the origin of all these events lay in Terra and its church, and that I had to look to Earth if I wanted to know the truth behind the past and the present."

Degsby had breathed his last just after being transferred from *Beryozka* to *Hamelin IV*. It felt more like protracted suicide. The color of his skin and the breakdown of his internal organs were sure signs of alcohol and drug abuse. Perhaps he'd been tortured by the pain, but to Julian it seemed he'd been submitting to that abuse as punishment for his apostasy. When the bishop was given a space burial, Julian couldn't help but feel for him.

"So, everything is on Earth," muttered Yang, turning his teacup in both hands and warily observing the squall clouds rising from the horizon of his heart.

"He also told me this: humanity must never forget its obligation and debt to Earth."

It seemed this was what Degsby had most wanted to say. Yang was still observing and analyzing the rain clouds but nodded at Julian's words all the same.

"It's a sound argument. But righteous awareness doesn't always lead to righteous action. Julian, our civilization began about seven thousand years ago in a corner of a small planet called Earth."

"In the East, was it?"

"Yes. Some theories postulate the existence of an unknown advanced civilization before that, but either way, the continuity of history tells us that the ancient world was the womb of our current space civilization."

As the failed student of history spoke, his thoughts as a strategist were working busily in his head. He couldn't very well discount what the bishop had said as delusional rambling.

"But even just on the surface of this one planet called Earth, the political, economic, and cultural center has shifted over time. Ever since humans have ventured into outer space, that center has unavoidably moved off planet."

Yang guessed that the Church of Terra's disciples were involved in extra-religious activities with the goal of restoring sovereignty of humanity to its rightful throne on Earth. That was what the deceased, using the grandest terms he allowed himself, had been trying to convey. He'd detected in Julian the secret fragment that he wanted him to know.

"Julian, compared to those who built the first towns on the banks of the Tigris and Euphrates, we haven't developed that much mentally. But, right or wrong aside, our knowledge has increased and our limbs have grown too much for us to return to our cradle. It's unthinkable that Earth should restore its supremacy by means of some conspiracy."

Despite thinking this way, there was nothing he could do about it.

"Then we should just leave Earth to its own devices?" Julian asked.

"No, I wouldn't go that far."

Yang urgently opened the directory of his brain, drawing a red line on a certain page.

"I'll have Bagdash look into it. Such things are more up his alley than fighting."

Thus, his intelligence staff, who'd been idling about for two years on Iserlohn Fortress, were given a significant task for the first time in ages.

"In the meantime, I'll have him get in touch with those from the Phezzan commissioner's office still left here on Heinessen. With his quick wits, he'll at least catch the tail of that poisonous snake."

"Captain Bagdash…"

What Julian had said was neither a question nor a confirmation, but a humble objection. Bagdash was a member of Yang's field staff headquarters, but his participation had no small pretext. Two years ago, when a group of militant diehards known as the Military Congress for the Rescue of the Republic brought about a coup d'état with the goal of establishing military dictatorship, it was Bagdash who'd smuggled them into Yang's fleet to assassinate him. But his intention had been readily detected, and Bagdash had betrayed his comrades to profess his loyalty to Yang.

"There's no one else."

Julian relented. By way of changing topics, he asked about Yang's strategic plot to bring down Reinhard von Lohengramm. Yang opened his heart to Julian in a way he hadn't when speaking to Chairman Islands.

"Even if I succeed, I wonder what kind of historical significance it'll have. What I mean is, while defeating Reinhard von Lohengramm by force and dissolving the empire will surely benefit the Free Planets Alliance, what will it mean for the rest of humanity?"

Julian had thought that getting rid of a dictator should benefit all of humanity for a long time to come, but Yang didn't buy into such reductive optimism. Yang rustled his unruly black hair.

"It would obviously be a major blow to the people of the empire. They'll demand a ruler of powerful reform, which will likely be followed by governmental breakdown. And if—no, *when*—things go bad, you can be certain there'll be civil war. The people will become victims of one another. It's a harsh story. Must we do this just to get some short-term peace for the alliance?"

"But why concern ourselves to that extent? I think we'd do best to leave the empire's business to the empire."

Yang was disappointed to hear this.

"Julian, don't ever think that just because you're fighting against another nation you shouldn't care about what happens to its people."

"I'm sorry."

"No, don't apologize. It's just that when you look at things through the prism of nationhood alone, your field of vision narrows and you lose sight of things farther away. You should really stop distinguishing between friend and foe as much as possible."

"Okay, I'll try."

"Things will only get harder from here, but they say it's always darkest just before dawn."

"That's a famous saying of our founding father, Ahle Heinessen, isn't it? He was cheering on his comrades when they escaped from the Altair star system in ships of natural dry ice to embark on a long march of ten thousand light-years."

"So it's said, but who knows if any of that ever really happened? It's something that any revolutionary or leader of a political movement could've said. But Heinessen saying it has more cachet than a nobody saying it. I doubt that Ahle Heinessen sought to be idolized, much less deified."

Yang shook his head. Although he had a violent aversion to any thinking that condoned national supremacy, here he was obediently showing his respect and affection for Heinessen's founder. He'd compromised a part of himself to protect his beloved democracy, but when he thought of how the results of his victory might affect the people of the empire, the wings of his heart grew heavy and damp.

IV

By the end of February in SE 799, year 490 of the imperial calendar, Yang Wen-li's fleet maneuvers were under way. Later described as the leading example of "the exquisite art of military operations," it would come to be widely known as an elegant tactical success but was unprecedented even at the conceptual level. That its actions were diversionary tactics and its final objective something else entirely would excite future historians.

As a military man of a democratic nation for whom authority wasn't some despotic ideal, Yang had faced numerous limitations and until now had always conceded to the superiority of Reinhard von Lohengramm's front lines. He was at last able to meet the empire head-on.

As for Reinhard, the first act had been entirely underwhelming. The reasons behind this would also be of great interest to historians, but even an unparalleled genius was prone to occasional lapses of judgment.

While construction of a military base on the planet Urvashi was under way, Reinhard gathered his highest leaders to draft and determine middle-term strategies. Senior Admiral Oskar von Reuentahl and Admiral Lennenkamp arrived with their fleets, bringing the total of soldiers to twenty million. Only Admiral Kornelias Lutz stayed behind on Iserlohn Fortress to establish sovereignty over the corridor. With nearly all the highest leaders of Reinhard's expeditionary forces gathered in the tactical meeting being held on the flagship *Brünhild* in Urvashi's satellite orbit, Mittermeier and von Reuentahl shook hands to celebrate their reunion.

The long-term objective of rendering Iserlohn Fortress powerless by passing through the Phezzan Corridor had already been achieved, and they'd reaped more than enough benefits by recapturing it. But there was little reason to be proud of their accomplishment when Yang's strongest fleet continued to roam freely.

Their current plan hung on two options. The first was to deploy all forces and make a direct hit on the enemy nation of Heinessen. The second was to capture and suppress the various other planets and leave the capital independent, thereby securing future supply routes from the imperial mainland. Reinhard's decision would determine which course the empire would follow.

In recent meetings, Reinhard had kept his own judgments to himself, and this time was no exception. He wasn't fully present, and the admirals' discussion was trifling to his ears.

"It's entirely pointless for us to be locked here in indecision. I say we attack the enemy capital in one fell swoop and bring about total conquest. Isn't that why we came all this way?"

Of course, there were opposing opinions.

"Now that we're here, we should avoid doing anything rash. Gaining total control of the capital doesn't guarantee the alliance will fall. There's a good chance of getting tripped up by rebellions in other sectors. We'd do better to subjugate the surrounding areas by cornering them physically and psychologically until they beg for mercy."

This vigorous argument didn't stimulate Reinhard's mind at all, and the meeting adjourned without a conclusion having been reached. The young dictator's head was heavy, and he had no appetite for dinner.

The next morning, Reinhard couldn't get out of bed. He had a temperature of over 38 degrees Celsius. The doctor rushed in rather nervously, but his fears soon melted like ice in spring when he diagnosed Reinhard with nothing more than a fever from overwork. Captain Kissling, the head of Reinhard's personal guard and the one who'd called the doctor, was just as relieved as he was.

When Reinhard, leaning his golden head on a pillow, thought about it, he realized that he'd been running around nonstop for more than a decade. Not that he looked back on this ascendency with any sort of self-pity. Compared to his rival, Yang Wen-li, Reinhard was far more durable in his industry. He'd always worked in both military and political spheres, where his judgments were always necessary and reasonable.

It was probably a good idea to take a rest occasionally. A weary body meant a weary mind. Although he forced himself to think and make decisions, it was impossible for him to be as on top of things as when he was healthy. He was impatient, but at some point he had to give in.

"You should take it easy today, and tomorrow if you can. Rest is the simplest, yet most effective, medicine."

Reinhard obediently took the doctor's advice, taking a lap around the sandman's park, and woke up close to noon. He pressed the intercom switch near his pillow to ask for water.

It'd been seven years since Reinhard had been laid up in bed with a fever. He'd had many fevers as a child. Every time, his sister Annerose would nurse him back to health. In fact, even when it wasn't a significant fever, he'd sometimes stay in bed just to feel the porcelain touch of her hand on his forehead.

"It's only a little fever. Go ahead and sleep if you want. Before you know it, you'll get bored and want to get out of bed, Reinhard…"

His sister was right. In the morning, he'd had enough of the feel of clean sheets, and when he was fed a lunch of vegetable soup by his sister's hand, his muscles ached for lively activity, and he fretted over how he might justify getting out of bed.

An academy student came in carrying a tray with a crystal water pitcher on it. Reinhard remembered his reddish-brown hair and dark-green eyes. In response to Reinhard's inquisitive gaze, Emil von Selle held the glass reverently and gave a deep bow.

"I've been ordered by Fräulein von Mariendorf to look after Your Excellency."

"You have knowledge of medicine?"

Reinhard was only teasing, but the boy answered in earnest.

"My father was a doctor. I've been thinking about going on to military medical school once I graduate from academy."

Reinhard noticed the boy had used the past tense.

"And what does your father do now?"

"He died three years ago in battle. He worked as a doctor aboard a cruiser but was blown away along with his ship in the Battle of Amritsar..." The boy's tone was neutral. "But Your Excellency has avenged him. I'd like to thank you, on behalf of my mother as well, for destroying the rebel navy at Amritsar."

Reinhard drained the glass of cold water in almost one gulp and spoke gently.

"Be sure to get your medical license as soon as you can, and I'll make you my personal physician when you do."

These words set the boy's eyes aglitter with deep emotion. Emil went red in the face and vowed to do his best for this young, elegant dictator who was the object of his admiration.

The doctor came in with Captain Kissling and, after again giving his unoriginal opinion that the fever was fatigue related, used an atomizing injector to treat him with a fever-reducing medicine. To the topaz-eyed Captain Kissling standing nearby, he seemed to be making a show of his loyalty to the master. Of course, if the doctor made any suspicious movements, Kissling was ready to kill him then and there.

Reinhard slept again, dreaming intermittently. First, his sister Annerose, as she was before being imprisoned in the emperor's rear court, stepped into the garden of his dreams. Wearing modest yet immaculate clothes, she was baking him an onion pie. That fragrant scent disappeared, and on the starry backdrop of the screen, a redheaded Siegfried Kircheis smiled at him. With that nostalgia came an idle complaint.

"If only you were alive, then I wouldn't have to deal with these troubles. You could've led my expeditionary force commands while I concentrated on domestic affairs in the imperial capital…"

Even as he uttered these self-indulgences, he was ejected from the land of sleep. As he blinked awake, babbling incoherently, a figure moved in silhouette beyond the thin curtain. He remembered that the boy Emil had been there all along. The young blond dictator assured him he was okay, but when he noticed that his forehead and neck were covered in sweat, he had Emil wipe it away for him. After politely carrying out his duty, the boy hesitantly wished him success in battle.

"Don't worry about me, Emil. When the abilities of both sides are the same, the outcome can go either way. Besides my own luck, I also get luck from my friend, who gave me his life and his future."

Reinhard momentarily closed his eyes at the behest of something formless.

"I carry on my shoulders the luck of two people, and so I'll never lose to Yang Wen-li. Worry not."

Reinhard was responsible for not only himself, but also the twenty million members of his expeditionary forces, as well as the twenty-five billion citizens of the empire. But at this moment, the sense of security given to him by this single boy was most precious to Reinhard for reasons he himself didn't comprehend.

CHAPTER 6:

ONE BATTLE AFTER ANOTHER

I

THE "TYRANNY OF DISTANCE" was a phrase used to indicate just how difficult unified rule of a human society that had grown by a third would be through military force alone. The one who'd pushed this policy was Münzer, who'd worked as Emperor Maximillian Josef II's chief justice. Maximillian Josef accepted his loyalty, discarded his plans of invading the Free Planets Alliance, and over two decades of peaceful rule never once mounted a foreign campaign.

But it was Kim Hua Nguyen who coined the term "tyranny of distance" when he was chosen to be the Free Planets Alliance's first ruler, an honor he staunchly refused due to his old age and blindness. He was a close friend of founding father Ahle Heinessen, who died en route during the Long March of 10,000 Light-Years. After establishing the nation, he didn't take public office, assuming instead the role of honorary president of the Heinessen Anniversary Foundation. When asked by governmental leaders about future defense policies, he answered:

"The distance between the imperial mainland and our commonwealth will become our greatest protective barrier. And while someone possessed of enormous ambition and genius will likely break through this barrier in due time, we won't have to worry about that for a century or more."

Nguyen had died in SE 538, 238 years before Reinhard was born.

"In short, distance militarily controls transportation, supply, communication, and command networks. These difficulties exist in proportion to the magnitude of that distance."

These conditions were common knowledge within the military, and in making light of them, both the empire and the alliance had experienced painful and shameful defeats.

In SE 799, year 490 of the imperial calendar, Reinhard von Lohengramm came along with enormous ambition and genius, forcing everyone to yield to his own tyranny of distance, and had seemingly broken through that protective barrier as Nguyen predicted. But when he considered supplies and communications with the imperial homeworld for a navy twenty million strong, he couldn't be happy winning only one battle. And while it was a fact that they were in an overwhelmingly advantageous position, history was filled with examples of mighty expeditionary forces losing to weak defensive ones.

This tyranny of distance, so far as human resources were concerned, had made a lasting impression. Purveyors of insurrection and sabotage found their spirits dampened by homesickness and war-weariness.

To those conquerors who vowed to extend their power "to the ends of the world," soldiers turned a blind eye.

"If you want to go so badly," they said, "why not go yourself? We'd rather go back to our hometowns and die among loved ones."

In ancient times, illnesses brought about by changes in physical terrain left their marks on the body, although no one could say that wasn't still true today. Being confronted with constellations different from the night sky they were used to was difficult for soldiers to reconcile. To Reinhard, traveling fifteen thousand light-years away from the capital of Odin was a flash in the cosmic pan. Then again, his soldiers' hearts had never flown so far as his. With Odin as his base of operations, and once the alliance expedition was completed during his subsequent reign, this tyranny of distance would follow him wherever he went.

"I'd just as soon make Phezzan the capital of the new empire."

Reinhard was given to this opinion recently. Once he'd conquered the alliance, his territory would be effectively doubled. To rule efficiently while maintaining a high sense of uniformity, the present capital of Odin was too far from the new territory. Relocating the capital to Phezzan would situate it at a nodal point between the old and new territories, sufficient for centralized rule as a hub of materials and information. If he could build bases like Iserlohn Fortress on either side of the Phezzan Corridor, it'd be impregnable. Originally, Odin had been the base for the Goldenbaum Dynasty, but that didn't mean that Reinhard had reason to inherit it uncritically. A new dynasty entailed a new capital. A simple capital that did away with the ostentatiousness of the old dynasty…

In the meantime, however, Reinhard had to concentrate on developing his base on the planet Urvashi, which would not be his future capital.

Yang Wen-li's first strike inflicted damage on a group of transport ships heading for Urvashi by way of Iserlohn. This was to have been the initial step toward making a permanent base of Urvashi. Two hundred and forty giant spherical containers, fully loaded with enough food and fuel, greenhouses and armory plants, all kinds of raw materials, and liquid hydrogen for twenty million people for a year, all guarded by eight hundred cruisers and escort ships.

The spherical containers had been made by boring tunnels through nickel meteorite, filling them with ice, and then sealing them at both ends before heating them up using sun reflectors. The moment the heat penetrated the center, the meteorite's large volume of ice turned into steam and expanded tremendously, leaving behind a giant hollow sphere with a thick nickel coating. Stuffed with cargo and outfitted with propulsion units, the spherical containers were complete. With no way for the containers to defend themselves, the convoy was a necessary measure.

In charge of this operation was a young rear admiral by the name of Sombart, who had personally requested to be assigned this duty. No matter how simple the task, he wanted to be known for something.

The young soldier had his mind set narrowly on war and tended to downplay the importance of supplies. Despite his youth, he was older than his master, but when Reinhard considered that the alliance forces were far from destroyed, he encouraged him to be on constant lookout, always maintaining communication with the main force, and to request reinforcements the moment he sensed any danger. Sombart puffed up his chest with pride.

"If I should fail, I will offer my unworthy life to Your Excellency, that I might confirm the justice of our entire fleet. You can count on me."

His boasting made veterans Mittermeier and von Reuentahl lift their eyebrows higher even than Reinhard's. Mittermeier offered to go, but Reinhard shook his golden locks. However important the supplies were, it seemed a waste of human resources to invest generals of von Reuentahl and Mittermeier's caliber in such an operation.

"Seeing as you've spoken so highly of yourself, I'll let you put your money where your mouth is," he said, and sent Sombart away.

Contrary to Reinhard's expectations, Sombart left brimming with confidence and in high spirits. Not that he wasn't without genius, but he wasn't exactly built to thrive under pressure. At the very least, he had the right amount of self-esteem and accuracy. He'd sharpened his nerves and his fangs, but it wasn't enough to rival the Yang fleet, which was lying in wait for its chance. When Vice Admiral Thurneisen's fleet came rushing out to meet the transport ships on imperial orders, Reinhard foresaw a crisis when communications grew intermittent. The containers were destroyed, precious cargo and all, and the escort ships were reduced to thirty, wandering around the battlespace in a daze like dogs who'd lost sight of their masters.

Although Rear Admiral Sombart had managed to escape death, he would only live for a few days longer. He returned in shame to an unforgiving Reinhard.

"It's only natural that the enemy should aim for our supply channels. Although I made it a point to stress that, and despite your arrogance, there's no excuse for damage coming to that precious cargo through negligence. You be your own judge."

Rear Admiral Sombart was ordered to kill himself by poison. The admirals said nothing. The reason Mittermeier and the others did not defend him was that martial law made no distinctions. It was heartless, but there was nothing to be done.

Even if it had the psychological effect of serving as an example to others, Reinhard convened his highest leaders to pronounce his verdict.

"I'm partially to blame for not formulating any concrete plans so far, but if we're going to achieve total domination, not just temporary invasion and capture, then we need to be more careful. I think it's time we eliminated the enemy's systematic forces once and for all."

The Yang fleet hadn't yet returned to the capital of Heinessen and was passing through the Bharat star system in search of other collection and supply bases. Reinhard's genius allowed him to see through to what was at the root of that basic strategy of changing collection and supply bases with each battle, but he also understood the difficulty of capturing and destroying the enemy even with that understanding of alliance tactics. In any case, he had to track down Yang's whereabouts. And when he did, he would mobilize all forces.

Reinhard nominated Admiral Steinmetz for the job. Admiral Steinmetz, taking his fleet, made immediate headway for Urvashi.

II

The ruination of the Imperial Navy's supply ships was a great success on the part of Yang's fleet. But it was just the first step toward the grander, more agonizing battle ahead. To lure out Reinhard von Lohengramm and face him head-on, he had to continue fighting and winning. By that prospect alone, his troubles were just getting started. The more he won, the more formidable enemies would stand in his way. It all bore a deformed resemblance to accruing interest on a debt, and by now Yang felt the situation was getting out of hand. Seeing him like this, Julian smiled.

"Every day, you're becoming more and more like Griping Yusuf II."

Julian stood by Yang's side as if it were the most natural thing in the world, when in fact, despite his promotion to sublieutenant, no order of job reassignment had been given, and so nominally he was still a military attaché on Phezzan and not Yang's subordinate. Yang only noticed it after starting for Heinessen. Julian had, of course, known all along but kept silent about it. Lieutenant Commander Frederica Greenhill deftly handled the situation, claiming that sublieutenant Julian Mintz was responsible for supplying the information he'd gathered on Phezzan to aid Admiral Yang's tactical decisions, and that was enough to secure Julian's position on board. Julian was grateful for it, too. Yang mumbled about it for a while but voiced no objection and eventually dropped the subject.

On March 1, Steinmetz discovered the Yang fleet much sooner than he'd expected. This was, unbeknownst to Steinmetz, because Yang had wanted to be noticed. But the location of his discovery was problematic. Midway between the Raighar and Tripura star systems, it was far removed from any known shipping routes. The reason for this was obvious from the data captured on Phezzan.

"We've confirmed the existence of a black hole. Its Schwarzschild radius is about nine kilometers, but its mass is sixty quadrillion tons to the ten billionth power, and the danger-zone radius is estimated to be, at most, 3,200 light-seconds, or 960,000,000 kilometers."

"Then I'm assuming we shouldn't get any closer than one billion kilometers?"

According to the operator, Yang's fleet was precisely toeing that one billion–kilometer line. Moreover, it had assumed a convex formation with the black hole at its rear.

"What could they be planning?"

As Steinmetz inclined his head slightly to one side, chief of staff Vice Admiral Neisebach dispelled his commander's doubts.

"Putting the danger zone at their rear limits our trajectories of attack. There's no way we can go around them. That must be their aim."

Steinmetz nodded. Neisebach's opinion was sound in its persuasiveness. Steinmetz ordered a concave formation. Both sides were forced to engage head-on.

At 2100 hours that same day, they were in range. First, Yang's fleet hurled sheaves of light at the enemy. The imperial forces returned fire, sending forth a dazzling cascade into pitch-black space. Slowly yet surely Steinmetz pressed forward, pushing the alliance into apparent disadvantage. The alliance began to retreat. Steinmetz steadied his racing heart, quietly spreading out both wings of his concave formation into a half encirclement.

A turning point in the battle came when, at 0530 on March 2, the alliance, cornered by the empire's half-circle formation, suddenly charged with fierce gunfire. Moments later, Yang's ships had breached the center of the Steinmetz fleet, spreading out on either side behind the enemy and driving them toward the black hole.

It was the perfect execution of a "breach and spread" strategy. Steinmetz's formation had completely backfired. He'd have done better to hold his advantage and charge the Yang fleet in kind. A more reckless commander would've done just that. But Steinmetz was top-notch and so had taken the safer way out, much to his chagrin. He'd been blind to the fact that Yang hadn't gone on the defensive precisely so that he could carry out this bold attack.

The Yang fleet had surrounded the imperial forces in a semicircle, concentrating consistent fire on a single point, thereby pushing the Steinmetz fleet into the black hole's gravitational field. The imperial forces surged like a stampede into a deadly event horizon—an abyss with a gravitational field reaching six hundred trillion times normal density. The Yang fleet's firepower came on strong and severe, and one imperial ship after another exploded into particles of light.

The operators of Yang's flagship *Hyperion* cheered with excitement. This only incited their commander's caution.

"Enemy at the rear! I fear a pincer attack."

The receiver of this report didn't show one-tenth of the excitement as the one giving it. Yang took off his black beret, ruffling his unruly black hair.

"When you say at the rear, how far are we talking? Time distance is fine."

The operator flew to the control panel, crunched some numbers, and estimated three hours, give or take.

Yang nodded once, put the beret back on his head, and crammed his disheveled hair under it.

"Then we defeat the enemy in two hours and use the third to make our getaway. Sound good?"

With a nonchalant tone that one might've used to suggest dinner after a movie, Miracle Yang ordered his entire fleet to intensify its fire.

Like a herd of cattle being chased off a cliff, the Steinmetz fleet fell prey to the black hole's gravitational field, which his ships were powerless to resist.

"Help, we're being pulled in!"

Such cries congested the Imperial Navy's communication channels before going silent. As the black hole's inescapable gravity sucked in the Steinmetz fleet, the central ships were pulled in in a straight line, while the surrounding warships were twisted and ripped apart like paper dolls by a fierce tidal force. Riding giant gravitational waves, they rushed through space against their will. Vanishing into the event horizon, they were nothing more than clumps of metal and nonmetal. Those within the ships who resisted the black hole's pull with all their might died of ruptured organs and broken bones before turning into balls of flame when the nuclear-power reactors exploded, all the while hurtling through a dark tunnel of extinction. It was a wondrous sight, like watching a group of fireflies dancing in the face of death, their light sucked in like the physical substance that it was. The victors became slaves to a strange feeling of unreality as each ball of fire went out, one by one.

Half of the Steinmetz fleet sank forever beyond the event horizon. Of the remaining half, many ships had been destroyed by gunfire, while those that managed to escape both the gravity well and the alliance attack and return to their comrades constituted no more than 20 percent of the entire fleet. This 20 percent, barraged by Yang's coordinated attack, barely made it to the Schwarzschild radius line and, riding its hyperbolic orbit, gained enough velocity to get out of range. Although the commanders had succeeded in breaking away, their faces were white, like those of the dead.

Following his successful pincer attack, Yang retracted his previous remarks. He suspended his plans for escape, determined to wage battle against the next wave of the enemy. Not only because there was a high chance of being attacked from the rear, but also because, putting together several pieces of intel, they knew that Admiral Helmut Lennenkamp was spearheading the reinforcement division. Anxious about leaving things to Steinmetz alone, Reinhard had wasted no time in sending backup. Lennenkamp had planned on being there in due time, never imagining that Yang would fell an enemy twice his size in a matter of hours. Lennenkamp would have to be equally swift.

"Mister Lennen, is it?" Yang muttered to himself, abbreviating the surname as he often did for his own convenience.

For a mere few seconds, he put a hand to his chin in deep thought before snapping his fingers—a sound that only he could hear, and even then only faintly. If not for the faith of those working under him, his commands would've been difficult to grasp and accept.

"Fire three volleys just before the enemy gets within range. After that, we'll retreat to the Raighar star system. But we'll do so slowly and systematically."

Even within the Yang fleet, no one understood the significance of this order, but no one questioned it either. After cutting through the infinite darkness with three aimless shots, they began their escape as if cornered by the advancing imperial forces. At first, the latter took the bait and upped their speed, but then Commander Lennenkamp suddenly ordered his men to fall back, and this they did begrudgingly.

That's when Yang, his eyes locked on the screen, ordered a full counterattack.

His timing was exquisite. Lennenkamp's retreat had given momentum to the enemy's attack. Flashes of light mowed down both the darkness and the imperial fleet in one go, lighting up screens and retinas alike with their explosions. Seeing the wall of light approaching his flagship, Lennenkamp lost the will to fight and retreated after all. At 1300 hours, after half of its forces had been driven away, the imperial fleet pulled itself back together, at which point Yang made his getaway in earnest.

"I wonder why the enemy retreated midattack. Had they kept going, they probably would've won," said Julian to the dark-haired young marshal on *Hyperion*'s bridge. Even to Julian, it was a mystery.

Lennenkamp, Yang explained, had been enticed by the Yang fleet in the battle over Iserlohn Fortress and had dealt him a hard blow. If Yang had learned anything from this exchange, it was that Lennenkamp would likely take any opportunity given to him as a trap and take precautions accordingly. If the alliance's retreat seemed deliberate, then no doubt Lennenkamp would be wary to give chase. Any simple commander hell-bent on revenge would've done the opposite. Yang had made clever use of this psychology.

"Yet again, many tens of thousands of widows and orphans will despise me for what I've done today. It's a little too heavy for me to bear it all. You only have to fall into hell once…"

Despite having made quick work of two imperial fleets in a single day, thick clouds gathered about Yang's expression.

"If the admiral is going to hell, then I'm coming with you. At least you'd never be lonely," offered Julian, speaking from the heart.

Yang's expression softened.

"Don't be silly," he said, laughing bitterly. "I was planning on sending you to heaven so that you could fish me up from hell. I want you to do as much good in this universe as you can."

Julian said he would try his best, even as he leapt with pride on the inside over Yang's victory. Julian had learned the psychology of both his strategies and tactics. It was precisely because both Steinmetz and Lennenkamp were not incompetent leaders that they fell into the psychological traps that Yang laid for them. Julian made a mental note that opponents of a certain degree of strength could also be the most predictable.

"In Yang's fleet, even a dozen lifetimes aren't enough when you battle two fleets in one day."

In the fighter pilots' waiting room of *Hyperion*, "Ace" Olivier Poplin, who'd risen to the rank of commander, was griping as usual. His friend Ivan Konev rebuked him.

"In your case, you'd need a dozen women for each of those lifetimes, so it's tough either way."

"That's not entirely true. For each of my lives, it's a dozen women who'd need *me*," Poplin said.

"Well, whenever you *do* die, those women will just move on to other men with their own virtues."

Having put his friend at a loss for an answer, Ivan Konev gave a sedate yawn.

III

The success of Yang Wen-li's back-to-back attacks against the Steinmetz and Lennenkamp fleets was a sharp blow to Reinhard's self-importance. Despite their prominence, the two admirals had been led around by the nose. His rage was incomparably greater than when his transport ships had been destroyed.

With his ice-blue gaze, Reinhard harshly admonished the two admirals kneeling before him. He refused to allow them to regroup their fleets and forbade them any further stake in the battlespace. Their comrades were even more relieved than they were to have gotten off so easily.

"I hope you've learned well from this. There are opponents whose level you cannot measure up to. Think hard about why I gave you your current positions, and start from square one."

Reinhard meant to reassign Lennenkamp as commander of Iserlohn Fortress and put Lutz in his place, but he was opposed by his private secretary, Hildegard von Mariendorf. Her reasons were threefold. First, if Steinmetz stayed behind while Lennenkamp was reassigned, the one being reassigned would think it unfair. Second, he'd already purged Rear Admiral Sombart, punishing him as an example to others, and doing so again in this case would harm overall morale. Third, everyone was sure to make light of the Iserlohn Fortress commander's duties. Reinhard saw the soundness in Hilda's argument and stopped his tirade against Steinmetz and Lennenkamp. Taking them both off the front line this late in the game would severely dampen their military strength. He could only accede to Hilda's better judgment.

Reinhard's ice-blue eyes seemingly emitted a piercing light, reflecting the storm raging inside him. He would need an entire day to calm that storm.

･ ･ ･
･ ● ･
･ ･
●

With their dreary interior design and furniture, the high-ranking officers' lodgings were already in place on Urvashi. For the first time in months, von Reuentahl and Mittermeier felt the touch of real earth beneath their feet and enjoyed a conversation over wine. After reminiscing about various battles, the topic inevitably turned to the crafty enemy general whose threat they were currently facing.

"His tactics are nothing short of magnificent. But I can't imagine that even Yang Wen-li would attempt to compensate for strategic shortcomings by racking up tactical victories. He must have something else up his sleeve."

Von Reuentahl looked at his friend's face, but his mismatched eyes were filled with doubt.

"What is it? Have you hit upon something?"

"Well…"

Mittermeier crossed his arms.

"Just say it, only to me."

The air in the room felt thick as mud, as it also had when they were struggling as low-ranking officers on the front lines. It was that very thickness that prompted Mittermeier to hesitate.

"It's something that Duke von Lohengramm said. Namely, that for the alliance to overcome its strategic disadvantage, they would have to kill him—that is, Duke von Lohengramm—in the battlespace. Their victory can come at no other price."

"Ah…"

In the glow of those mismatched eyes, there was the slightest flicker. Something about it made his friend uneasy.

"So, while it appears Yang Wen-li is insistent on a tactical-level victory, you're saying this is all a ruse to bring Duke von Lohengramm out into the open so he can battle him head-on."

"It all makes sense, if you think about it."

"That it does."

Von Reuentahl nodded while Mittermeier poured wine into their glasses.

"If Duke von Lohengramm should fall, we lose our leader, the object of our loyalty. The question then becomes, 'For whom do we fight?' It's everything our enemy could hope for."

"The matter of who would succeed him has yet to be settled."

"Whoever does succeed him, he'll never have absolute rule on par with

Duke von Lohengramm." Mittermeier's tone, like the flicker in his friend's eyes, was complex. He knew that von Reuentahl's abundant reasoning power came with its own irrational baggage. It wasn't just the philandering, which gave an impression of underlying recklessness, but also that, when they worked together as men of ambition in troubled times, a scent of exceeding danger wafted about him. He was probably the only one who knew this, or so Mittermeier thought, but von Reuentahl wanted to take care of himself. He didn't think he should be wasting his talents drilling useless holes in level ground.

Whether he knew his friend's innermost feelings or not, von Reuentahl looked at the empty wine bottle longingly.

"Is that all we have? I could go for another."

"Sadly, since our supply ships were destroyed, our suppliers have been less generous. We can't have only high-ranking officers enjoying themselves."

"Running out of wine and beer is one thing, but if our meat and bread rations fall short, it'll affect our soldiers' morale. No starving soldiers have ever won a war."

"Either way, we'll need to fight before we get to that point."

This meant that Reinhard would be forced to face Yang Wen-li head-on after all. Until now, he'd built up an advantageous position, and while he was hoping to be within hailing distance of the alliance's capital, an instrumental duet between impatience and uneasiness was resounding in corners of the empire's most veteran brains.

It was during this interim that imperial forces rolled out their third victim. Once again, Admiral August Samuel Wahlen would be ground to defeat by the Yang fleet.

Wahlen was of a staunchly different opinion about an empire spending its days idly waiting for the next supply shipment. He came to Reinhard with an operational plan of his own.

"According to information gathered on Phezzan, the alliance has eighty-four supply bases in its territory, and material stockyards besides. Seeing as our supply convoy was attacked, I say we take an eye for an eye—attack their supply bases and pillage whatever we can."

Reinhard agreed with this plan not for the sake of some small greed but because he was no closer to making a final decision, and Wahlen's plan at least showed initiative. He needed more time, and in any event, he couldn't squander an opportunity to elevate the morale of his men with the prospect of more supplies.

On the other hand, since the empire's stronghold was on the planet Urvashi, assuming he was observing them, Yang would know with a fair degree of certainty whether they were on the move. To that end, the Yang fleet had disappeared somewhere not far from Heinessen, leaving Reinhard at a loss to where he should focus his surveillance. This handicap put even the empire's most competent generals at a considerable disadvantage.

As the Wahlen fleet set out to attack the alliance's supply base in the Tassili Stellar Region, their passage was blocked by the Yang fleet from the direction of Tassili. Again, Yang made a show of his appearance and would've been disappointed if it had been ignored.

Seeing as the transport ships were never built for combat, it only made sense to position them in the center of the fleet to protect them from attack. Yet Yang had placed the supply containers in front, while the warships followed like servants attending their queen. The formation had no way of retaliating against a frontal attack. In Wahlen's mind, such careless inattention to basic protocol meant they were looking to pick a fight.

When the imperial forces assumed their tightest concave formation and rushed forward, the alliance stopped them in their tracks. What followed was a disgraceful spectacle. If the alliance forces were to engage, their own containers would get in their way. If they spread out in battle array, they'd be too thin to oppose a concave formation. Their feigned confusion brought out the first shot from the imperial forces, at which point Yang's fleet fled as gallantly as it could. Although intentional in every respect, it seemed so genuine that Yang's chief of staff, Vice Admiral Murai, couldn't help but comment on it.

"Our fleet has gotten pretty good at faking retreat."

The Wahlen fleet pursued the alliance forces, dispelling the disgrace of their comrades Steinmetz and Lennenkamp in the process, but the commander refrained from continuing their attack, ordering his ships instead to seize the cargo as planned. Wahlen wasn't one to let belligerence get the better of him. Because the transport ships were long gone, more than eight hundred containers, precious cargo and all, fell into the hands of the imperial forces without incident. The alliance's ungainly goose had surrendered them its freshly laid golden eggs.

But when Wahlen's fleet absorbed the large cluster of containers into its center and started back, singing a victory song like the Vikings of yore, the alliance forces reappeared, hot on their heels.

"Retreat while continuing to protect the containers," ordered Wahlen.

He positioned his ship at the tail end of the fleet, leaving the head of the formation responsible for counterattack. Their coordinated formation and firepower made the alliance forces falter, and for a moment the alliance started to fall back in seeming confusion. They held their distance and kept timidly on their tail.

"They just don't know when to give up. I suppose it's only natural, seeing as we've taken their precious cargo…"

Whereupon countless beams of light shot out from the spherical containers. There was no escaping being fired upon at such close range and density. One of the destroyers was obliterated, while a cruiser and two more destroyers suffered massive damage. It was enough to plunge the imperial forces into chaos.

"They've hidden troops inside the containers! So that's their little game, knowing we needed the supplies?"

Wahlen clicked his tongue, ordering his men to give up on transporting the containers and to instead exterminate the unruly parasites that had infiltrated their bowels. A container, twined in threads of energy beams converging from eight directions, exploded in a momentary convulsion. The first of many.

A ball of white-hot light blanketed the imperial soldiers' field of vision as a chain of explosions ensued and giant clusters of fiery jewels appeared at their centers. The price of one of those jewels was the lives of tens of thousands of soldiers.

Each container had been outfitted with a rudimentary automatic firing system and payloads of liquid helium. And when their energy beams converged with the containers, the imperial forces triggered giant, deadly explosions by their own hand. The turbulence of heat and light tore them apart from within. The ship navigators went white-knuckled at their control panels trying to avoid collisions with their fleet mates, but their efforts were rewarded with a fierce attack as the alliance charged them at full force.

The Wahlen fleet had brought about mayhem in both form and spirit, and was completely beaten into submission by the gunfire of Yang's sudden assault. Tens of thousands of energy flails whipped down on the imperial forces, who screamed and writhed in pain. Each burst of light was like a spray of blood jetting out from the imperial forces' wounds. Wahlen's ships, crew and all, blood and metal, vaporized, looking something like a chain of miniature suns.

"Human beings have their own value," said Vice Admiral von Schönkopf by way of criticizing his commander's strategy on the bridge of Yang's flagship *Hyperion*.

Julian Mintz was staring at the violent dance of light and shadow without a word. Yang had figured that the imperial forces would place the containers in their midst, surrounding them with their ships, and had gone so far as to install the self-firing mechanisms to increase his chances of trapping Wahlen.

Despite wanting unilateral destruction, Yang couldn't bring himself to join hands with his cheering subordinates in optimism.

"Duke von Lohengramm's anger and pride will have reached a critical mass by now. He doesn't have the resources to sustain a drawn-out conflict. Any day now, he'll come at us with everything he's got, and with perhaps even fiercer determination and even grander tactics than anything we've seen."

All eyes were on Yang, who noticed that he'd just spoken aloud words he'd meant to keep to himself. It wasn't easy trying to prevent the wall around his heart from cracking.

IV

The latest blow to the imperial forces was the most serious yet. Rounding up every survivor he could, Wahlen returned alive, but as he knelt before the young imperial marshal and apologized for his thoughtless loss, Reinhard summarized his coldhearted anger in one word:

"Enough."

Reinhard then stormed out of the room. The admirals left behind dropped their shoulders, their expressions of relief reflected in each other's eyes.

"Even someone as tactically sound as Wahlen was deceived," they groaned.

"No, it's precisely *because* he's so skilled that he was deceived. The same goes for Steinmetz and Lennenkamp on that point."

They weren't just making excuses. A more hotheaded man would've forgotten the containers altogether and gone after the enemy. In which case, he would certainly not have fallen for Yang's tricks. Wahlen had tripped himself up by his own reasoning. And yet, Wahlen's loss didn't necessarily mean he hadn't reaped at least one stalk of wheat. Just as they were about to be stampeded from all sides, he'd regrouped his fleet, all the while tracking the Yang fleet's postbattle behaviors, thereby confirming that the Yang fleet, which had emerged from Tassili, had disappeared in the direction of the Lofoten Stellar Region.

Yang Wen-li was changing fleet gathering points and supply bases after each battle, moving from one to another as he fought.

Now that reality had confirmed the genius of Reinhard's intuition, the empire's veteran generals were at a momentary loss. This meant that Yang had no central base of operations, instead proceeding nomadically and with tactical confidence.

"This is problematic. That means the whole of alliance territory has effectively become their base," muttered Fahrenheit, a mixture of disgust and admiration in his light-blue eyes. It was, in other words, a guerilla war being waged by a regular navy, and the Imperial Navy had no choice but to fight an enemy that had no headquarters. The more than ten thousand light-years they'd slogged through to get here didn't seem so long after all.

In retrospect, Yang had given up Iserlohn Fortress too easily. They'd predicted he wasn't too attached to it as a hardware base but had vague fears regarding his thoroughness.

Mittermeier kicked the floor with the heel of his shoe.

"It's just one fleet."

A profound amount of emotion was folded into this low voice. Admiration and humiliation, astonishment and anger all made for a seething soup.

"With just one fleet, he's toying with our multiple forces! He can appear anytime, and anywhere, he pleases."

Although the imperial forces were aware that the alliance had upward of eighty-four supply bases, predicting which one Yang would take next was difficult, and in this instance, knowledge was more a source of confusion than clarity.

"When we were fighting those profligate sons of the high nobility in the Lippstadt War two years ago, we thought there was no one so incompetent as them. But that was a terrible misjudgment on our part. No matter how resourceful Yang Wen-li is, it serves us right for being deceived by a single fleet."

Fahrenheit responded to Mittermeier's sigh with a glint in his light-blue eyes.

"I'd just as soon destroy all eighty-four supply bases without occupying them. At least then the Yang fleet would be immobilized by hunger."

"An empty proposition," said von Reuentahl bluntly. "Deploying our forces now would leave our military base in the Gandharva star system ripe for the picking. And even if we could gain control of all eighty-four, we'd be foolish to spread our forces so thin. So far, all Yang has done is take us out one by one."

"Are you suggesting, Admiral von Reuentahl, that we just stand back and watch his mischief unfold?"

Fahrenheit's tone was pointed. The heterochromatic admiral kept his cool, parrying that sharp tongue.

"Not at all. All I'm trying to point out is that he runs away every time we catch up with him. Moving around aimlessly would only give him more opportunities to toy with us."

"But it's not like we have enough resources to lay low for a while."

"Which is why we must be the ones to lure *him* out. We'll set a trap to surround and destroy him. It's the only way. Now we just need to figure out what kind of bait he'll respond to."

"Fail to bring him down this time, and we'll never win."

Müller's sandy eyes were filled with solemn light.

That the concern of the empire's leaders was aimed more at Yang Wen-li than at the alliance's capital and government was an undeniable prejudice. As they saw it, an attack by Yang Wen-li posed more of a real threat than anything the alliance government might have done. Whenever a military division operated independently of its own government, the power and authority of opposing conquerors was unsustainable.

"There must be a pattern to Yang's movements," said the hot-blooded and ambitious Vice Admiral Thurneisen.

If only they would analyze the patterns, they might just figure out to which base he was headed.

"What are you, an idiot?" said Wittenfeld. "Who knows how many years that would take? Are we to wait until he has exhausted every one of his supply bases?"

Paying no attention to Thurneisen, now red in the face from anger, the commander of the Schwarz Lanzenreiter turned back to Mittermeier and the rest.

"While Yang Wen-li is prowling around like some cat in heat, I say we ignore him and attack the enemy capital directly," Wittenfeld declared.

His opinion wasn't entirely off the mark, despite the vulgarity with which he expressed it.

"And as our men withdraw to the empire, an unharmed Yang Wen-li will emerge from his current supply base, recapture the capital, and rebuild the alliance. Which means we'd have to go Odin knows where to defeat him."

Mittermeier's tone, although restrained, rather provoked Wittenfeld.

"You're all as afraid of Yang Wen-li as a lamb is of a wolf. How do you intend to prevent future generations from mocking us?"

Mittermeier kept calm against these harsh words. "What I'm afraid of isn't Yang Wen-li himself, but the distance we're putting between the war front and our homeland. If you can't understand that much, then we have nothing to talk about."

Wittenfeld was silent, because there was indeed nothing more to say. And while communications were completely stable between the empire and Phezzan for the time being, the supply situation was erratic at best. None in Reinhard's faction was so foolish as to think a war could be waged without supplies.

Before a conclusion presented itself, an order came from Reinhard.

"Calling all admirals. I've decided on our strategy."

Chief of Staff von Oberstein was curious about the details of Reinhard's plan, but the blond-haired youth gave only cryptic assurance.

"One month from now, Yang Wen-li's fleet will be wiped from outer space. I'm looking forward to it."

Von Oberstein took his leave, unsure of what had so dramatically restored his master's confidence.

ᘁ

The hall in which the admirals had assembled was utterly bare of decoration. Had their supply fleet not been vanquished by Yang, a little more concern for interior design might've been given, but for now the only elegance in the room stood before them in the form of a young dictator, even if the words that came from his lips were acrimonious.

"I ask you, why did we brave this long march of ten thousand light-years?! Was it to draw a line under Yang Wen-li's name? No, it was to draw a line *through* it! Did your military pride sprout wings and fly off somewhere?"

Several admirals, as if hearing the cry of thunder very near them, went rigid at the sight of Reinhard clad in his elegant black-and-silver uniform. On hearing the words "draw a line under Yang Wen-li's name," Admirals Wahlen, Steinmetz, and Lennenkamp cast their gazes downward, as if some invisible hand were pushing the backs of their heads. Only Wahlen lifted his head back up determinedly, looking his young master in the eye.

"We have harmed Your Excellency's inviolable name, and the depth of my remorse for failing you knows no bounds. Despite, no, *because* of this, I offer myself in whatever capacity you may need me. I hope you will allow me to make up for my transgressions with a fresh victory."

"I expect nothing less. But it's time I came to the fore and settled this once and for all."

Reinhard's eyes were drawn to another admiral.

"Von Reuentahl!"

"Yes, sir."

"You will take your fleet to the Rio Verde Stellar Region, where you will attack the local supply base and secure the area."

As von Reuentahl swallowed his answer and looked back at Reinhard, the young dictator smiled slightly.

"Do you see? It's all a ruse. The rest of you will take your respective fleets and go off on your own. And when Yang Wen-li sees that I've been left alone, he will come out of his cave into the open. That's when we'll nab him."

The admirals exchanged glances.

"Then Your Excellency will become a decoy, taking on Yang Wen-li's attack with your fleet alone?" asked Neidhart Müller, speaking for all present.

The glint in their young master's eyes was answer enough.

Müller suddenly raised his voice.

"That's far too risky. Please, let me at least stay behind as your vanguard."

Reinhard smiled.

"Nothing you need to be worried about. Do you think I'd lose to Yang Wen-li with the same number of troops, Müller?"

"No, that's not what I meant to…"

Seeing that Müller was at a loss for words, Mittermeier stepped forward on his behalf.

"That's not what worries me. Yang Wen-li may be a renowned general, but at the end of the day, he's nothing more than a fleet commander. Doesn't it make sense that Your Excellency should battle him on an even playing field? I beg you to reconsider."

That voice was also shot down by the young dictator.

"Indeed, your speech has merit, but from what I hear, Yang Wen-li has risen to the rank of marshal. And because I'm a marshal of the empire, I'd say that makes us equals."

"No one in the universe is your equal," shouted Thurneisen ardently, but because he proposed nothing concrete, Reinhard only nodded curtly. In the artificial eyes of von Oberstein, and in the mismatched eyes of von Reuentahl, the colors of derision ran high. They both glanced at Thurneisen.

"Brownnoser," they said, flatly.

Mittermeier cleared his throat.

"Very well. Since Your Excellency has already decided, it's not our place to interfere. But if you could just let us in a little on your thinking, it would put your humble servants at ease."

"Then let me wipe away one of your insecurities."

Reinhard turned his ice-blue eyes to the boy, Emil, waiting in a corner, and asked for some wine. The admirals were surprised to hear him speak so gently, his tone more akin to a request than a command. They noticed that Reinhard had a thick stack of paper on his desk.

Bound by invisible chains of nervousness, Emil brought over a bottle of red wine and a wineglass. He filled the glass with wine and reverently held it out for Reinhard. Perhaps the admirals were more relieved than he was that he didn't spill a single drop.

As Reinhard waved his hand, which was so finely wrought it seemed for all the work of a sculptor summoning his greatest passion and concentration, he poured the wineglass's crimson contents as wet light over the stack of paper.

The collective gaze of the admirals focused on the paper, now stained as if with blood. Their gaze was so hot it seemed the paper would burst into flames when their focal points perfectly aligned. Reinhard's fingers picked up one sheet of paper. Then another sheet, and another, until a wave of understanding swept over Mittermeier and von Reuentahl. When he finally lifted the first clean sheet, the young dictator scanned the room.

"Look closely. The paper is thin, but overlap many sheets of it, and they absorb all the wine. I plan to use this strategy against the brunt of Yang Wen-li's attack. His forces will never be able to penetrate every layer of my defense."

Reinhard was only speaking metaphorically, but the long-serving veteran generals clearly grasped the sheer artistry of their master's plan.

"Once we've neutralized his assault, all of you will double back with your fleets and surround him, annihilate his forces, and force his surrender."

The admirals saluted in silence. Once again, their young master had proven his genius.

Reinhard's chief secretary, Hildegard von Mariendorf, requested a formal meeting after dinner to propose how they might avoid a head-on attack from Yang. Hilda's cropped blond hair glistened in the light as she made her case.

"I say we decline to give the Yang fleet the benefit of our attention, take Heinessen, and force the alliance government's surrender. If we can then make them order Yang Wen-li to stop his futile resistance, we will have achieved your goal of conquest without firing a single shot."

"But then, from a purely military standpoint, I will have lost the war."

Hilda was silent.

"No, I cannot do that, fräulein. There's no way I'm losing to anyone. My popularity and the faith people have in me both stem from the fact that I'm undefeated. It's not because of my saintly virtue that I gain the support of soldiers and civilians alike."

Hilda was surprised to see a pall of self-deprecation flicker across Reinhard's face. She wondered if the sharpness of this young man's intelligence wasn't also the seed of his discontent.

"As you wish, then. I will join you aboard the flagship."

"No, Fräulein von Mariendorf. You weren't built for war. Nor can I bear to see it bring you even the slightest dishonor. I would rather you stay here on Gandharva and wait for my good news. This war will be nothing like what happened the other day. There's no room for spectators."

Hilda started to protest, but Reinhard cut her off.

"On the off chance that anything happened to you, it would fall upon me to apologize to your father, Count von Mariendorf."

Hilda said nothing more. A sublieutenant by the name of Alois von Liliencron was assigned to lead a convoy of twenty ships for her.

The boy Emil, who came to prepare Reinhard's bed, blamed Yang Wen-li. All this running away without fighting was pure cowardice. The young blond dictator shook his beautiful head with a smile.

"You're wrong, Emil. Generals gain their renown only by knowing when and how to run. A wild animal living in constant attack mode is nothing more than a foil for those who hunt it."

"But Your Excellency has never run away from anything, right?"

"I would if it were necessary. I just haven't needed to." His was a quiet, remonstrating tone. "Emil, don't try to learn from me. No one can do what I do. It would only bring them harm. But if you learn from a man like Yang Wen-li, then at least you won't be a foolish general. Not that it matters, seeing as you're going to become a doctor someday. I'm just rambling now."

Why was Reinhard letting this boy trespass the corridors of his heart? Indeed, why was he *making* him? Reinhard, in his own way, was finding an answer, but he didn't know whether it was correct. Maybe it was a form of reparation, but Reinhard himself didn't want to recognize it as such.

"I can't live any other way. Maybe that's not quite true, but I was set upon this path from a very early age nonetheless. I began to walk it so that I might take back everything that was taken from me. But…"

Reinhard went silent. Emil couldn't even imagine how Reinhard had intended to finish that sentence. Reinhard looked back at the boy with distant eyes.

"Time for bed. A child needs time to dream," he said instead, echoing words once spoken to him by his elder sister Annerose. With Siegfried Kircheis, who'd come to stay the night, he was rambling on in his narrow bed, when his sister had called in from the door: "Time for bed. Children need more time to dream than adults."

As Emil bowed respectfully and made to leave, Reinhard's heart contracted at the very thought of his archnemesis. He stood by the hard glass window, enjoying a panorama of the night sky, and spoke to himself.

"This is what you've always wanted. And now that I'm giving it to you, you'd better show yourself, Miracle Yang."

Reinhard von Lohengramm shot his ice-blue gaze into the multitude of twinkling stars. They were the eyes of one fighting his way to supremacy. Putting forth his chest, wrapped in black-and-silver cloth, he pressed his palm to the window. Feeling the reverberation of his own pulse on the glass, the blond youth flashed something less than a smile on his elegant face. A feeling of complete exaltation filled his body, causing every cell to throb.

For a moment, he was happy. A year and a half had gone by since losing his greatest ally. And now, he was about to face his greatest enemy.

Reinhard needed that enemy. No matter how many lights glittered in the night sky, there was no reason for any of them to shine without something to reflect them.

On April 4, Wolfgang Mittermeier took his fleet and headed for the Eleuthera Stellar Region. Five days later, von Reuentahl's fleet attacked Eleuthera and the neighboring Rio Verde Stellar Region.

The young admiral with the mismatched eyes stood on the bridge of his flagship *Tristan*, staring at the receding planets.

"All fleets will turn back to surround and destroy Yang Wen-li's fleet. That's the plan, is it?" He spoke these words only to himself. "A splendid strategy. But what happens if we don't all turn back?"

CHAPTER 7:

I

IT ISN'T EASY TO PINPOINT when the so-called Vermillion War began. If we take Yang's successive victories over three imperial fleets as the first act, then it was already under way in February of IC 490. In addition, Reinhard's operation to treat every Free Planets Alliance sector as a trap, by which he tried to confine the Yang fleet as if in a giant spider's web, was put into effect on April 4, when the Mittermeier fleet first started for the Eleuthera Stellar Region. Yang knew this but ordered a march to the Gandharva Stellar Region on April 6 and by the tenth had touched base with Wiliabard Joachim Merkatz, who'd been invited as secretary of defense of the legitimate imperial galactic government."

When Merkatz came to see him off, the exile government's prime minister, Count von Remscheid, was visibly upset. He rebuked Merkatz for acting like a veteran general who was abandoning him. Merkatz wasn't the type to respond to every distortion and misunderstanding.

"What would be the point for me in staying here? Either for Your Excellency the Count's sake or for His Majesty the Emperor? I'd much rather seek out the possibility of joining the Yang fleet and defeating Duke von Lohengramm once and for all. Your Excellency, I'd hoped you would condone my actions for that reason."

Count von Remscheid was silent. He felt ashamed of himself for not making mention of the child emperor.

When Merkatz left the prime minister's office, Bernhard von Schneider welcomed his superior with a salute. A group of tired men in military uniform accompanied him. Von Schneider smiled bitterly and turned back to his men.

"This is all that's left of the legitimate imperial government forces. They're prepared to join Your Excellency for the long haul."

Merkatz looked around at the faces of these "government soldiers." Of different ages and builds, the youngest was a boy not yet twenty, who was clearly uncomfortable in a baggy old uniform he'd probably inherited from his father. The oldest looked to be of Merkatz's generation. The one thing they did have in common was their countenance, in which he detected a fragile combination of loyalty, bravery, and self-satisfaction. Merkatz gave up on trying to dissuade them. It was obvious they were going to follow their determination no matter what. Thus, seven divisions were added to Yang's fleet.

Merkatz wasn't the only one who would be joining this band of irregulars. Admirals Morton and Carlsen, both of whom had tangled with Reinhard and had been forced into defeat, had regrouped their severely depleted soldiers and piggybacked on the Yang fleet, but the fact that they'd done this without waiting for the Ministry of Defense or Joint Operational Headquarters to approve their petitions was proof that military order existed in name only.

It was under these circumstances that the character of the alliance's volunteer soldiers on the eve of a "final decisive battle" came to be debated, but the so-called volunteer soldiers, despite being possessed of fighting spirit and bravery, were thought to be a "disorderly mob" when it came to supplies and communications. And while the partisans could potentially become valuable assets beyond their abilities, it was difficult to imagine that they'd be able to effectively muster enough power in a decisive head-to-head between such giant fleets. Even during the civil war of the Military Congress for the Rescue of the Republic, the number of hot-blooded volunteers had been staggering. With so much confusion going on in the background, Morton and Carlsen's command abilities were exactly what Yang desired.

He also discovered the existence of a few irregulars around him. The man accompanying Julian Mintz, his enormous frame looming behind Yang's ward, was Ensign Louis Machungo.

When Lieutenant Commander Frederica Greenhill brought over the latest data on the Imperial Navy's movements, Yang widened his eyes at the enormous man.

"Who the hell is that?"

"What do you mean, 'Who the hell is that?' That's Ensign Louis Machungo."

"I know that. What's he doing on my ship?"

"He's here for Julian, of course. A most splendid bodyguard."

In putting it so simply, Frederica silenced Yang, who'd been grumbling about separating the public from the personal. Machungo had secured his seat.

Reading over the data brought to him by Frederica in his private room, Yang sighed as he felt the sun setting over the horizon of his soul. All data suggested that Reinhard von Lohengramm's main fleet, followed by the fleets of his veteran generals, had left the Gandharva Stellar Region. Yang felt compelled then and there to aim for total control of Gandharva.

"What a despicable man," Yang muttered on the inside.

Yang felt those words turning into a slow drip of cold fear, percolating through every cell of his body.

Either the scope of Reinhard von Lohengramm's conceptual abilities or the elaborateness of his planning would've been difficult for any ordinary person to handle, but the young blond dictator had taken both to extremes.

While Reinhard dispatched his admirals far away, feigning isolation of his main fleet, the fact that he was trying to lure the alliance into an enormous trap was well within the realm of Yang's foresight. But he had never imagined Reinhard would leave the Gandharva Stellar Region. When Reinhard's admirals were as far as possible from the main fleet, Yang was already planning to seize the opportunity to gain victory in a short yet decisive battle before they could swing back around and engage him. But Reinhard had moved his main fleet. Yang's computer predicted, by the velocity and angle of Reinhard's movements, that when his admirals were farthest from the main fleet and had reached the threshold of a return maneuver, Reinhard would be in the Bharat star system, where Heinessen would be visible with his naked eye. To prevent Reinhard's penetration of the Bharat star system, and the sectors surrounding the capital from turning into a battlespace, Yang would need to fight Reinhard earlier than he'd anticipated. Likewise, Mittermeier and von Reuentahl were sure to turn back sooner and closer than planned to the prospective battlespace. With Reinhard before him and von Reuentahl and Mittermeier at his rear, Yang wasn't deluded enough to think he could win. His plans for victory had been deduced by the empire, and because supreme commander Reinhard would necessarily be his main target, for the first time he could put his finger on the fifty-yard line.

"And what of the other fifty…?"

For once, Yang wasn't in the best of tactical positions. He had to win, but until his admirals came rushing back to the battlespace, Reinhard would need to hold the war front. Considering Reinhard's character, he surely valued "winning" over "not losing," but such assertiveness and proactivity went hand in hand with his bottomless ingenuity. He was no mere bullfighter running wildly around the arena. Yang had to find a way to win over this most heroic of opponents.

"I have no other choice, do I?"

Yang smiled bitterly to himself. He'd never been fond of this "must do" attitude. Although not everything his heart desired came true, he wanted to stay on the path of independence and spontaneity as much as possible. In the footprints of his life, the dust of regret was already accumulating.

"If only someone else could do this for me."

Of course, there was no such person. Others had always forced upon him ingredients he was hopeless to cook, after which he was made to stand in the kitchen until he managed a meal.

Noticing a reserved knock, Yang opened the remotely controlled door to reveal a flaxen-haired boy with a nervous expression on his face.

"May I come in, Marshal?"

"My door's always open for you. Come in."

The boy, who had risen to the rank of sublieutenant four years earlier than his guardian, saluted and entered the room. He combed back the flaxen bangs that fell annoyingly over his shapely face. He took a seat and Yang asked what was the matter.

Julian bent forward.

"What do you think of Duke von Lohengramm dispersing his fleets?"

"What do I think, indeed."

"Then if you don't mind me airing my thoughts, it's obviously a setup. He's sending us an invitation: Come and attack me, now that I've openly sent my admirals in different directions and left my base empty. If we go after him, we'll be falling right into his trap."

"What kind of trap?"

A mist hung over Yang expression, but the hot sharpness of Julian's gaze dispelled it. Without looking away from Yang, he spun his words in one breath.

"When our fleet approaches their stronghold, the enemy will be timing our every move. Every fleet will turn around, corner us in their giant net, and annihilate us. *That* kind of trap."

Yang took off his black beret with its white five-pointed star and fanned his face. At such times, he didn't know how to praise the accuracy of the boy's insights.

"You've known all along, I take it? Even I can see it. And yet you're purposefully taking the bait."

Yang ruffled his black hair in silence. Julian leaned in closer. Yang was unable to share the boy's zeal.

"Man, usually it's the younger ones who insist on going all out while the older ones try to hold them back, but here it's the opposite. You think I'm going to lose to Duke von Lohengramm?"

"Don't think you can shut me up with that kind of talk. It's unfair."

After a moment of silence, Yang admitted he was wrong and hung his head.

"Sorry about that. You're right. That was an unfair way of putting it."

"No, I was out of line. I'm sorry."

Yang uncrossed his legs and righted himself.

"Listen, Julian. My motto has always been never to fight when there's no chance of winning. I'm not about to go against that logic this time around."

"So there's no chance of winning?"

"Honestly speaking, not really."

Yang returned the beret to his head and stuffed his disheveled hair under it. He wanted others to understand the facts of the situation, but only on a need-to-know basis.

"Still, we only get one shot at this. Given that Duke von Lohengramm has accurately divined my aims, he *is* sending me an invitation. If he was purely self-interested, he'd forget about me altogether and strike Heinessen. Maybe that would be more efficient, but he'll never do it, because he has accepted my rude challenge."

"Then you'll engage him in grand-scale battle?"

Yang thought it over with some difficulty.

"No, I'm not that much of a romantic. All I'm wondering now is how I might use Duke von Lohengramm's own prideful romanticism against him. Honestly, I wish there was an easier way out of this."

Julian opened his mouth to say something but then closed it. It was never in his interest to make Yang uncomfortable. But Julian wondered if there truly wasn't an easier way. Why else would he have felt so compelled to ask about it?

"In any case, don't go overboard."

Yang nodded, seemingly satisfied.

"I'll be fine. It's not my habit to do more than what's required of me. I appreciate your concern."

II

On April 11, the day before leaving the base, Yang gave his officers and men half a day's reprieve. It was a custom to do this before any war, and Yang adhered to it strictly.

"This is a message from your commander. As of today, you are free to do as you wish until 2400 hours. Here's to having no regrets."

This message, communicated by Vice Admiral Murai, prompted hopeful yet somehow empty cheers. Ludmila, now serving as their base of operations, was a small planet of barren rock, and without even meager recreational facilities to keep them entertained, having freedom of time didn't mean having many choices in how to spend it. Olivier Poplin took one look at his friend Ivan Konev and shrugged his shoulders.

"Heinessen and Iserlohn weren't so bad, but what sort of freedom can we possibly exercise in a place like this? Oh well, guess I'll go find someone to share a night of passion with. What about you?"

"I'll be sleeping in my room."

"You're brave for saying something so idiotic out loud."

"Idiotic?"

"Assuming you were joking, yes. More so if you meant it."

"You do like your jokes, that's for sure."

Being on the receiving end of Konev's nonchalance, Poplin puffed his chest out a little.

"One cannot live on jokes alone, but I'd never want to live without them, either."

"Your very existence is a joke."

"I think you've stepped outside the bounds of sarcasm there, Mr. Konev."

"Not really. That's just the jealousy of an unpopular man talking. Please think nothing of it, Mr. Poplin."

The two ace pilots exchanged cynical smiles and went their separate ways.

When Yang Wen-li invited her to his private room, Lieutenant Commander Frederica Greenhill knew exactly how she was going to spend her "Cinderella liberty." As she touched up her light makeup and walked in, Yang turned to the reinforced glass table, unsure of how to react, and welcomed her. He politely offered her a seat.

With one finger, Yang Wen-li was capable of mobilizing a giant fleet of tens of thousands of ships in battlespaces all across the universe. And yet, this young man, who had originally aspired to be a historian, wasn't the main actor in every scene of this drama called life. In some, he was the ham actor who couldn't wrap a tongue around his lines to save his life. In this instance, he managed, by no small effort, to get the engine of his mouth running, and called his guest's name: first as "Lieutenant" before correcting it to "Lieutenant Commander" and then to "Miss Greenhill." Each time he provoked a response in his beautiful aide but made no effort to continue. Not out of spite, but cowardice. It took him more nerve than it did to fight enemies ten times his size. He called her a fourth time.

"Frederica."

This time, the young hazel-eyed woman gave no immediate reply. It was practically groundbreaking for him to call her by her first name. She widened her eyes, at last answering with a yes, by which she regained her own faculty to speak.

"It feels like we've gone eleven years back in time."

Frederica smiled tenderly.

"The marshal hasn't called me by my first name since you saved my life on El Facil. Do you remember?"

Yang Wen-li felt embarrassed and shook his head like some cheap automaton.

He'd been a twenty-one-year-old sublieutenant when he'd evacuated the many civilians of El Facil, then completely surrounded by the Imperial Navy. Even as he was helplessly scratching his head over it, what he did next opened the first page of "Yang's Miracle." When Frederica brought him his lunch, the young sublieutenant sincerely said, "Thank you, Miss Greenhill," to the fourteen-year-old girl, who smiled reflexively and told the young officer, more like a scholar in the making than a military man, to call her Frederica. The "Rescue of El Facil" sparked their friendship. The destination of that friendship was still beyond the scope of their vision. Yang was now standing at a crossroads, and it wasn't easy for him to break out of this stalemate.

"Frederica, when this war is over…"

Yang had organized his thoughts this far but failed to coordinate his emotions and intentions, so the words came out incoherent and disjointed.

"I'm seven years older than you and, how should I put this, well, I'm not the easiest person to live with, and I've got many faults besides. Now that I think about it, I'm not sure I'm qualified to be asking you this. I even considered pulling my rank somehow. It's probably untoward of me to be asking you this on the eve of battle…"

Frederica held her breath. Without letting her confusion show, she understood where Yang was going with this. She felt her pulse getting faster.

"But I'd rather regret saying it that regret not saying it. Ah, this is so embarrassing. I've been talking about myself the whole time. My point… my point is, I'd like for us to get married."

Yang had broken through, emptying his lungs in one go. It required no small amount of stamina to shrug off his indecisiveness. Frederica felt wings spreading and taking vigorous flight in her heart. She thought for what seemed like forever over her answer to this proposal.

"If we combine our yearly pensions, we wouldn't have to worry about feeding ourselves, even when we're old. And…"

Frederica was searching for the right thing to say, but her superior memory betrayed its owner. Her words had gone somewhere on vacation.

"My parents were eight years apart in age. Perhaps I should've mentioned that earlier."

Frederica was beside herself, thinking that if she didn't say something, Yang might mistake her silence for some definitive statement. Looking at Yang, she could see he didn't share her joy. For all the fame that being the youngest marshal in the history of the Alliance Armed Forces had brought him, this young military man who didn't look the part even in uniform was unsettled beneath the bangs sticking out from his beret.

"Um, what is it?"

Yang struggled to express what he was feeling. His was the face of an academy student being given an oral exam. Such seriousness was most unbecoming of him. He took off his beret and spoke with discomfort.

"You haven't given me your answer. Will you marry me?"

"Eh?!"

Frederica opened her hazel eyes wide and blushed at her own carelessness. All he'd wanted was a yes or no. Everything she'd said had indiscriminately bypassed that hurdle. After reining in her ecstatic heart, Frederica gave her answer.

"It's yes, Your Excellency," she said. "It's yes, Your Excellency," she repeated, prompted by the absurd doubt that only she had heard her own voice and that Yang hadn't. "Yes, I'd be honored…"

Yang nodded awkwardly, again struggling to put words together into a coherent sentence.

"Thank you. What I mean is…how should I put it…I, uh…"

In the end, Yang said nothing.

Julian Mintz entered Vice Admiral Alex Caselnes's private room as if by gravitational pull. Caselnes was suspicious and smiled once he knew the reason. He mixed a thinly watered-down drink and offered it to the boy.

"I see. Yang finally bit the bullet, eh?"

Julian nodded and drank vigorously, choking as it went down. The ice cubes in his glass clinked together. Caselnes grinned and filled his own glass in kind.

"It's basically an auspicious occasion. Shall we drink to it?"

Julian eyed his glass and went red in the face, and not just from the alcohol. He apologized for having so rudely drunk before sharing a toast. Caselnes dropped some ice into Julian's glass, pouring him a drink that was slightly darker in color than the first. After making their toast, Julian asked:

"You said it's basically an auspicious occasion. What did you mean by that?"

"Auspicious for Yang, because he actually found someone to be his bride. And a first-class one at that. And while I might question Lieutenant Commander Greenhill's tastes, she's marrying someone she loves, which is truly something to celebrate. You can have a funeral by yourself, but it takes two for a wedding."

"Then why did you say 'basically'? Do you have reservations?"

Caselnes avoided an immediate reply and poured himself a third glass. Taking the drink in hand, he answered without putting it to his lips.

"For the same reason you drained your glass before we toasted."

Julian was silent.

"I can only assume you've got a thing for Miss Greenhill."

Julian went completely red. The ice cubes danced as he slammed his glass back on the table.

"I want nothing but the best for them! Really, I love them both. It's only natural they'd end up…"

"I understand."

Caselnes did his best to keep the boy calm.

"Another round?"

"Yes, watered down."

The vice admiral obliged the boy's order.

"Maybe it's not my place to say, but the mechanisms of love and the human heart can't be solved with arithmetic. There's no magic formula. You're young enough to move on from this. But when it gets more serious, your love for one thing comes at the expense of your love and respect for other things. It's not a question of good versus evil. You just can't help it. Honestly, I'd be a little worried if you were head over heels at this point. You're a smart kid, and of good character to boot. Then again, flames have a way of flaring up in the most unexpected places."

"Yes, I understand."

"Hmm, well, I'm glad you do, even if it's only in your head," said Caselnes, who saw right through Julian. He changed the subject. "But I wonder, will they still call each other 'Admiral' and 'Lieutenant Commander' even after they're married?"

"No way—they'd never do that."

Caselnes made a stern face at Julian's knee-jerk response.

"When my wife and I got married, she called me Commander Caselnes at first. It was all I could do not to salute every time."

Julian laughed, but it was obvious to Caselnes he did so mostly out of courtesy.

"Let's save this discussion for after our victory. And what will you do, Julian, once they've married? You could always live with them."

Julian's breath was hot with alcohol and other things. He put his empty glass back on the table and coughed a few times.

"I wouldn't want to interfere with their newlywed life. How does the saying go? 'Those who disturb the love of others should be killed by a horse's kick.' I'd only get in the way."

Julian was trying to make light of it, but if Yang and Frederica did get married, he knew he would need to distance himself from them.

In Julian's chest, the image of a planet he'd yet to see was taking shape. It was a modest planet revolving around a small sun, situated on the outskirts of imperial territory. This planet, Terra, was the third in its solar system. It had once been humanity's only inhabited world. When he'd heard that name come out of Bishop Degsby's dying mouth, Julian knew he had to go there at least once.

Julian had no way of knowing what awaited him on Terra. If the blade by which he might rend the veil of history was hidden there, then he had to take hold of it. Mixed with the cream of this desire, the black coffee of his foresight was no longer just that.

Either way, he saw value in going there for the pure sake of it. Julian had nowhere near the perceptiveness of Yang, who had no choice but to approach the past and the future differently. But what Julian lacked in insight he would make up for in action. If he did have a life after this war, and Yang's marriage to Frederica became a reality, he would take that as a sign to set off for Terra.

"To your happiness," muttered Julian under his breath, stuffing his aimless thoughts into a drawer and locking it.

Caselnes watched him closely, his expression a mixture of curiosity and sympathy.

III

The Yang fleet left base and set a course for the Vermillion star system.

"Suddenly, we've become one big extended family. I don't envy Yang for having to oversee it all."

Caselnes was speaking to Julian as an "irregular" himself. After losing Iserlohn Fortress, his position as administrative director had gone with it, but until his subsequent duties were decided, we would ride the flagship *Hyperion* with authority. The reduction of distance between them and their destination was directly proportional to the increase of his anxiety.

When they arrived at the outermost perimeter of the Vermillion star system and saw on-screen its faint sun hanging like a small fruit in early spring, the alliance's leaders could almost hear their own veins constricting.

"Such a pathetic sun," cursed Vice Admiral Attenborough.

In his nervousness, the faintness of that lone fixed star made him uncomfortable. No matter how vividly that star shone, he would've found a way to criticize it.

"If we don't manage to block Duke von Lohengramm this time, we'll have nowhere else to go."

More than an ordinary realization, this was a decided reality, and so Julian couldn't quite sympathize with what the staff officers were saying. Their eyes, in accordance with some silent pact, were focused solely on their commander. Seeing Yang enjoying his conversation with Merkatz with such composure slightly lessened their emotional burdens. So long as their commander was alive and well, they could expect a miracle.

Even as marshal, Yang's military getup hadn't changed. His black beret—embossed with a white five-pointed star—black jacket and half boots, ivory scarf, and slacks were all the same. Only the star rank insignias had increased by one. The meaning of what that one star symbolized seemed major, but it had brought about no noticeable change in the behavior of the one it honored and made Yang seem like no more of a military man than he had before.

Merkatz, standing by Yang as his advisor, was wearing the black-and-silver uniform of the Imperial Navy. On his middle-aged body, insignias overlapped one another. He was, quite naturally, a man of warrior-like qualities more than military, and even in Frederica Greenhill's highest esteem seemed more like Yang's superior.

The skirmish between both sides opened with a silent competition of reconnaissance. The alliance divided the 125 billion cubic light-seconds surrounding the Vermillion star system into ten thousand sectors, which were covered with two thousand vanguard patrols. Chief of Staff Murai oversaw the entire operation, far excelling his black-haired commander when it came to these meticulous tasks. Yang felt justified in this allotment of duties, since any practical diligence left in him had been destroyed by his taxing evacuation of El Facil eleven years before.

In the thirty minutes leading up to battle, the level of their anxiety rose with every continued silence until the imperial forces arrived on the scene. A petty officer within Lieutenant Chase's FO2 reconnaissance division was the first to make the discovery.

"Lieutenant, look!"

The officer's voice was restrained in volume, his tone anything but, and was enough to make the lieutenant nervous. A billowing multitude of lights threatened to overtake the pitch-black expanse, swallowing the weak light of the stars behind them in silent approach.

The lieutenant switched on the FTL, his voice and fingers trembling.

"This is the vanguard reconnaissance, division FO2. We've spotted the enemy's main forces. Current position is sector 00846, heading for sector 1227, 40.6 light-seconds out. They're closing in fast!"

On the other side, the Imperial Navy's enemy-search network had discovered a small nest of mice roaming ahead of them. Vice Admiral Rolf Otto Brauhitsch, who had fought in the Battle of Kifeuser under Siegfried Kircheis, was the first to receive images from their recon satellite, along with a report from their small patrol group.

When asked by his subordinate whether they should seek and destroy, he shook his head.

"It'd be a small win at best to attack a recon fleet. Let's not waste our time. We're better off trying to determine the direction of their return, along with the position of the enemy's main forces."

Brauhitsch's command was spot-on, for while the alliance's FO2 recon division was making the enemy's position known to its allies, the opposite was also taking place. Because they weren't taking the most direct course back to their base of operations, the trajectory of their path was easily discerned by tactical computer.

When he received Brauhitsch's report, Reinhard had been gazing at the ocean of stars spread out on the overhead display from the bridge of his flagship *Brünhild*. His fair face took on a paler hue in the light of stars raining upon him, like some white porcelain image at the bottom of a river. The others around him hesitated to speak, holding their breaths as they immersed themselves in their respective duties. It was Senior Admiral Paul von Oberstein who broke that sacred silence by announcing the enemy fleet's approach to the young imperial marshal.

"We'll most likely make contact in the Vermillion star system."

From the start of their mission, Reinhard had agreed with von Oberstein's deductions on all fronts. Since time immemorial, battlespaces were most often chosen based on implicit agreements between enemies and allies alike. In this case, and for that reason, Reinhard had no doubt as to why Yang Wen-li had chosen the Vermillion star system as his decisive battlespace.

"So, it'll be here after all."

Although the blond-haired youth muttered these words without much admiration, when he called for his chief aide, Rear Admiral von Streit, he ordered a rest for all divisions. Reinhard smiled at his surprised aide.

"There's no reason to think the battle will begin anytime soon. Let us gather our nerves while we still can. Let them do as they will for three hours. They can even drink if they want to."

When the aide took his leave, Reinhard remained seated in his commander's chair and closed his dark eyelashes, giving himself over to the expanse of his heart.

All troops were granted an unexpected rest on the alliance side as well, while their highest leaders took to chatting in the conference room over coffee. Yang took a sip from his cup. He didn't know the first thing about coffee. Neither did he care about its quality.

"Not that I need to remind you, but Duke von Lohengramm is a genius without parallel. If we face him on equal terms, we'll have hardly any chance of winning."

"You're probably right," Yang said.

Von Schönkopf was being frank. It wasn't taboo within Yang's fleet to imply retreat or surrender.

"That said, you're not as bad as all that. This year alone, have you not led not one but *three* renowned imperial admirals by the nose?"

"I got lucky. Maybe not *just* lucky, but lucky all the same."

Yang spoke the truth as he saw it. Despite having destroyed three imperial fleets already in this war, going head-to-head with Oskar von Reuentahl and Wolfgang Mittermeier meant that Reinhard von Lohengramm would be unable to compose his victory song as planned. Although he didn't think he would lose, a succinct victory would be easier said than done. Insofar as he was in the scouting stage, it was unthinkable that Reinhard himself and the Imperial Navy—these two matchless things—would be thrown into the mix at this point, and for that reason he had no intention of trying his luck further. To be sure, he'd succeeded so far, but that didn't mean the goddess of fate was smiling down on him still. Rather, by those consecutive victories he felt like he'd used up his three wishes.

Merkatz eyed his commander, young enough to be his son, with gentle eyes, but said nothing.

"The enemy's formation is narrow but makes up for that in depth and density. I'd say they're planning a central piercing attack."

Deputy Chief of Staff Patrichev's crossed arms were practically the size of Yang's torso. Although intent on transcending his desk work to become a frontline commander since the days when the Yang fleet was called the Thirteenth Fleet, this jovial and dynamic man had been consistently stationed by Yang at headquarters.

"You aren't worried about letting them run free?" chimed Olivier Poplin.

But Patrichev understood Yang's strategy.

"Makes sense to me," he intoned in his operatic bass, although he wondered how much of a relief it would be to the soldiers.

As the chain of discussions pulling their mental equilibrium to its limit slackened, and the staff officers left the room, Walter von Schönkopf stayed behind. Yang momentarily looked away before speaking up.

"Do you think we can win, Vice Admiral?"

"That depends on whether you truly want to win."

Von Schönkopf's tone was deadly serious. Yang was in no position to discount that.

"Every fiber of my being wants to win."

"Wanting isn't enough. If you don't *believe* it, then how are you ever going to get others to believe?"

Yang was silent. Von Schönkopf's incisive tongue had cut him to the core.

"Whether you're a career soldier with his heart set only on winning or an ordinary man of ambition who desires power without knowing how much, you're a worthy adversary. And while I'm on the topic, if you were a man of unwavering conviction and responsibility who believed in his own righteousness, you'd be all too easy to agitate. But the fact is you're someone who, even in the heat of battle, doesn't believe in his own righteousness."

Yang gave no answer.

Von Schönkopf tapped his coffee cup and went on.

"He who is sure to win in a fight, although he doesn't believe in himself, lives, from a spiritual point of view, an unpardonable existence. That's the definition of a hopeless man."

"Even the worst democratic government is superior to the best autocracy. That's why I fight Reinhard von Lohengramm on Job Trünicht's behalf," Yang said. "I think that's conviction enough."

Even as he opened his mouth, Yang confirmed the truth of von Schönkopf's keen insight by not believing a single word of what he'd just said.

Back on ancient Earth, as the democratic empire of Athens warred with the despotic empire of Sparta, the independent nation of Mílos had assumed neutrality, affiliating itself with neither faction. Upset with Mílos for refusing subordination, the Athenians invaded, treating Mílos as their enemy. They slaughtered civilians, annexed their territory, and toasted their own actions as a victory for democracy. This ugly paradox set a bad example for the future. Had this invasion and the subsequent mass killings arisen out of an insane despotic ruler's ambition, they'd still have had hopes of being saved. Only cases in which the people were harmed by rulers they themselves had chosen were truly hopeless. People had the peculiar habit of sometimes applauding those who disdained them. Rudolf von Goldenbaum, on his way to the throne, surely got there by riding on the shoulders of his people. That was a consequence of the "worst democratic government." It was impossible for Yang to believe everything he himself had said. Even so, he thought, while the collapse of an autocracy might bring about the best democracy, the collapse of the worst democracy had, oddly enough, never brought about the best autocracy…

When their rest was over, preparations for war were carried out at once. Relaxed minds suddenly came alive with the power of ignited engines. Already various enemy-seeking channels had announced the presence of a giant enemy ahead, setting off an alarm in the heart of every officer.

"Distance from the enemy: eighty-four light-seconds."

The operator's voice was beamed to all ships, and with it cold hands to grip the soldiers' chests. Their breathing and pulses quickened, body temperatures rising.

"They're getting closer, little by little."

"Obviously. What would we do if they were moving away from us?"

Conversations between fellow soldiers at gunports and turrets were a yin-yang of nervousness and uneasiness. If they allowed the guns to overheat, they'd blow flame and burn each other up completely.

Yang, per usual, sat on top of his commander's desk, tented one knee, and kept his eyes on the main screen. But then his gaze wandered of its own accord over the high leaders—first to Merkatz, then to Murai, von Schönkopf, Julian Mintz, Machungo, Frederica Greenhill, and Patrichev in turn, not lingering for a moment—before returning to the screen. Frederica, feeling both great reassurance and slight discouragement, looked at the young marshal, who'd taken off his black beret and was ruffling his unruly hair. He belonged to her now. But not only to her. Compared to the more than ten billion people of the Free Planets Alliance who had their own faith in him, hers was modest at best. She felt overambitious for wanting to share a future with him.

Yang put the beret back on. Frederica braced herself and focused on the screen. Nothing else mattered until after they survived the war.

"Enemy forces are breaching the yellow zone."

The operator's voice was dry and formal at first. Then it spiked.

"They're completely within firing range!"

The gunners were ready, fingers poised at their firing buttons. They held their breaths, waiting for their commander in chief's orders. Yang took a breath, raised a hand, and swung it downward ten times as quickly as he'd lifted it.

"Fire!"

Tens of thousands of glowing dragons charged through space. Before these could reach their prey, the Imperial Navy's own dragons were loosed from their cages, rushing down on their opponents. Fang clashed with fang, exploding in dazzling offshoots of light.

At 1420 on April 24 of SE 799, year 490 of the imperial calendar, the Vermillion War had begun in the most mundane way.

IV

Bursts of light filled outer space with their soundless cadence. A fresh sword cut through this white-hot maelstrom, scattering ships like flailing shadows. Not thirty minutes after hostilities commenced, the war had plunged into a fierce fight.

The Vermillion War had opened on such an ordinary note that both Reinhard von Lohengramm and Yang Wen-li were worried that the other had some clever scheme up his sleeve. In anticipation of the other's next move, each could only take his first steps using extremely conventional tactics.

Reinhard had been planning an unprecedented "deep defense" tactic against Yang's offensive. Yang, of course, had his own ideas. But neither of them put these into operation, so as not to give the other a head start. This epic light show was therefore far from what either side had wanted. But the battle was on. Like raging wild horses who despised the rider's reins, they stampeded wild and free. Yang was frustrated by Reinhard's actions enough that he needed to concentrate a good amount of his nerves on orbital corrections.

Changes in the tide of battle were precipitous and disorderly, and neither Reinhard nor Yang could handle all of them. By the time orders were received, situations had changed drastically, making those orders meaningless. When reports from the Imperial Navy's front lines begged further instructions, lightning flashed in Reinhard's ice-blue eyes.

"Each division will respond as needed! What's the point of having mid-ranking commanding officers? Do I have to do everything around here?!"

The alliance fared worse. When commanders on the front lines requested detailed instructions, Yang sighed.

"Take that up with the enemy, why don't you. It's not like I have any power to choose in this situation."

Their highest commander's mental disturbances were rather entangled in the climaxing ferocity of conflict. Beams and missiles clashed in hostility, destructive and defensive powers alike vying for superiority. In cases of superior destructive power, they broke through energy-neutralizing magnetic fields and armor, gutting ships by the turbulence of their lethal heat. In cases of superior defensive power, their enormous energy scattered in vain, harming only the weakest prey in their waning path. As both armies were toyed with by surging waves of energy, they hurled every projectile at their disposal. Even as ships suffered hits to their very bowels by nuclear fusion missiles, they were lasering through enemy ships in return.

The empire's rainbow-colored onslaught exploded all around Yang's flagship *Hyperion*. The first to go was the cruiser ship *Narvik*, which after being hit dead center split into equal halves, while the others lit up their corner of outer space with balls of light.

Apprehension came over the swarthy, virile face of *Hyperion*'s captain, Commander Asadora Chartian.

"Your Excellency! Our flagship is too far forward. I fear we might become the target of concentrated fire. Requesting permission to fall back."

Yang turned his dark eyes, brimming with trust, to the captain.

"I leave control of this ship to its captain. Do as you see fit."

Within ten minutes, Yang regretted those remarks. A division of imperial forces, lacking communication lines with other fleets, was leading a new charge. "Why are we retreating? I can't very well command this way," Yang cried out. The moment Yang saw a gap, he reinforced one of the beams holding up his tactical canopy. Yang leaned forward and gave his command to Frederica.

In the end the command lacked conviction, but the moment the first imperial formation aimed its gunports at the enemy, a second formation came in from behind for the kill. The collision-avoidance systems of both fleets responded quickly, sending them flying in all directions. Navigations officers cursed gods and devils alike, clinging desperately to their control panels.

The chaos was short-lived, but for Yang it was enough. Each of the alliance ships turned toward the enemy's unexpected dance and at once unleashed its main battery. Points of light appeared everywhere, negating each other's borders as they grew into a larger collective sphere.

This left a giant hole in the imperial formation. It was a deformed mixture of energy and nothingness, a gargantuan maelstrom of high-frequency waves that denied the very existence of life.

Back on the flagship *Brünhild*, Reinhard was fuming.

"Just what the hell does Thurneisen think he's doing?!"

The communications officer cowered at Reinhard's voice, struggling to establish contact against the electromagnetic waves jamming his communications. The operators, too, were sweating over their attempts to distinguish the jumble of signals from both sides. They confirmed that Thurneisen had abandoned his post.

"Such a hero."

Von Oberstein's artificial eyes glowed indifferently.

"His voice travels far, but his eyes only see what's in front of them. You should cut him loose."

"If I'm still around when this battle is over, I'll take your warning to heart," Reinhard spat out. "But right now, I need his strength to get through this. Get me Thurneisen!"

A communications shuttle, carrying a transmission capsule with Reinhard's orders, left *Brünhild*'s hold. This aggravated Reinhard even more.

By going ahead on his own, fueled only by his own belligerence and ambition, Thurneisen had upset Reinhard's plans on a tactical level. Reinhard would have to drag him by the neck and restore order to his fleet. Rushing into a war of attrition like this risked playing into Yang's hands.

Reinhard's apprehensions proved correct. Yang was in a bad spot but had cleverly changed tactics, inviting concentrated fire from other imperial fleets besides Thurneisen's into his concave formation. The exquisiteness of his timing earned him a look of astonishment from Merkatz, and the imperial forces, as if being sucked through a straw, broke ranks and scrambled to neutralize the alliance's barrage.

"Fire!"

It was an attack of formidable density and accuracy. Like wild cattle driven by madness, the imperial forces rushed into an invisible wall. Light and heat billowed, and soldiers once filled with courage and exaltation became instant human wreckage. Chains of explosions extended in every direction, bringing forth a craftsmanship of light every bit as brilliant as humans could make. Inside those jewels were figures of life and death that were anything but graceful and magnificent.

Some people evaporated in an instant. Others burned down the steep slope into death, leaving a trail of futile screams behind. Soldiers blinded by the flash bumped into fleeing comrades, inadvertently plunging their faces into exposed wires and dying in showers of sparks.

Cruelty had never been their aim in fighting. But now they understood that justice and faith craved blood above all. In order make the justice proclaimed by their highest commander a reality, until their faith was satiated, many had soldiers burned alive, torn limb from limb. If only their sovereign had renounced justice and faith, those soldiers who watched as their entrails spilled out from open wounds would never have had to die in fear and pain. But rulers would continue to insist that justice and faith were more important than human lives, even as they hid behind their own authority, far from the battlespace. If anything distinguished Reinhard from such cowardly rulers, it was that he always stood on the front lines.

"Mother, mother…"

These were the last words of a soldier whose legs were blown off by the blast and who dragged his upper body across the floor with both hands as blood gurgled from his mouth. Another soldier, drenched in his own blood, tripped over him. One of his ribs cracked, and the lights went out in the young soldier's eyes.

Cruelty and tragedy were by no means exclusive to either side. The alliance, having sustained severe return fire, was also suffering the consequences.

Uranium-238 bombs fired from electromagnetic catapults pierced the hulls of alliance warships, radiating superhigh heat. Soldiers embraced by arms of flame let out strange screams as they rolled around on the floor. The floors themselves were already red-hot, and splattered blood evaporated into white smoke on contact. Orders to abort fell on deaf ears. As those still alive, covered in blood, warded off tendrils of flame and smoke, they ran for airtight doors as fast as their bodies would allow them. The blood spilling from their wounds kissed the floor, sending up plumes of fresh steam, while the heat burned the soles of their feet through the bottoms of their shoes. There was another explosion as giant hands of hot wind knocked down more soldiers. Shards of metal and ceramic flew at high velocity, slicing through their necks, helmets and all. Headless corpses fell atop comrades who'd just managed to get up, giving rise to more screams. Hands were hideously burned the moment they touched the floor, leaving skin behind when they were pulled up, their exposed flesh resembling purple gloves. Even as the bay doors closed, blocking off this hellish scene, the gates to a hell of slaughter were opening before the eyes of those still alive.

Time demanded a sacrifice in proportion to its passage. The destruction grew only fiercer and greater in quantity. Both the empire and the alliance were helpless to save themselves from plunging into the depths of a boiling sludge.

CHAPTER 8:

I

AT THE OUTSET, 18,860 ships and 2,295,400 soldiers on the empire's side and 16,420 ships and 1,976,00 soldiers on the alliance's participated in the Vermillion War. The numbers were roughly the same, and considering that the alliance's supply lines were shorter and that the imperial forces, now on the defensive, had reserves to fall back on, they were evenly matched. If anything, the alliance was, for lack of a better term, "not at a disadvantage."

But the Imperial Navy had the enormous reinforcements of Mittermeier, von Reuentahl, Müller, and Wittenfeld to look forward to. The alliance, on the other hand, didn't have a single coin left in its vault. If they were defeated here, not a single soldier would be left stationed on Heinessen. The fate of the Free Planets Alliance hung on whether one man, Reinhard von Lohengramm, could be brought down.

The weight of the situation was enough to crush the heart of the alliance's high commander. Despite fraying at the seams over the enormity of his responsibility, he was anything but weak. Yang's defiance took root in the realization that there was a limit to what human beings were capable of. If Yang Wen-li couldn't win against Reinhard von Lohengramm, then no one in the alliance could.

At the same time, he wanted nothing more than to avoid the painful sight of soldiers dying in fear. Yang knew such casualties came with the territory, but the mental pictures of destruction and bloody spectacle were enough to make the ersatz historian's heart run cold. Now, as before, he couldn't help but wonder whether he was even worthy of pursuing the joys of domestic life. This had been the biggest reason behind his reluctance to reciprocate Frederica Greenhill's feelings before. And while it seemed he'd finally overcome that, his heart was still lagging behind. Of course, if Yang gave up on these pleasures, then the dead would have no reason to come back to life…

The Vermillion War would, for generations to come, be worthy of special mention for the enormity and precision of its tactical machinations, and for the legendary marshals who clashed under its fateful banner. By the close of the battle's first act, Yang and Reinhard had already coproduced and directed unfathomable carnage, and now both sides were gearing up for a reluctant war of attrition. Despite sensing they were on a one-way track to catastrophe, they were at last successful in bringing the fighting under control, closing the curtain on an hour's worth of mutual killing that otherwise threatened to go on endlessly. Their discernment and judgment in handling this situation proved their prodigiousness, if only passively.

"Man, what a mess," Yang sighed as he ran his eyes across incoming data.

That the inherent coldheartedness of tactical science could so efficiently kill one's own men was, this time, made clearer to him by the valuable military forces he'd wasted. He was in a sour mood.

"If only we had more men. Ten thousand…no, five…even *three* thousand more ships would be enough. If only…"

Yang sighed again, knowing full well the futility of such groundless reasoning. As he ruffled his black hair, he pulled himself together and went back to the drawing board.

Those other than the commander had their respective duties. The military doctors and nurses had mobilized their entire medical network to treat the wounded. Faced with a choice between humanity and efficiency, they favored the latter, and their methods were in some ways cruel. First, they numbed patients' pain receptors with paralysis gas, then cut off the affected parts and replaced them with artificial organs and skin. Limbs damaged beyond repair were removed with laser scalpels, then switched out for artificial limbs equipped with hydrogen batteries. Such measures were first carried out only in cases where living cells couldn't be regenerated by electron radiation, but because half the time the body didn't accept them, those more gravely wounded who then regained consciousness screamed in protest when they couldn't detect their limbs properly. But no matter how much they cried to get their own appendages back, those amputated parts had already been incinerated. There was no way to preserve them hygienically. Thus, the number of soldiers who came out of the war as partial biomechanoids was comparable to the number of those less fortunate.

Early on April 27, the war underwent its first major change when, after regrouping his forces, Yang ordered a blitzkrieg.

It was rare for him to become so proactive against a progressive enemy. Usually, Yang moved only when the other side did and preferred taking his opponents by surprise over attacking them head-on. Likewise, when Reinhard was informed of an alliance blitzkrieg, he acted out of character for one so dynamic by ordering an orthodox counterattack.

Future historians would speak of these events as if they'd been there:

"And so, the Vermillion War had begun in earnest. Reinhard von Lohengramm's forces had made the first strike, while Yang's adopted a deep defensive posture. Each by his own merits tried his best to turn the tide of the war in his favor by coaxing his opponent into action."

But when all was said and done, whether actively or passively, Reinhard could only have done his best within the confines of the arena. Each had his own reason for acting the way he did.

The Yang fleet attacked the imperial forces in a planned conical formation. From the alliance's opened gunports, tangible and intangible energy alike rained down on the enemy with the force of Shiva's hammer. The imperial fleet's retaliation was just as fierce but was not enough to stop Yang's advance. Explosions bloomed in profusion all around them.

Any destroyers hit directly were subsumed by variations of white, orange, crimson, blue, green, and purple that disturbed the optic nerves, scattering as countless fragments in all directions. Clashing bundles of energy sent out light and heat, rocking ships with their turbulence. Tens of thousands of fire arrows battered ships as enormous amounts of air and soldiers were sucked out through those breaches into the darkness.

Had all of this been accompanied by sound, it would've driven the combatants insane.

The Yang fleet's concentration technique had never had much of an effect in the past, but this time was an exception. His relentless maelstrom of light beams dealt severe damage to the imperial side, causing plenty of fear and confusion. Reinhard's forces seemed about to retreat, before quickly abandoning that option to cut a horizontal path. But Yang was one step ahead of them.

In trying to make a detour while avoiding fire, the imperial forces had drawn the worst lot. They attempted to disperse themselves like a giant river flowing out from a ravine onto the plains, packing tightly together while sustaining concentrated enemy fire.

Such an efficient attack was worthy, in Yang's mind, of being carved on his gravestone. The gunners, even without perfect aim, managed to create one explosion after another, rendering an oil painting of blood and flame in outer space. Just one of those explosions meant the demise of thousands of human lives.

The imperial forces were unilaterally knocked back, their ranks broken, their formations scattered. Yang wasn't going to let this chance slip through his fingers. His concise yet powerful command was conveyed to all forces.

"Charge!"

The Yang fleet's conical formation plunged forward at full power and broke through the Imperial Navy's line formation like a steel sword piercing a bronze shield.

The operator let out a whoop of excitement.

"Breach successful! We're through!"

Again, despite the cheers filling the bridge of the flagship *Hyperion*, Yang was anything but moved by their delight.

"It's too thin," he said, sounding more like someone complaining to his butcher than a scrutinizing military leader. Julian understood where Yang was going with that statement. The imperial forces' defense formation shouldn't have been so easy to break through.

"We can expect more enemies at any moment."

The commander's prediction came true not half an hour later. At around 1200 hours, another line of defense appeared, showering them with gunfire.

As the Yang fleet continued forward at great speed, persisting with the concentrated fire that was its specialty, it drilled numerous holes in the empire's defenses, mowing down imperial ships at point-blank range. Commodore Marino's division even succeeded in cutting off the head.

Commodore Marino had served as *Hyperion* captain before Commander Chartian had succeeded him. His skills as captain weren't necessarily comparable to those as fleet commander, but he straddled both roles nonetheless. Like a carpenter working an awl, his division had bored through the imperial formation. But before their cheers could even settle, more points of light appeared before them, spreading to either side in a macabre gesture of welcome.

"They just keep coming. How many layers of defense do they have? Is this an old-fashioned petticoat or something?"

The cursing commodore looked around at his staff officers in disgust, but none responded. As the balloon of their triumph deflated, a thin mist of uneasiness and fatigue hung in the air.

The Alliance Armed Forces opened their gunports all the same, never slowing their charge, and attacked the third formation. After a brief yet violent battle, they'd literally torn it to shreds. Again, there were cheers—that was, until they sighted the fourth formation.

II

It was April 29, and Yang Wen-li's swift attacks had broken through the empire's eighth defensive formation. But a ninth had spread before the alliance: tens of thousands of points of light lined up together, ready to attack.

"Such thickness and depth…"

Yang was impressed. When the imperial formation had counterattacked, Yang had successfully predicted it would assume a deep defense pattern, but he hadn't expected it to be so dense. Here was a living example of the saying, "Reality is always greater than imagination."

Merkatz crossed his arms.

"It's like we're peeling away the layers of a pastry. One by one, these defense formations keep on coming."

"There's no end to them."

Chief of Staff Murai shook his head.

Rear Admiral Walter von Schönkopf twisted his lips into a cynical curve.

"It's too late to stop now. Shall we peel away the ninth layer, or…?"

Yang returned his gaze to Merkatz and nodded, having gotten the answer he was looking for. They were past the point of no return. Knowing that the water was getting deeper and the mud thicker, the alliance had no choice but to walk into the center of the lake. Duke Reinhard von Lohengramm was pulling the alliance by an invisible tether, and his manipulation thereof felt magnificently ominous. But how was Duke von Lohengramm observing the progress of this battle, and where was he hiding himself, waiting for his moment to strike?

"Your Excellency…"

This reserved voice came from Julian's mouth.

"Did you have something to say?"

"Yes, Your Excellency. I think I know what Duke von Lohengramm means to do."

Yang slightly furrowed his brow and looked at the flaxen-haired boy. Yang was harsh with him like this on occasion, if only to avoid the appearance of a ward's favoritism.

"He's good at keeping up appearances. But a light-year separates what Duke von Lohengramm thinks and what he does."

"Yes, but in this case, I'd say that distance isn't even one light-*second*."

The staff officers' gazes converged on Julian. Yang waited a moment before pressing for an explanation.

"Duke von Lohengramm's goal is to exhaust us, both physically and psychologically. This is especially proven by the fact that every time one formation is broken through, another one takes its place."

"He's right, you know," muttered Merkatz.

Yang gazed at the boy in silence. Julian was enunciating every word carefully, as if to confirm what he was saying for himself.

"They're not coming at us head-on. Our sensors would've picked up on that if they were, and Duke von Lohengramm would have a hard time keeping an eye on the battle's progress. Presumably, there's nothing at all, and hasn't been from the start, between our forces and Duke von Lohengramm. Instead, I think the enemy's forces are positioned on either side of us, like thin cards." Julian took a breath and stated his conclusion. "In other words, they're shuffling their deck right front of us. If only we could circumvent this, we might be able to engage Duke von Lohengramm's main fleet."

Julian had expressed himself with incomparable lucidity and accuracy. When the boy finished speaking, Merkatz nodded first.

"I see. That makes sense. You've certainly thought this through."

Yang sighed. It was possible for Duke von Lohengramm to have moved all divisions from the sides to the alliance's fore, all while keeping a direct eye on the state of the war. Even so, thought Frederica Greenhill, she wondered whether Yang's sigh was directed at Reinhard von Lohengramm or Julian.

Just then, a report came in from an operator. A group of the empire's single-seat fighter walküren was fast approaching.

"Have Poplin's and Konev's squadrons engage," Yang ordered.

Already thinking of the next short-term tactic, he moved off his desk into the chair and put on his black beret.

⁘ ⁘ ⁘

As 160 spartanians and 180 walküren flew past each other at high speeds between the large warships, they transitioned into an all-out dogfight.

Olivier Poplin had been called many reprehensible things, but a coward wasn't one of them. He sallied forward, ensuring that those who trembled at his approach would be the first to go down.

"Whisky, Rum, Vodka, Applejack, all units are go. Don't get swallowed up by the enemy. You swallow them."

Poplin had, appropriately enough, named his squadrons after types of alcohol. Following his customary signal call, he gave them the green light to branch into eight directions.

Although Poplin's squadron was known for its three-as-one formations, the fleet captain was having too much fun taking out enemy craft solo. He appeared reckless, when in fact he penetrated the multitudes of enemy targets with such speed and vigor that with every beam he fired he reduced one or two ships to a flower of light. His enemies were taken aback by his peerless skill, but two of the walküren, their pilots spurred on by courage and ambition, ferociously taunted their large prey with arrows of fire and snapped at his heels.

"You think you can provoke me? You're half a century early for that," Poplin laughed derisively.

As his pursuers corkscrewed behind him, he dashed through space toward an enemy warship. Ignoring the photon-bomb tracers dangerously caressing his craft, he shot up suddenly just before impact. He climbed to the top of the ship, just centimeters away from the body, and performed a roll.

The two walküren in pursuit were no match for his skills. One of the pilots crashed into the hull of the ship, scattering in an orange ball of light. The other attempted to replicate Poplin's steep climb but got too close to the ship's hull and was sucked out through a hole torn in his craft after churning up too many sparks of friction.

"Guess I can't count those two among the ones I've shot down. Konev is totally going to outdo me this time."

Poplin didn't have much time to boast, as his subordinates were embroiled in a fight the likes of which they'd never encountered. The imperial walküren, under Commander Horst Schüler, with eighty kills to his name, was employing his own three-as-one strategy against the alliance, capturing and destroying spartanians in tandem with tightly knit fire. As the spartanians were drawn within their firing range, they evaporated, one by one.

Poplin rallied his pilots, amazed at how sharply their numbers had dropped. The status report from Lieutenant Moranville was filled with bitterness.

"Team Applejack is down to two. Everyone else was killed in action... everyone else..."

Suddenly his voice grew weak and drove an ominous wedge into Poplin's chest.

"What's going on? Do you copy?"

The voice that came back wasn't Moranville's. The only common feature they shared was a feeling of overwhelming exhaustion.

"This is Warrant Officer Zamchevsky. I'm all that's left of team Applejack."

Poplin audibly sucked in his breath and let it out, smashing his piloting console with his right fist.

That the renowned Poplin fleet had lost almost half of its ranks made the alliance shudder, but an even stronger impact was waiting in the wings. Upon returning, Poplin was downing a whisky in the officers' mess, still in his pilot's uniform, when Konev's vice commanding officer, Lieutenant Caldwell, came walking in with a weary-looking pair.

"Hey, what happened to your boss? I want to see his face looking more depressed than me."

Lieutenant Caldwell stopped in his tracks, his face a study in bewilderment and hesitation, and answered in a heavy voice.

"As of now, I'm acting commander of the Konev squadron, Commander Poplin."

With a face that was a poster of displeasure, painted and framed, the ace pilot tossed back another glass.

"I'm in no mood for roundabout explanations. What's happened to your commander?"

The lieutenant resigned himself and gave an unambiguous answer.

"Killed in action, sir."

Poplin glared at the lieutenant with a light in his eyes that resembled an urge to kill. The dissonance of innumerable conflicting emotions was the only thing that kept an angry bellow from roaring out of his chest.

"How many did it take to bring him down?"

"Sir?"

"I asked you how many it took to bring him down. Ivan Konev would never have gone out from a single shot. How many imperial ships did they need to take him out?"

The lieutenant looked at the floor like someone accused of wrongdoing.

"Commander Konev wasn't killed in a dogfight. He was fired upon by a cruiser."

"I see."

Poplin stood up from the table. Lieutenant Caldwell reflexively took half a step back.

"The imperial forces needed a cruiser to put away Konev, did they? Then they'll need at least half a dozen battleships for me."

Poplin laughed, but his laughter put the lieutenant in mind of a heat thunderstorm. Poplin threw something, which Caldwell caught. The lieutenant watched the ace pilot, who betrayed nothing of his drunkenness, leave the officers' mess before looking at his own hand. There, clutched in its grip, was an empty bottle of corn whisky.

After successfully breaking through the imperial forces' ninth layer, Yang Wen-li announced a change of strategy. For once, he was truly drained by this ongoing succession of battles.

"Duke von Lohengramm's tactic is to chip away at our forces by a most extreme form of deep defense. It's just as Sublieutenant Mintz has said. Going on any longer like this would be foolish, but stopping would buy them time, and so either way we play into his hands. Our only chance at victory is to demolish the enemy's multilayered formation."

After such a stale introduction, Yang presented the fruits of his mental labors to his staff officers and instructed them on his new strategy.

Thus, on April 30, the war underwent its second dramatic change.

III

At this stage, Reinhard, in an apparent state of lethargy, was devoting himself to sustaining Yang's attacks as a means of whittling away at his penetrative power. Facing Yang head-on was just one part of his strategy to capture the whole of FPA territory. When his generals fell back from the sectors to which they'd been dispatched and flooded the Vermillion Stellar Region, the first battle welcomed its magnificent climax. The preparations for said climax were relatively simple.

To sustain Yang's assault, Reinhard had prepared upward of twenty-four defensive formations. In the same way that he'd symbolically poured wine over a stack of paper for his generals' edification, he planned on depleting Yang's military power one layer at a time. Reinhard had put everything into this strategy, which filled Yang with insuppressible admiration. The military forces of a temporarily breached defensive formation dispersed to either side and took a roundabout path back to their allies in the rear, where they formed a new defensive barrier. Thus, Yang was faced with the prospect of a never-ending battle, winning over and over against a limitless defense.

Reinhard's strategy was a well-oiled machine. Not only did it stop Yang in his tracks, it inspired Yang to retreat some eight hundred thousand kilometers away, where he concealed his fleet behind a small group of planets that would be difficult to probe. Before long, a report confirmed that a sizable fleet had fallen back and was moving to the alliance's starboard side, or the imperial forces' port.

A gloom passed over Reinhard's ice-blue eyes. It was unthinkable that Yang Wen-li would disperse his forces without good reason. His purpose in doing so was undoubtedly to spread out Reinhard's forces in kind, but the problem was whether Yang had dispatched his main force to begin with. The artificial-eyed chief of staff, Paul von Oberstein, interrupted his master's train of thought.

"Considering how openly they did it, we can assume it's a decoy, but it might not be. Either way, it'd be foolish to spread ourselves too thin."

Reinhard nodded, but that gesture took on hues that were more of deferment than approval. He didn't have the greatest of expectations for von Oberstein as a tactician. The artificial-eyed chief of staff might have been an excellent strategist and politician, but when it came to genuine combat, he couldn't hold a candle to Reinhard's refined genius.

Reinhard noticed he'd been fiddling with the pendant on his chest. If the redhead whose likeness slumbered inside that pendant were still alive, he surely would've had some good advice for Reinhard. Since losing him, Reinhard had carried out all battle plans himself, from page to stage, as it were. The enormity of what was lost to him was as deep as the foolishness of having lost something he shouldn't have lost in the first place.

"What say you, Your Excellency?" urged von Oberstein.

At this, Reinhard dragged his heart back to the ground floor of reality. It still took him a few moments to give his order.

"Turn all divisions portside. The enemy is using this as a decoy to move its main forces. We block their way and hit them where it hurts."

For once, Reinhard lacked total confidence. The thought of whether he should modify his first attack method was patrolling his brain. If Siegfried Kircheis had been by his side and proposed such a thing, he would've followed it without question. His inborn ambition, however, was a necessary reaction against the passive measures he'd taken thus far. He was also tempted by the prospect of taking down Yang Wen-li without leaning on the military forces of his admirals. He believed that he'd read deeply enough into Yang's tactics. He'd have to hand over the reins eventually, even if only for one battle. Still unable to control the chaos in his heart, Reinhard turned to a positive plan.

Save for the small number of fleets under Reinhard's direct control at headquarters, the imperial forces reorganized their battle formations, advancing quickly on the enemy by detouring portside. Turning from total defense to offense put the young admirals in high spirits.

But when the imperial forces had the enemy within firing range, they were astonished, for what they thought was the alliance's main force was a group of two thousand decoys pulling meteorites to trick the radar into thinking they were more numerous. While this decoy fleet was luring the empire's main forces, the alliance's own jumped out from their hiding spot in the small planetary cluster and went fiercely after Reinhard's headquarters.

The alliance forces charged with all their might. If they missed this chance, then defeat was inevitable. Dusty Attenborough and the rest shouted at their subordinates while stamping their feet on the floor, piercing the empty, defenseless space like an arrow.

By the time the imperial forces noticed what was happening, the alliance had already crossed behind them and was closing in on Reinhard's headquarters. The speed of their charge impressed even the Gale Wolf, Wolfgang Mittermeier.

Thurneisen, Brauhitsch, Aldringen, Carnap, and Grünemann tried their best to turn back but were showered by fire from the decoy fleet, sustaining significant damage. Not that they cared much about that, for even as they were being hit from behind by the decoy fleet, the imperial forces were attacked by rows of alliance ships from the fore.

If this was successful, the imperial forces were sure to be hit by an acute flank attack. Yang Wen-li's forces were at their exquisite best. Although the imperial vanguard groups fired beams and missiles at random, when they inflicted damage on the alliance's starboard side, the alliance broke formation and surged to port, making it seem as if their center would break. Convinced of this, Thurneisen and Brauhitsch raged to recover from the humiliation of being attacked by the decoy, and charged in tandem.

Change was quick. Just as they were convinced they'd successfully broken them, the imperial admirals were dumbfounded to learn that they were under siege by the alliance. The bend in the alliance formation was in fact the hollow of a deformed concavity that the alliance had formed in response to the imperial offensive. If the imperial forces confronted them head-on now, they'd be stuck in the middle of the formation. The imperial forces were unlikely to make that foolish mistake. The optical illusion that convinced them they were attacking the enemy's side had groomed them to be tactical victims of Yang Wen-li's supernatural abilities.

Gunfire from the decoy fleet blocking off the rear also intensified, and the alliance attacked from all sides.

Innumerable striations skewered the imperial fleet, and knives of light minced its warships. Surrounded and immobilized, the imperial forces rolled down a steep slope into death and destruction amid dazzling explosions of light.

"Aldringen's fleet is being decimated."

This report, filled with danger and fear, was met with a deep ocean of silence by the flagship *Brünhild*. More bad news poured in.

"Brauhitsch's fleet is dissolving its battlefront."

The operator giving these reports fought for control over his voice. Reinhard had known all along that the ongoing destruction wouldn't be restricted to the fleets or battlefronts but would also include the legendary invincibility and glory of his authority.

"I've been cheated," Reinhard mused to himself.

A shadow of self-deprecation ran down his pale, beautiful face. If the encirclement was perfectly successful, his defeat was likely, but he was damned if he wasn't going to crush Yang Wen-li before that happened. With nothing more than an imperfect encirclement and an awkward dispersal of forces, he and his men had become sitting ducks.

"Did we win all these victories only to lose in the end? Kircheis, is this as far as I was meant to go?"

Gripping the pendant in his white hand, he asked himself these silent questions within his bottomless loneliness. His redheaded friend gave no answer. Neither could Reinhard make him.

The imperial forces were on their last legs, just waiting for the moment when they would fall like an enormous evergreen oak struck by lightning.

Reinhard's chief aide, Rear Admiral Arthur von Streit, walked up to his young master. Known as a man of sincere reasoning, he gave counsel, doing his best to maintain determination in the face of catastrophe.

"Your Excellency, a shuttle will be ready for you shortly. Please, you must escape while you can…"

Reinhard stared back at his aide. At that moment, the cold glint in his ice-blue eyes was beautiful enough to make the one they regarded catch his breath.

"Don't overstep your bounds. I've never heard of any strategy that involves running when it isn't necessary. Since when do cowards triumph?"

"Forgive me for speaking out of turn. But fleeing the battleground at this point doesn't mean you'll lose. Once we've gathered all the admirals' forces, we can jump back into the arena for a return match."

The golden-haired youth was stubborn, forgetting what he himself had persuaded Emil of the other day.

"If I'm killed by Yang Wen-li here, that's all I will amount to. What kind of supreme ruler will I be then? Those I killed will mock me from hell to Valhalla. Do you *want* me to become a laughingstock?"

"Your Excellency, don't take your precious life so lightly. We'll start afresh. Please, get out while you can," implored Captain Günter Kissling, of Reinhard's personal guard, with his topaz eyes.

But Reinhard's expression, retaining its porcelainlike solemnity, rejected his appeal. Von Streit shifted his gaze to Kissling. Although it went against his master's intentions, he silently hinted that he should escape from the flagship. Kissling nodded.

At that moment, the three protective warships in front of *Brünhild* became victims of concentrated fire. One of the ships was hit in its power core and vanished in a ball of flame. Another was split in two, while the last spit out a torrent of debris from its open wound and staggered out of firing range.

Their explosions flashed across the screen, shocking those inside *Brünhild*. Enormous volumes of released energy kicked at *Brünhild* like a pack of wild horses, violently rocking the imperial flagship. Everyone on the bridge, save one, fell to the floor. Only the young, golden-haired dictator managed to avoid falling over by virtue of his unbelievable balance and agility.

And then, a strange thing happened. There was a lull in the alliance's fierce tirade. As Reinhard tried to help up the boy Emil, he threw a sharp glance at the screen. The maelstrom of light beams vanished, and the screen reverted briefly to the darkness of space.

"It's Müller's fleet," the operator shouted. "Müller has come to our aid—we're saved!"

Those last words expressed for all the true feelings of the bridge, and were answered by a chorus of approval.

IV

There was a reason why, among the imperial generals dispersed to carry out Reinhard's grand encirclement, Neidhart Müller was the first to go on the offensive. Having been ordered to seize the Lucas Stellar Region distribution base, which was relatively close to Vermillion, he'd planned on going back to fight once he was finished with that task. The base appeared fortified, and would therefore require a few days to subjugate. But when Müller arrived at the Lucas Stellar Region, word came that the base would be welcoming them without resistance.

It was the one responsible for the base, a man by the name of Aubrey Cochran, who handed everything over to the empire. Of course, his many subordinates insisted that the materials therein were too precious to give up. They were about to irradiate and render useless eighty million tons of grain, twenty-four million tons of edible meat, sixty-five million tons of domestic animal feed, 2.6 million carats of diamonds for industrial use, 38.4 million tons of liquid hydrogen, and comparable stores of rare metals, fuel, and petroleum products. But Cochran refused, explaining his reasoning thusly.

"Were the supplies amassed here for military use, that would be one thing, but they're all for civilians. No matter how our leaders and political system may change, the lives of the people mustn't be destroyed. Maybe I'll be called a traitor, but that'll be my cross to bear."

The extremists among his men, having no intention of handing over their resources to the empire, forced themselves upon Cochran, but others held them back. In the end, the Lucas Stellar Region supply base was surrendered to the empire without incident. At first, Müller detested Cochran for what he deemed selfish and traitorous actions. Later, after learning of Cochran's reasoning from his men, he was impressed and invited him to join his own staff officers. He thought of giving him the important office of supervising supplies and finances.

Cochran turned down the offer. Thinking himself a coward, he was worried how others might see him and how he would never be able to stop people from saying he'd sold off their resources to the enemy just to secure a post. He was promised that the resources would be used only for civilians and that he and his men would be allowed to return to Heinessen. Once reassured of this, Müller left quietly. But Cochran's good faith was betrayed. After returning to Heinessen, according to his former subordinates' indictment, he was arrested on suspicion of abetting the enemy and sent to a remote POW detention camp to await punishment. Amid political and military chaos, his existence might've been forgotten if not for the efforts of one man. Two years later, when the Bharat star system uprising was ending, Neidhart Müller would dispatch his men in search of Cochran's whereabouts and rescue him from death by malnutrition in the detention camp. Cochran would subsequently come to work as head accountant under Müller, but that's another story.

Neidhart Müller's return and rescue brought about the third sea change in the Vermillion War.

Without his acute flank attack on May 2, the alliance might very well have captured Reinhard von Lohengramm before the day's end, or so future historians, who couldn't resist the temptation to dramatize their subject, would unanimously conjecture. Since the previous day, Yang Wen-li's tactical command had been almost infallible, momentarily surpassing even Reinhard's. But he, too, was about to meet with an unavoidable setback.

The Müller fleet's appearance revitalized the imperial forces. They opened their gunports, determined to vanquish the alliance with all the energy at their disposal, and showered their formidable opponents with beams and missiles.

Flowers of light bloomed amid rows of alliance ships and disappeared to reveal barren, dark holes. As they were being herded into a disadvantageous position, the alliance forces fired back, crushing the imperial flagship.

Rear Admiral Dusty Attenborough of the alliance, reaching the limits of his stamina, continued his frontline command without sleep or rest.

"Our commanders shouldn't give up and run away just because one imperial fleet has joined the fray. I'd like to see what else Miracle Yang has up his sleeve," remarked Attenborough as he stroked his stubbled chin.

Müller's fleet had quickly left stragglers behind and arrived in the battlespace with 60 percent of its forces—hardly worthy of being called a fleet. This was a small success for Yang.

To him, Müller's appearance smacked more of chance than calculation. Among the imperial admirals, he thought that Wolfgang Mittermeier, he of incomparable rapidity, would've arrived ahead of the rest, and Yang had planned on taking down Reinhard before that happened. As of that moment, the income and expenditure of his plans were well-balanced. If the situation continued as it was, victory was within his grasp. But not without a new plan.

Yang muttered to himself as he fanned his face with his beret.

"I really got ahead of myself by ignoring Müller…"

He hadn't planned on making light of the Imperial Navy's youngest admiral, but he'd ended up doing just that.

The first to take the brunt of Müller's offensive was Admiral Lionel Morton.

It was a most severe attack. Morton's fleet, which at the start of the battle totaled 3,690 ships, was reduced to 1,560 after an hour. Their losses in that hour amounted to 57.7 percent—a figure that, while perfectly accurate, would look doubtful in the eyes of military historians.

Of course, the imperial forces paid no small compensation, either. The alliance's encirclement held its form, hitting the advancing imperial flagship with everything it had, unleashing currents of explosive light and energy all the while. But at this moment, Müller excelled Yang by the sheer force with which he'd surged into the arena.

"Admiral Morton has been killed in action."

Upon hearing this mournful report, Yang briefly closed his eyes. Noticing the sure colors of despair and weariness in his youthful face, Julian and Frederica exchanged glances.

The remainders of Morton's fleet, having lost their commander, and under intense fire, barely managed to hold their ranks and regroup with Yang's main fleet. Müller, having killed Morton in action, forced his way between Yang and Reinhard and appeared to shield his master from enemy attacks with his own body.

"He's a first-rate commander. Reads the situation well, fights well, and protects his emperor well."

Yang wasn't the only one with the bad habit of praising his enemy's strength. Reinhard was similarly afflicted, and it wasn't uncommon for his mentality and sensitivity as a military man to do a full one-eighty into utmost respect and adoration for his enemies and contempt and hatred for his comrades.

But this time, there was no leeway for admiration. The violence of Müller's attack was too much for the alliance to absorb as the imperial forces bored their way into their midst. Flashes and flares rained down on the alliance forces in a storm of superheated flames. Lethal striations lanced in every direction, for a moment lighting the dark path to death, playing a silent requiem for their victims.

"Müller has done well," muttered Reinhard from the bridge of *Brünhild*, now saved from retreat. He wiped his beautiful face with the towel handed to him by Emil and literally caught his breath.

∪

The alliance forces had been made to stand at the precipice between life and death. Had Müller been able to muster his entire fleet, he would've pushed them over that precipice.

None of which meant the imperial forces had the upper hand on all fronts. To be sure, the fighting going on between the alliance and the imperial forces hemmed within its unbroken ring of entrapment had taken up an overwhelming amount of time and energy. Both the Aldringen and Brauhitsch fleets were no more than military wreckage, while the Thurneisen, Carnap, and Grünemann fleets had little strength left to break through the encirclement. Thurneisen's hands were occupied with defense, and Grünemann, having suffered serious injuries, relinquished command to his chief of staff.

A full twenty-four hours later, Carnap, too, had succumbed to the power of the alliance's siege, and after accumulating enough losses contacted Reinhard's main fleet to request reinforcements. When he heard this from the communications officer, the young dictator swung his luxurious golden locks.

"I have no surplus forces. Let them die as they are. If he wants to say something, I'll hear him out in Valhalla."

Reinhard wasn't just being coldhearted. He truly had not one spare soldier or ship to his name.

Carnap, on the other hand, didn't take too kindly to this advice.

"Die as we are, he says?! So be it. And if I die first, I'll reach Valhalla ahead of you and make you my errand boy, Reinhard von Lohengramm!"

Carnap rose from his commander's chair, giving orders to all depleted fleets under his command to attack with all the speed at their disposal. Had their efforts been focused on a single point, or had the encirclement broken, the Yang fleet might've collapsed. Carnap's decision was only natural, but it gave Yang a valuable opportunity.

"Open fire, as accurately and efficiently as you can."

Yang made it a point to stress that last part, because the alliance was beginning to run low on energy supplies. He had a corner of the encirclement sustaining fire from both sides intentionally opened.

The imperial forces were pleasantly surprised. And when those inside the encirclement attempted to escape from within it, the outer imperial forces tried to burst in to save their comrades. Both sides rushed toward the same point of empty space, congesting the area as they did. This left the Yang fleet easily able to brandish its special skill—concentrating fire on a single point.

Carnap evaporated along with his fleet, which left a vast graveyard of shining light in space to show for its last stand.

Thus, the state of the war changed for a fourth time.

Neidhart Müller saw his foremost fleet engulfed in flame. Colorful tornadoes reflected in his sandy eyes. The severity and strength of the alliance's destructive power at the last moment was nothing short of marvelous. The flagship was damaged in six places, enough to breach its nuclear fusion reactor, forcing crew members to take cover.

"Your Excellency," implored Commander Guzman, beads of sweat forming on his pale face, "please abandon this ship. Its fate is sealed."

Müller gently nodded his head in reluctant agreement, but he didn't simply want to abandon ship.

"All right, then, we'll move our headquarters elsewhere. What's the closest battleship?"

Upon learning it was *Neustadt*, Müller nodded.

"You're coming with me in the shuttle."

That order alone prevented the captain from committing suicide. Reinhard's feet were inevitably bound by the chains of his own search for glory, but Müller, who had once suffered a great defeat at the hands of Yang, had learned to be flexible in the face of certain doom. He entrusted himself to the shuttle and left his flagship to die.

But when Müller changed flagships, the alliance homed in on *Neustadt*'s center, rendering it inoperable. Five minutes after Müller and his men had made their escape, it vanished in a ball of flame.

"Am I lucky or unlucky?" said Müller with a bitter smile.

He moved his headquarters to the battleship *Offenburg*, and two hours later to the battleship *Helten*. Müller did so not out of cowardice, but as proof of his determination to continue fighting tenaciously even in the heat of a losing battle.

Thus, Neidhart Müller would be greatly renowned in future generations as the admiral of three different ships in the same war. But his valor and devoted fighting style weren't enough to stave off Yang Wen-li's onslaught. His future biographers would forever stress how this one human being fought with such quiet determination and outstanding powers of judgment, struggling through so many dangers in his attempts to grab the tail of victory. Yang overcame the extreme danger of Müller's involvement in the war and formulated a new battle plan, which he carried out to perfection.

But on May 5, the fifth sudden change of the war took place. Its cause was something in the alliance capital of Heinessen, 3.6 light-years away from the battlespace. On this day, at 2240, an FTL was sent to Yang. Chairman of the alliance High Council Job Trünicht had ordered an unconditional cease-fire. When the order was received, the alliance's battery was just about to get Reinhard von Lohengramm's flagship *Brünhild* in its sights.

CHAPTER 9:

I
A CEASE-FIRE.

Yang Wen-li had his hands wrapped around the empire's neck when the order came and was just preparing to administer a fatal squeeze when he was thrown back into a corner by his own government.

"What are those bastards on Heinessen thinking!"

It wasn't a question, but a violent anger manifested in verbal form.

"Have our superiors also gone crazy?! We were just about to win. No, we *have* won! Why must we stop now?!"

With an angry roar, Attenborough threw his beret to the floor, as he had been hoping to get within hailing distance of Reinhard's flagship *Brünhild*.

Back on *Hyperion*, Walter von Schönkopf spoke sharply to Yang.

"Commander, I have something to say."

Yang turned around and lightly shrugged his shoulders.

"I know what you want to say, so keep it to yourself."

"If you know, then let's proceed as planned."

Von Schönkopf's eyes were burning as he pointed at the main screen.

"Ignore the government's orders and launch an all-out assault. Do that, and you'll have taken control of three things: Duke von Lohengramm's life, the universe, and history as we know it. Man up! Press on, and you'll pave your own road through history."

When he closed his mouth, the calm after the storm gripped everyone on the bridge of *Hyperion*. People followed the sound of each other's breathing, trembling from the elevation of their own pulses. Von Schönkopf had said something he shouldn't have said. As a child, he'd fled the empire with his grandparents to become a man of high stature, climbing up on his own abilities and merits to the rank of vice admiral in the Alliance Armed Forces by the age of thirty-five. With all eyes on him, he'd plucked a forbidden fruit from its branch.

But how sweet that forbidden fruit was, filled with the nectar and aroma of conquest, hegemony, and glory. Not only Yang, but also those around him could almost taste it.

Yang was uncomfortably silent. Not the calm after a storm after all, but what Frederica Greenhill likened to sunlight during Indian summer. Yang didn't break open the cage of that silence so much as gently push it open with his words, by which he deepened Frederica's convictions.

"There's that course, yes. But those clothes aren't my size. Tell all fleets to retreat, Lieutenant Commander Greenhill."

Wolfgang Mittermeier had gained total control over the alliance supplies and communications base in the Eleuthera Stellar Region and was just about to head back when he welcomed an unusual guest on May 2. An unidentified vessel was picked up by the ship's enemy-surveillance network, but when it was ordered to stop, what came back was totally unexpected.

"We're friendly forces seeking an audience with the commander."

The Countess Hildegard von Mariendorf stepped out onto the floor of the battleship *Beowulf*, greeting a wide-eyed Gale Wolf with a smile that was a mixture of physical fatigue and mental vitality. The combination of her cropped blond hair and men's uniform gave the strong impression of a beautiful boy.

"Fräulein von Mariendorf, what a pleasant surprise."

Prior to this, Hilda had secretly left the Gandharva star system and reached the outer rim of the Vermillion Stellar Region. Half by persuading high-ranking officers to defend her absence and half by coercive ex post facto approval, she had borrowed a speed cruiser. Then, just after the battle began, and after watching Yang's first major assault from a distance, she had reached the Eleuthera Stellar Region as fast as humanly possible. Having not a single soldier to save Reinhard, she felt compelled to enlist the aid of an ally she could trust. She didn't want to risk an FTL missive at such great distance, because this place was squarely in enemy territory and the danger of being intercepted was too great.

"Hmm, so you're saying it's too late to head for the Vermillion Stellar Region?"

"Yes, I doubt even the fast legs of the Gale Wolf would make it in time to save Duke von Lohengramm."

Mittermeier offered a brief, bitter smile, and asked the obvious question.

"Then what do you propose? I'm guessing you have a backup plan in mind, fräulein."

Hilda nodded.

Today was May 2, she explained. Even leaving for the Vermillion Stellar Region right away would put their arrival at four days later, on May 6. And they couldn't travel in just one ship but would need to pull a grand fleet of them. After observing the situation from a distance, she could guess what would happen next. Yang Wen-li's attack was unusual, and strong signs pointed toward Reinhard's eventual defeat. And by the time they reached the battlespace on May 6, it would be useless to attack an enemy already on the verge of winning. Even so, the distance between here and the alliance capital of Heinessen in the Bharat star system was shorter than that to Vermillion and could be traversed conservatively in forty-eight hours. Consequently, by making a sudden change and attacking a likely defenseless Heinessen, bringing about the surrender of the alliance government and forcing them to command Yang to cease fire, they would save Reinhard from certain defeat.

Hilda was unaware that Neidhart Müller had reached the battlespace at Vermillion three days ahead of schedule.

"In fact, I proposed this once already to Duke von Lohengramm, but he refused it outright, saying that fighting and winning were all that mattered. While I do think his values are sound, if we lose, then everything goes back to zero."

Mittermeier tested the waters of an insensitive question:

"Do you think Duke von Lohengramm will be defeated?"

It was a question that, had it been posed to Müller by Reinhard himself, would've shut him up completely. Without hesitation, Hilda looked the Galactic Imperial Navy's most renowned general in the eye.

"Yes, if things continue as they have been, Duke von Lohengramm will experience the first, and final, defeat of his life."

At least Mittermeier couldn't help but acknowledge the bravery and dynamism of this twenty-two-year-old woman. All the same, he jokingly compared her to the goddess Athena.

"I understand you on that point. There's just one problem, fräulein."

Mittermeier only sniffed the aroma of his coffee, returning the cup to its saucer.

"That is, whether Yang Wen-li will follow a cease-fire order from his government. From where he stands, the fruit of victory is ripening before his very eyes, so why would he feel compelled to throw it away for a cease-fire? Doesn't he have much more to gain by ignoring the order and taking that fruit for his own?"

The soundness of what Mittermeier had pointed out wasn't lost on Hilda. Who in their right mind would give up on a fight that was 99 percent won for a cease-fire? If he ignored the order and kept on fighting, he'd seize not only a military victory. Indeed, if the government crumbled within that time, he could easily seize its authority for himself as a hero devoted to the salvation of his nation. Surely no one would relinquish such an opportunity. Then again…

"The possibility has crossed my mind. But I've concluded that an order to cease fire will be effective against Yang Wen-li. He's had more than enough opportunities to seize power based on his might and military acumen alone. But he passed up every one of those opportunities and has contented himself with being a soldier, defending borders."

Mittermeier was silent.

"It's possible Yang Wen-li is someone who feels with every fiber of his being that there is something more valuable than power. And while I do think it's a commendable trait, we must use it against him, underhanded as that seems."

"Either that, or he might suddenly develop a taste for power and ignore the government's order altogether. This opportunity is much bigger and more tempting than any he's been faced with before."

"Yes, it's quite possible. Are you saying, then, that my proposal isn't worth implementing?"

"No," said Mittermeier, shaking his head. "Very well, Fräulein von Mariendorf. Let's give it a shot. It's not like we have any other choice."

The rapidity of his decision, thought Hilda, was also commendable for the deftness with which he'd assessed the situation.

"Thank you very much. Your approval means a lot to me."

"But I'm not doing this alone. I'd like to request a comrade to accompany me. Surely someone as intelligent as you can understand why, fräulein."

Hilda nodded. She understood Mittermeier's fastidiousness as a military man. If Mittermeier didn't betake himself to save his master Reinhard in the battlespace and captured Heinessen by himself, people would say he let, or seemed to let, his master die for his own military and political ambitions. Such a burden would be unbearable for Mittermeier. It was precisely because she thought the Gale Wolf was such a man that Hilda had chosen him as the target of her persuasion. Her judgment on that front was favorably rewarded.

If she understood Mittermeier's meaning, Hilda had something to ask him, despite knowing there was no need to ask it.

"So, who will accompany you to share in your achievement?"

"He's in a nearby star system and easy enough to reach, a man whose abilities can be trusted. Oskar von Reuentahl. Do you object, fräulein?"

"No, I think he's an obvious choice."

Hilda wasn't lying, but neither was she giving voice to everything that was on her mind. She herself wasn't quite clear on why she'd chosen Mittermeier and not von Reuentahl. She'd never been one to put too much stock in intuition. If a police officer's intuition was always correct, then no one would ever be falsely accused. Likewise, if a military man's intuition was always correct, no one would ever lose. But her choice was founded on intuition, and as such had nothing to back it up.

II

Mittermeier changed course for the alliance capital of Heinessen. His men were perplexed to learn they'd be linking up with the von Reuentahl fleet. Karl Eduard Bayerlein, who served under Mittermeier, lowered his voice.

"I wonder what Admiral von Reuentahl will think of this. Mightn't it turn the imperial forces against each other?"

"You've got quite the literary imagination there," teased Mittermeier, but because the silent pause that preceded those words was short yet pregnant, it fell flat.

He may not have had that much information, but this young man named Bayerlein sometimes demonstrated an exceptional ability to predict the future. While he was valuable for not being a simple grunt worker, he was slightly bothersome to Mittermeier for his inability to balance emotions and reason.

"Von Reuentahl is a friend, but I'm not so mild mannered a person that I would keep a half-wit as a friend for ten years. You're free to think what you like, but don't say or do anything to cause useless misunderstandings."

"Yes, my apologies. I was out of line."

Bayerlein bowed his head deeply, but inside the shuttle on his way back to his flagship, he called one of his men and gave the order to prepare for war. When the flustered subordinate asked why, Bayerlein said irritatingly:

"Isn't it natural for a soldier to always be ready for a surprise attack? We're in enemy territory here, not the playground behind your primary school back home. There's no taking a nap beyond the watchful eye of the teacher."

Seeming to let slip something of his own childhood, he terminated the communication.

Even he thought he'd gone too far. He knew full well that his superior Mittermeier, whom he respected, was close friends with the renowned commander von Reuentahl. Whatever had made him think they might turn on each other? He was gripped by this embarrassing thought. To think that he'd said such a thing out loud and not gotten lambasted for it! Maybe he should weigh down the wings of his imagination. But even as he considered this, for some reason Bayerlein didn't think to rescind the order he'd given.

．・　・
　・　　　●
　・
　　　　・

When Hilda's proposal went out over the FTL hotline through Mittermeier, Oskar von Reuentahl took some time to think it over. Even an intelligent man equipped with ironclad nerves such as his was hard-pressed to reply at once.

He'd thought to himself, "What if I don't come back?" when leaving for Gandharva, but if he didn't come back, the other admirals would steal his thunder, and the value placed on him by his master would only plummet. None of this felt real. But the situation suddenly progressed as if it were beckoning him.

Chief of staff Bergengrün had already come to report that Vice Admiral Bayerlein's division, within the neighboring Mittermeier fleet, had taken strict defensive measures that were unnecessary under the present circumstances.

Von Reuentahl fell silent, a sharp light reflected in his mismatched eyes. He knew that, among those under Mittermeier's immediate authority, Bayerlein was the youngest and most determined commander. Wondering why he would act as if an enemy were nearby, he considered interrogating Mittermeier. But von Reuentahl thought he had the answer. If von Reuentahl not only refused Hilda's proposition but defended himself against it, did that mean he would have to fight Mittermeier? Having observed Mittermeier's behavior, von Reuentahl didn't believe his friend had made an indication to that effect. If it was up to Mittermeier, his temperament wouldn't allow him to remain silent. Did this mean that novice Bayerlein had done this of his own volition…?

Von Reuentahl's mismatched eyes appeared placid on the comm screen, but Hilda saw the storm raging in their bottomless abyss. At least this time she knew her instincts had been on target, and she felt her uneasiness deepen accordingly. Had she, rather, brought about the unintended result of making men possessed of uncommon ambition and talent realize what an ideal opportunity this was? If they were made aware that there wasn't enough time to save their master in the battlespace, perhaps a daring ambition might sprout in men who'd had no such ambition before. Feeling as if she'd done something foolish, Hilda was getting restless.

But von Reuentahl, as if seeing through her apprehension and discomfort, smiled without a word and nodded deeply.

"Understood. I will do as you say and go along with Fräulein von Mariendorf's proposal. I will order all fleets to attack Heinessen but will go there to discuss the finer details. Once we've merged fleets, of course."

If I were to summon Mittermeier here, he thought, *Bayerlein might overreact and think I was taking him hostage.* Von Reuentahl pondered that point.

There was no need to make things difficult. Von Reuentahl labored to rein in his heart, which was prone to escaping from the hands of good reason. Fräulein von Mariendorf was wise and abundant in stratagems. But not everything progressed in accordance with this daughter of the empire's thinking.

III

Mittermeier and von Reuentahl, Twin Ramparts of the Galactic Imperial Navy, led a fleet of thirty thousand ships, breaking into the Bharat star system on May 4. By the next day, they'd reached Heinessen's planetary orbit, throwing its citizens into panic by their obstruction of the twinkling stars. For the first time in its history, the people of Heinessen saw the Imperial Navy with their own eyes.

Amid the confusion, Mittermeier's announcement hijacked the planet's communication network.

"This is Senior Admiral Wolfgang Mittermeier of the Galactic Imperial Navy speaking. The airspace above Heinessen is under our control. I come demanding a peace treaty with the Free Planets Alliance government. I therefore ask that you suspend all military activities and rescind all arms. Failure to do so will result in an indiscriminate attack on Heinessen. You have three hours to give your answer. In the meantime, enjoy this little demonstration."

Mittermeier's threat weighed heavily on the ears of its recipients. Moments later, one of the imperial ships fired on a single point six thousand kilometers below on the planet's surface.

A flash and thunderous roar filled the atmosphere. Its light blanched the fields of vision of soldiers and civilians alike, fading just as quickly amid a reverberation that beat their eardrums mercilessly. An orange ball of light tore at the black silhouette of Joint Operational Headquarters and sent pieces of it soaring high into the air. As half of these fragments were sent floating in a roaring shock wave, one of the soldiers taking cover on the ground spoke in a trembling voice.

"How dare they! A low-frequency missile!"

The direct hit of that missile was enough to decimate the aboveground portions of the Joint Operational Headquarters building. The Gale Wolf spoke to Hilda, who was watching it all unfold on-screen.

"That should do it. Those in power don't bat an eyelash when civilian houses are destroyed, but destroy a government building and the blood drains from their faces."

"Then you're trying to avoid bringing harm to civilians."

"Well, I *was* born as one, so…"

Hilda looked favorably upon Mittermeier's bitter smile.

"Admiral, could you please send one more message? Tell them if they surrender, we swear on the name of the galactic prime minister Duke von Lohengramm that not even the highest ranking among them will be prosecuted. I think that should be enough to lead them to a decision."

"Normally that would be a bad idea, but in this case it just might work. I'll convey the message."

Mittermeier had complete faith in Hilda's counsel.

The landscape below was reflected on the giant screen. Deep underground, in a safe place far removed from ordinary citizens, a meeting of the National Defense Committee was already under way. High officers of the government and military were lined up, their faces pale as if hewn from tundra. At this very moment, "Marshal" Dawson, director of Joint Operational Headquarters, was staring at the screen with vacant eyes.

Awakening from an unseasonal hibernation, chairman of the High Council Job Trünicht, who'd convened the meeting, broke through the mire of silence.

"Here's my conclusion…"

Trünicht's voice was, of course, by no means jovial, but it was also strangely lacking in any grimness befitting the circumstances. Like his expression, his voice seemed to be that of a mechanized doll wearing a mask.

"We will accept the Imperial Navy's demands. Seeing as they've declared an indiscriminate attack against the entire population, we have no choice."

As Chairman Islands of the Defense Committee made to protest, Trünicht needled him with his glance.

"Have I been officially recalled? Certainly not. That means all responsibility and qualifications to hand down the decision to end this conflict lie with me. All I'm trying to do is carry out that responsibility to the best of my ability."

"Please stop this."

The Defense Committee chairman's voice was trembling more from shame than anger.

"It's not within your rights to abuse the institution of democratic government to bring down its spirit and stain its history. Do you alone mean to let two and a half centuries of democratic history since our founding father Ahle Heinessen go to rot?"

As Trünicht lifted both corners of his mouth, his face seemed even more masklike.

"Aren't we self-righteous, Islands. Maybe you've forgotten, but I remember it well. That night, when you came to my house to bribe me with an expensive silver dinnerware set, begging for a cabinet minister position."

Those present had rarely heard such malice from his mouth before.

"Not to mention the donations and kickbacks you received from all those self-interested companies. Did you not siphon from your election funds to buy that summerhouse? Did you not go gallivanting with your mistress on the public's dime? I know all about it."

Numerous beads of sweat seeped out from the Defense Committee chairman's broad forehead, and not from heat.

"I'll admit, I'm a third-rate political contractor. I have you to thank for having been able to reach my current position. I'm in your debt. Which is why I can't stand by and watch your name left in history as the statesman of a ruined nation. Please reconsider. Maybe we'll die here, but if Admiral Yang should kill Duke von Lohengramm, the alliance will be saved. I wouldn't wish misfortune upon a single soul, but that's the reality. If Duke von Lohengramm dies, the imperial forces will go back to their homeland, and as they're fighting for hegemony over the next era, Admiral Yang Wen-li will rebuild our national defense system. Those political commanders who succeed us will cooperate with him in turn."

"Hmm, Yang Wen-li?"

If a voice could be poison, then so would Trünicht's have been.

"Think about it. Had that fool Yang Wen-li not destroyed the Artemis's Necklace that once protected this planet, we could've saved ourselves from imperial invasion. That things have come to this is entirely his fault. A great commander? He's just an imbecile who can't see the future."

The commander in chief of the Alliance Armed Forces Space Armada, Marshal Bucock, spoke for the first time.

"I see. So, if we still had Artemis's Necklace, this planet alone would be protected. But what about the other star systems? So long as this planet, and your authority on it, are safe, you couldn't care less about the war raging on in other star systems."

The voice of the old admiral, now in his seventies, while far from strict, nevertheless erected a granite wall against Trünicht's reckless remarks.

"The point is, the alliance's days are numbered. Its politicians play with power. Its soldiers, as seen at Amritsar, are absorbed in speculative enterprise. They preach democracy yet make no efforts to protect it. Even its people have relinquished politics to fewer and fewer hands and have stopped trying to shape the state altogether. The collapse of a despotic government is the sin of its rulers and senior statesmen, but the collapse of a democracy rests on the shoulders of every citizen. Although you've had any number of chances to run from your seats of power legitimately, you've chosen to abandon your authority and responsibility by selling yourselves over to a rotten politician."

"You're done with your speech, I take it?"

Job Trünicht smiled faintly. Had Yang Wen-li seen that, surely his former impression of a feared and hated man would've resurfaced.

"Yes, I'm done. Now's the time to act. You just wait and see, Chairman Trünicht. I will stop you with everything I've got."

The old general rose from his chair, his entire being brimming with determination. Since no one present at the meeting could carry a weapon, the old admiral was unarmed, but without hesitation he tried to approach the young chairman thirty years his junior.

Voices arose from all around. First of restraint, then of confusion as the doors of the underground conference room gave way to more than ten men storming in. They weren't military police, but they held charged particle rifles and their faces were blank, like highly trained soldiers. Half of them formed a human barrier around Trünicht, while the remaining half pointed their guns at the others.

"The Church of Terra…!"

The petrified old admiral's exclamation turned everyone present into living fossils. Their gazes were locked on the men's chests, across which a slogan had been clearly embroidered: *Terra is my home. Terra in my hand.* The church's unmistakable mark.

"Lock them away," ordered the chairman sternly.

*　　　　　*　　　　*

"The Free Planets Alliance government has accepted the Galactic Empire's bid for peace. As proof, they're immediately ceasing all military activity."

When they received word from the surface, Hilda, von Reuentahl, and Mittermeier were watching the screen over coffee in *Beowulf*'s conference room, which now served as their joint headquarters in Heinessen's orbit.

Mittermeier reverently bowed his honey-complexioned face.

"Fräulein von Mariendorf, your resourcefulness is worth more than an entire fleet. I only hope you'll exhibit more of the same on Duke von Lohengramm's behalf."

"Much obliged. But I couldn't have done it without your cooperation. Please, both of you, be his wings and lift him up. Help him in all public matters."

That was, of course, a hope aimed mainly at the heterochromatic admiral.

"Honestly speaking, I didn't think things would go this smoothly. Bravo."

Von Reuentahl smiled but, deep within, felt the sun darkening. He'd anticipated the possibility that the alliance government might be unaware of the surrender. Now that the democratic government's headquarters, its stronghold, had come to embody justice in opposition to tyranny, he'd thought it had the moral backbone to wager its life in the name of self-protection. But to the leaders of the alliance, the fate of their democratic government mattered little if they had no power to show for it. In any event, to von Reuentahl, the matter was settled.

"Indeed, I was worried the alliance's pathetic leaders would ignore the risks to their own lives and wondered what we would do if they refused our demands."

Mittermeier shrugged his shoulders. Hilda nodded. Although they could count this as a success, it wasn't without its pangs of dissatisfaction.

"To think that something taking a hundred million people a century to build might be destroyed by one man in a single day…"

"This is what they mean by the death of a nation."

After voicing this not particularly original sentiment, Mittermeier looked back at his nearby comrade. Von Reuentahl's mismatched eyes were reflected on the dark surface of his untouched coffee. He lifted those eyes and spoke.

"The Goldenbaum Dynasty of the Galactic Empire, the Free Planets Alliance, and Phezzan. We've witnessed firsthand the destruction of three major powers that, between them, ruled the universe. If I might borrow an expression from Vice Admiral Thurneisen: Future historians are sure to envy you."

And yet, even as Hilda and Mittermeier voiced their agreement, on the watery surface of each heart, a small, inextinguishable ripple was spreading its rings.

IV

In the Vermillion Stellar Region, far removed from the alliance capital of Heinessen, the ripples of soldier's hearts were peaking in raging waves. In accordance with Yang's orders, fleets turned back and the fighting stopped, but the soldiers couldn't see past their anger and desperation over the absurdity of having to accept a cease-fire just shy of total victory.

"What the hell is wrong with the capital? Letting themselves get besieged by the empire…"

"We've surrendered. Unconditionally. A peaceful surrender. We put our hands up and asked for help."

"And what's to become of the FPA?"

"What's to become of the FPA, he says! We'll just become part of the empire. Maybe we'll be given a semblance of autonomy…but just that, a semblance. Not that it'll last for long."

"And then what?"

"How should I know?! Go ask that blond brat, Duke von Lohengramm, seeing as he'll be the one calling the shots from now on."

Not only were some mad, but others were grieving over this change of events. Some soldiers turned to their friends in tearful appeals.

"I thought we stood for justice. Was justice ever meant to kneel to a dark, despotic power? This world has gone off its rocker."

All the same, not many agreed with that naive doubt.

"Our government acts only to serve the enemy."

At first, such voices of denunciation were few and far between, but then they spread like wildfire throughout every fleet.

"That's right, our government officials have betrayed their own. They've gone against the faith and hopes of their own people."

"Those bastards are nothing but traitors. Why should we obey their orders?"

Some blamed their communications officers. Why had they complied with that order? If only they'd feigned ignorance for two or three hours, they could've captured and killed Duke von Lohengramm by now. How could they have just bent over backward like idiots and transmitted it so honestly?!

In this storm of disavowal, a small bud of affirmation timidly poked out its head.

"But my family is on Heinessen. If we refuse to surrender and suffer a full-on assault…My family has been saved because the government surrendered."

There was nothing more to say. He glanced around, and saw how his comrades-in-arms had changed their expressions. At least some were beginning to realize it took great courage to voice one's humanity in a sea of indifference.

"Let's ask Admiral Yang to maintain true justice and tell him we don't want him to go along with this outrageous cease-fire…"

"Right on, let's do it!"

Julian Mintz hurried toward the observation room amid uproar. He wanted to speak with Vice Admiral von Schönkopf. Von Schönkopf stood at the window with a whisky flask in his hand. In his eyes, which reflected a dark stillness and the starry waltz within it, hung a mist of loathsome despair. Julian stopped and for a while said nothing, his eyes grave, fully knowing of the vice admiral's despair.

"Vice Admiral von Schönkopf…"

Von Schönkopf turned and greeted the boy with a raise of his flask.

"Ah, since you've gone out of your way to see me, can I assume, as you and I think alike, that you believe Admiral Yang should ignore the cease-fire?"

Julian responded with a reserved yet uncompromising expression.

"I understand what you're feeling. But if we did that, we'd set a bad historical precedent. If we allow our military commanders to ignore governmental orders for the sake of their own convictions, the most important tenet of democratic government—namely, the ability to control military power on the people's behalf—would never be realized. Do you think Admiral Yang capable of setting such a precedent?"

Von Schönkopf's lips curled into a cynical smile.

"Then let me ask you this. If the government orders the slaughter of a nonresistant population, should the military comply with those orders?"

Julian shook his flaxen head vigorously.

"Of course not. When something calls into question one's dignity, I think one must be a human being first, a military man second. In which case one must disobey, no matter the government's orders."

Von Schönkopf said nothing.

"Which is why, except in the most extreme cases, one must act first as a military man of a democratic nation and go along with whatever the government tells him to do. Otherwise, even if one resists for the sake of humankind, one will be criticized for acting out of self-interest."

Von Schönkopf fiddled with his flask.

"Boy—no, Sublieutenant Julian Mintz—what you say is perfectly true. And while I understand it on a theoretical level, I had to say what I did."

"Yes, I know."

Julian was being genuine. His objection to von Schönkopf was an objection of reason to his own emotions.

"Admiral Yang has no political ambition whatsoever. And maybe he has no political talent, either. But he would never, like Job Trünicht, manipulate the nation as his personal possession, treat politics as an accessory, or betray the people who place their hopes in him. Compared to history's greatest politicians, Admiral Yang's abilities won't likely be of much significance, but right now, we have only Job Trünicht to compare him with."

"Yes. I think so, too."

Julian loosened the scarf around his collar. He was having a little difficulty breathing. Agreeing with himself was much harder than agreeing with someone else.

"But Chairman Trünicht was chosen to be sovereign by many who believed in him. Even if they were disillusioned, it's the people's responsibility to correct their own disillusionment, no matter how long it takes. Career soldiers should never attempt to correct people's mistakes by force.

Doing so would only bring about a repeat of the Military Congress for the Rescue of the Republic coup d'état that took place two years ago. The military would lead and rule the people."

Von Schönkopf brought the whisky flask to his mouth but put it back down halfway.

"The Galactic Empire might very well demand Admiral Yang's life as the wages of peace. And if the government responds by condemning him to death, what then? Do we willingly go along with that?"

The boy's face blushed.

"I would never let that happen," he declared. "Never."

"But I thought one must go along with whatever the government orders?"

"That's a question for the admiral. This is a question for me. I've no intention of yielding to Duke von Lohengramm and following the orders of his government. The only orders I follow come from Admiral Yang. If the admiral accepts the cease-fire, then I must accept it as well. Nothing else matters."

Von Schönkopf capped his whisky and looked at the seventeen-year-old sublieutenant, deeply impressed.

"Julian, I spoke out of turn. You've really grown up. I should follow your example and accept what I should accept. But there are certain things one just can't abide, no matter what. You're right about that, too."

The air in the flagship *Hyperion* conference room was so oppressive it seemed half-solidified. One standing and stretching his spine proudly within that invisible fluid was Guest Admiral Merkatz's aide, Bernhard von Schneider. His sharp eyes were aimed squarely at Yang Wen-li.

"There's nothing we can do about the cease-fire. It's the government's decision. But if you think for one minute I'm going to watch the FPA make Admiral Merkatz a scapegoat for your own protection, I cannot abide by such egotism."

"Von Schneider!"

"No, Admiral Merkatz, Commander von Schneider speaks the truth."

That was all Yang said. He said nothing bad about the alliance government. To begin with, since there was just cause in surrendering to save the people from indiscriminate attack, he couldn't afford any criticism. Even if it was obvious what the government's true feelings were...

"I'd like for Admiral Merkatz to step down from the fleet," Yang went on.

These words stirred the fluid air, and the staff officers with it, into a frenzy of shock and apprehension.

"I have no way of predicting the future. But, as Commander von Schneider has said, it's not far-fetched to think the alliance government might hand him over to curry imperial favor. I'm a man of the alliance, and as such am bound to go along with my government's foolish measures. You, on the other hand, have no such obligation. If you don't abandon this sinking ship, I'll be very upset."

Yang hesitated for a moment.

"Please take some warships with you. As well as whatever fuel, provisions, and men you might need, of course."

The fluid churned again.

"Should it face defeat, there's no way the Alliance Armed Forces will maintain military power at the same level it did before. If the ships are going to be destroyed eventually by the Imperial Navy anyway, I'd just as soon hide them. We could say they've been obliterated in battle or self-destructed. They'll have a hard time verifying either way."

"I'm grateful for what you say, Admiral Yang. But do you really expect me to escape for my own safety and leave you to take the heat?"

When Merkatz said this, Yang flashed a certain expression. Julian and Frederica recognized it as a smile of satisfaction.

"I thought you might say that. It's not like I'm asking you to retire, Admiral Merkatz. Rather, I have something more audacious in mind. For the sake of the future, I want you to preserve the most essential part of the Alliance Armed Forces. I want you to be our 'mobile Sherwood Forest,' as in the Robin Hood legends of old."

After a few seconds, the oppressive atmosphere in the room was suddenly lifted. Those who understood Yang's words looked at each other with exalted gazes. There was hope after all! Amid the commotion, Yang stroked his face, thinking he'd done something conceited. At least he'd gotten his point across.

And then, a sonorous voice of declaration:

"I'm with you."

Everyone's gazes fell on Olivier Poplin. The Alliance Armed Forces' preeminent ace pilot didn't care how important the meaning of his statement was.

"The 'Free' in Free Planets Alliance refers to independence. I've no lingering affection for an alliance reduced to a possession of the empire. It's like a woman without self-respect: unattractive. Requesting permission to accompany Admiral Merkatz, sir."

Most people who heard the metaphor thought it was just like him to use it. They felt their hearts starting toward a slightly brighter horizon. It was much easier to follow than take the lead when someone took the first step. At least they knew it wouldn't be a lonely journey.

"And I as well, with Your Excellency von Schönkopf's permission…"

The Rosen Ritter's second commander, Captain Kasper Rinz, also stood up firmly.

"As the son of a refugee, I won't stand to be subordinate to the empire any longer. Allow me to accompany Admiral Merkatz. That being said…" Rinz looked at the black-haired marshal. "Someday, I want Admiral Yang to lead us all. So long as you're alive, you have the Rosen Ritter regiment's loyalty."

"This is the first step toward militarization, pledging loyalty to neither nation nor government, but to one man. Only bad can come of this," said Alex Caselnes benignly, at which one person laughed.

Feeling his stance being questioned, Caselnes answered.

"I'll stay behind. Or should I say, I *must* stay behind. If too many generals disappear, the Imperial Navy might get suspicious. I'll remain here with Marshal Yang."

Von Schönkopf, Fischer, Attenborough, Patrichev, Marino, and Carlsen chose to follow Caselnes. Merkatz opened a window of words to something he'd long kept locked inside and bowed to Yang.

"When I was exiled here, I put my entire future in your hands. Whatever you tell me to do, I'll happily do."

"Thank you. I'm indebted to your efforts."

The staff officers took a temporary recess, leaving Frederica Greenhill behind with Yang. *And to yours, above all*, his eyes said.

"Sorry, Frederica," said the young black-haired marshal awkwardly when they were alone. "If someone else did the same, I'd surely think them foolish as well. But I can't live any other way. And to make matters worse, I've forced my dearest comrades into a tight spot…"

Frederica reached out a white hand, fixing the unkempt scarf peeking out from his collar. She smiled, his dark eyes reflected in her hazel.

"I don't know whether what you're doing is right or not. But there's something I do know. I'm crazy about you."

Frederica said nothing more. There was no need. She'd always known the kind of man she'd fallen for.

While there were those in the Imperial Navy who weren't surprised by the sudden cease-fire, Reinhard wasn't one of them. Upon receiving chief of staff von Oberstein's report, the young blond dictator recoiled as if his self-importance had been wounded.

"What's the meaning of this?"

Reinhard's voice was more than incisive; it was diamond plated. Having this unpardonable reality pointed out to him, he felt contempt and rage, even if it was good news clad in showy dress.

"The alliance has stopped its advance. And that's not all. They're requesting a cease-fire."

Von Oberstein guarded himself against an appearance of his master's violent side.

"This is madness. How did it happen so suddenly?! One more step—no, half a step—and those bastards would've won! What justifiable reason could they have to abandon certain victory?"

Waiting for his master's ripples of emotions to subside, von Oberstein explained the situation.

"You mean to tell me victory has been handed over to me?"

Understanding the situation, Reinhard's elegant limbs, clad in black and silver, sank into his commander's chair.

"A pathetic development. Have I been given a victory that was never mine to begin with? As if I were some sort of charity case being given a handout…"

Reinhard laughed in a way he rarely did. It was a laugh lacking in magnificence and vitality. The laugh of a lifeless statue.

CHAPTER 10:

"LONG LIVE THE EMPEROR!"

I

IT WAS 2240 ON MAY 5, SE 799, IC 490. After nearly twelve days, the Vermillion War came to an end. The forces that had participated on the imperial side numbered 26,940 war fleets and 3,263,100 men. Of those, 14,820 fleets had been destroyed and 8,660 had suffered major damage, bringing the total damages to 87.2 percent. A total of 1,594,400 were killed in action and 753,700 were injured, for a casualty rate of 72 percent. Those forces that had participated on the alliance side numbered 16,420 war fleets and 1,907,600 men. Of those, 7,140 fleets had been destroyed and 6,260 had suffered damage, bringing the total damages to 81.6 percent. A total of 898,200 had been killed in action and 506,900 were injured, for a casualty rate of 73.7 percent.

Historians have reached no consensus on whether the empire or the alliance won this war. That the casualty rates on both sides exceeded 70 percent was unusual from a military perspective, and the pointlessness of quibbling over a fraction of a percent determining the outcome was lost on no one. It was, for all intents and purposes, a draw.

Those who asserted the alliance's victory gave the following reasons:

"In the Vermillion War, the strategic leadership of alliance commander Yang Wen-li had always surpassed that of imperial commander Reinhard von Lohengramm. From the beginning, they were evenly matched, and Duke von Lohengramm's magnificent deep defense seemed to have been a success, but once it crumbled, the war's outcome was entirely in Yang's hands. Had he not been ordered to cease fire by a government under enemy threat, history would have recorded him as the unequivocal victor."

Those who advocated an imperial victory rebutted as follows:

"The Vermillion War was but a trivial episode in the grander-scale war that Reinhard von Lohengramm had plotted with the goal of conquering the Free Planets Alliance and unifying the entire universe. Drawing the enemy's main forces into his battlespace, with a detached force he attacked the enemy capital and forced their surrender by an unabashedly superlative strategy used since time immemorial. The Imperial Navy achieved its battle objectives, while the Alliance Armed Forces lost. In terms of who won, one need only resist the temptation to romanticize and look directly at the results. The answer is clear."

There were, too, those who flaunted justice.

"The alliance may have won in the battlespace, but the empire won beyond it."

"The empire may have won strategically, but the alliance won tactically."

Many such theories were put forth, but no matter how one sliced it, each had its own persuasive power. This war would spawn countless books in the future and provide sustenance for as many historians.

The mental states of the war's actors were clear, for neither side considered itself to be the supreme commander or winner. Reinhard couldn't rid himself so easily of the shame of being handed his victory. Yang, on the other hand, from the point of view of his own military thinking, respected a strategic victory far more than a tactical one and held no conviction in his success. Perhaps they were overestimating, but each valued the other's success more than his own. Both sides were becoming painfully self-aware of a superiority complex.

The Imperial Navy's highest commander and imperial marshal, Reinhard von Lohengramm, held audience with the Alliance Armed Forces commander of Iserlohn Patrol Fleet, Marshal Yang Wen-li, at 2300 hours on May 6, nearly twenty-four hours after the cease-fire had gone into effect.

During that time, on both sides the strongest human urges of appetite and sexual desire were overtaken by a desire to sleep. Throughout the twelve-day war, lulls of alternating naps and tank bed sessions were never enough to put their frayed nerves at ease. And now, released from the fear that a one-hour nap might turn into an eternal one, the imperial heroes and the alliance's wise generals alike were able to enjoy a deep and replenishing rest at last, although not without the aid of sleeping medication.

Meanwhile, around the battlespace, the imperial leaders—including Schwarz Lanzenreiter fleet captain Wittenfeld, Fahrenheit, Wahlen, Steinmetz, and Lennenkamp—who arrived to the battle too late, fled. Having already received reports of the cease-fire, and given how distressed they were over their shame and frustration, it was a necessary measure.

At 1900 hours on May 6, Yang Wen-li woke up and couldn't get back to sleep. He pulled himself reluctantly out of bed, surrounded by forty thousand imperial ships, perfectly unharmed. As he gazed at that multitude of overlapping lights with admiration, Yang took a shower, washed his face, and took care of his necessary grooming.

"There's something quite odd about drinking tea while surrounded by forty thousand enemy ships."

Yang leisurely let the steam of his black tea waft over his face. It had been a long time since he'd tasted the sweetness of Julian's Shillong leaf brew. Only his closest associates—Julian, Frederica, Caselnes, and von Schönkopf—shared his dinner table. Without the prospect of an imperial massacre looming over them, it felt almost like a gathering with friends. Nonetheless, Yang's audacity and stolidity were admirable, and his guests relished the opportunity to observe them in such close quarters.

By that time, the sixty-ship fleet under Merkatz's command had already left the battlespace, escaping the eyes and ears of the empire. Those same sixty ships included eight warships—among them *Shiva*, *Cassandra*, and *Ulysses*—four mother ships, nine cruisers, fifteen destroyers, twenty-two weapons transports, and two manufacturing ships. And while all of them were in reality unharmed, according to falsified data they'd been obliterated in the battlespace. Those on board were land troops and battleship personnel totaling 11,820 men. Captain Rinz, Commander von Schneider, and Commander Poplin, for their part, were on record as having been killed in action.

Inside the imperial flagship *Brünhild*, an exquisite accord of solemnity and elegance showed the extent to which its functionality as a warship was unharmed. Yang drew gazes of frank admiration from everyone.

"So that's Yang Wen-li, huh?"

Small waves of exchanged whispers washed on the shore of Yang's ears. He had the feeling he'd disappointed them. And who could blame them? Yang was a far cry from Reinhard, who was the most elegant noble youth of all time. And unlike Karl Gustav Kempf, whom he'd consigned to oblivion by his own design, Yang was hardly a man possessed of heroic appearance. Neither was he the coolheaded prodigy type. Then again, he didn't fit the scraggly bumpkin mold, either. At least, those who saw him seemed to think him handsome—Frederica Greenhill, for one. All in all, he was probably more acceptable as a young scholar confined to being a lecturer due to his lack of political connections. While at first glance, he looked to be twenty-seven or twenty-eight and of essentially medium build, his muscles sagged from the weight of a prolonged battle that had also left him scrawny. His unruly hair and beret didn't peg him as a military man at all. In any case, his appearance gave no strong impression to others of one who'd accomplished as much as he had.

A tall young officer with sandy hair and eyes turned to Yang and performed a salute.

"I am Neidhart Müller. It's a privilege and an honor to meet Your Excellency Yang, highest commander of the Alliance Armed Forces."

"Not at all, the honor is all mine…"

Yang offered an artless response as he exchanged salutes. He attempted no further answer.

He seemed to have made enough of an impression on Müller that the latter couldn't continue to hold feelings of defeat or enmity. There was a brief period of silence, but Müller, out of respect to one so decorated, broke the tension with a smile, as if his heart had been settled.

"If only you'd been born on our side of the galaxy, I would've wanted to study tactics under you. It's too bad that'll never happen."

Yang's expression also softened.

"Much obliged. I, too, wish you'd been born our side of the galaxy. If so, I'd probably be taking an afternoon nap right about now."

Yang wasn't just being polite. He was speaking the truth. A man of Müller's caliber would've made a brave fleet commander, and would've considerably reduced Yang's troubles.

Müller smiled, saying it was unfortunate indeed, and led Yang to Reinhard's private chamber. A young topaz-eyed officer stood before the door. After saluting Müller in silence, he opened the door and let their guest inside. And so, Yang Wen-li, black beret in hand, came face-to-face with Reinhard von Lohengramm in the flesh.

The mighty dictator's private room seemed far from luxurious, but that was probably because its master was already so magnificent. When the golden-haired youth stood up from one of the facing sofas, Yang felt it almost strange to hear no music. Yang had now seen, within reaching distance, a living legend, the figure of a youth who'd monopolized the favor of history and the gods. Yang had never seen anything so regal as his imperial uniform, silver against black.

Returning to his senses from a momentary stupor, Yang saluted. As he did so, unkempt bangs fell and covered his eyes. He brushed them back and tried his best to make up for his salute with another. Reinhard didn't seem to mind. He nodded to Kissling past Yang's shoulder. The door closed behind Yang, leaving the two of them alone. Reinhard's elegant lips resolved into a smile.

"I've been wanting to meet you for a long time. At last, my wish has come true."

"Thank you."

Another artless answer, but he didn't feel like competing with this blond youth's eloquence. He took a seat on the sofa Reinhard offered and put the beret back on his head, feeling that his hair was unrulier than ever. A boy who looked young enough to be in grade school opened the door and brought in a coffee set made of silver. Before long, a fragrant steam was wafting above the marble table. As the boy withdrew, eyeing his master with admiration and their guest with interest, Reinhard lifted a cup in one flowing motion.

"Our fates are intertwined. Do you remember, three years ago, at the Battle of Astarte?"

"I received a message from Your Excellency. You bade me well, until the next war. Thanks to you, I've made it out alive from some close calls."

"I never got a response from you."

Reinhard smiled, and Yang, won over, smiled back.

"Pardon my rudeness."

"That's not the loan on which I seek your interest…"

As Reinhard suppressed his smile, he returned the cup to its saucer without so much as a clink.

"How about it? Will you work for me? I understand you've been appointed the rank of marshal, but I'd like to appoint you as *imperial marshal*. Surely that's more than enough to entice you over to our side. Right here, at this very moment."

Yang asked himself: *It might seem crazy, but without an answer prepared, can I really resist such an invitation?*

"It's an undeserved honor—one I'm afraid I must refuse."

"Why?"

Although Reinhard didn't seem the least bit surprised, it was only natural to ask.

"I don't see how I could be of any use to Your Excellency…"

"Are you really that modest? Or are you trying to say I lack charisma as a master?"

"Not at all."

Yang's tone grew slightly stronger, and he wondered how he might explain it so as not to hurt the blond youth's feelings. Surprisingly, he wasn't afraid of angering the dictator—rather, he felt it was a crime to refuse his kind offer.

"Had I been born in the empire, I would've gladly served under Your Excellency, even without Your Excellency's invitation. But I was raised on a different water than the people of the empire, and I hear that drinking water one isn't used to can ruin one's body."

Thinking it was a poor metaphor, Yang put the coffee to his lips to buy himself some time. Although devoted to his favorite black tea, Yang could tell that the highest-quality beans and craftsmanship had gone into making this black liquid he now ingested. Unfazed by Yang's refusal, Reinhard lifted his own cup.

"I don't believe your water necessarily agrees with you. Given the nature of your accomplishments, I'd say you've been held back more often than rewarded."

He couldn't very well say that he should receive a pension as well, and so Yang shamelessly gave a solemn answer.

"I myself feel that I've been sufficiently rewarded. Besides, I like the way my water tastes."

"So, your loyalties lie only with democracy. Is that what you're saying?"

"Yeah, I guess so."

It was a barely impassioned answer, but Reinhard put down his cup and diligently pursued the argument.

"But is democracy so great, I wonder. Didn't the republican government of the Galactic Federation give birth to Rudolf von Goldenbaum's deformed child?"

Yang was silent.

"What's more, the one who sold your beloved—or so you think—Free Planets Alliance over to me was the very ruler freely elected by an alliance majority. A democratic government is a body which, by free will of its citizens, looks down upon its own system and spirit."

Yang had heard enough and felt compelled to respond.

"Forgive me for being rude, but you might as well say we should devalue fire because it causes so much destruction."

"Hmm…" Reinhard twisted his mouth, but not even that was enough to spoil the blond youth's beauty. "Perhaps, but is not the same true of autocracy? While tyrants do occasionally appear, you cannot deny the merits of a government built on strong leadership."

Yang looked back at Reinhard pensively.

"But I can."

"How so?"

"The right to harm the people is up to the people themselves. Put another way, the people have always been responsible for granting authority to the likes of Rudolph von Goldenbaum and even to far less significant players like Job Trünicht. You cannot blame anyone else. That's the crucial point here. The crime of autocracy is that the people can displace the evils of their government onto someone else. Compared to the enormity of that sin, the good deeds of a hundred wise rulers' good governments are insignificant. What's more, if we can think of a ruler of such sagacity as Your Excellency as being rare, then your deeds, good and evil alike, are just as explicit."

Reinhard looked as if he'd been lied to.

"Your assertions are as daring and original as they are extreme. I'm reluctant to concede. Just what are you trying to convince me of?"

"Nothing at all," said Yang, bewildered.

And he was indeed bewildered. He had no intention whatsoever of persuading or cornering Reinhard. As was his habit, Yang took off his beret and ruffled his long black hair. It was futile to oppose Reinhard's elegance, but he'd hoped to be at least a little more composed.

"I'm only putting forth the antithesis to your assertion. The way I see it, if one form of righteousness exists, then so must its opposite in equal measure. That's all I was trying to say."

"So righteousness is never absolute and cannot exist alone? Is that what you believe?"

Yang hated this talk of belief.

"It's only what I think. And who knows—maybe somewhere in the universe there is a sole, inimitable truth, and a simultaneous equation that elucidates it. But my hands will never reach that far."

"In which case my hands are even shorter than yours." Reinhard smiled somewhat cynically. "Truth has never been necessary. All I need is the power to do however I please by whatever means I please. It's the power to get on without following the orders of someone I despise. Have you never thought that way? Is there no one you despise?"

"The only ones I despise are those who would glorify war and stress the importance of patriotism even as they shelter themselves in safety, urging others to fight their battles for them while leading comfortable lives back on the home front. Being under the same flag as such people is an unbearable agony."

Yang was more than cynical; he was bitter. Reinhard observed him closely. Noticing this, Yang cleared his throat. "You're different. You've always stood on the front lines. Forgive me for saying so, but I cannot suppress my admiration."

"I see. So that's the only thing about me you deem acceptable. I'm flattered, really." Reinhard laughed musically, but his expression grew suddenly transparent. "I once had a friend. We made a pact together to hold the universe in our hands, at the same time swearing that we'd always gain our victory by fighting on the front lines…"

Although Reinhard hadn't given a proper noun, Yang guessed who it was. That friend was Siegfried Kircheis, the man who'd died saving Reinhard from an assassin.

"I would've sacrificed myself for that friend under any circumstance," said Reinhard, brushing back the luxurious golden hair falling over his forehead with his white fingers.

Perhaps he regarded Yang as a piano keyboard and was playing his requiem.

"In reality, he was always the one to be sacrificed. I presumed upon him and took advantage of him, to the point where he finally gave up his life for me…" His ice-blue eyes glistened through his declaration. "If my friend were still alive, you can be certain that right now I'd be facing not your living self but your corpse."

Yang didn't answer, because he knew his answers meant nothing to the golden-haired youth.

Reinhard took a small breath and changed the subject. He seemed to have dragged his heart back into reality.

"A while ago, I received a report from my commanders occupying your capital. It seems to have come from your superior, the commander in chief of the Alliance Armed Forces Space Armada. He has asked that all military responsibility be placed on him and that I not charge anyone else with a crime."

To this, Yang reacted.

"That sounds like something commander in chief Bucock would say. But I would implore Your Excellency to reject such an entreaty. What kind of people would we be to let him shoulder that burden alone?"

"Admiral Yang, I'm not one to hold a grudge. And while I did do just that against the high nobility of the empire, to me you're all worthy opponents. I had no choice but to imprison the director of Joint Operational Headquarters as the one most responsible. But when the fires of war die down, the futile shedding of blood isn't something I enjoy."

In Reinhard's expression was a noble pride, and Yang naturally bowed to the perfect honesty of his words.

"Incidentally, what will you do if I give you your freedom?"

Yang answered without hesitation.

"Retire."

For a moment, Reinhard regarded the black-haired admiral nine years his senior with his ice-blue eyes, nodding assent despite himself.

The meeting was over.

Inside the shuttle on his way back to the flagship *Hyperion*, Yang couldn't help immersing himself in thought. What Reinhard had pointed out regarding democratic rule was too harsh. *A democratic government is a body which, by free will of its citizens, looks down upon its own system and spirit...*

On the surface, it was the hardest of carbon crystals—to create a diamond, the pressure of enormous geological features was necessary. Likewise, the most precious thing about the human spirit was its essential resistance to authority and violence in the name of freedom and emancipation. Perhaps the ideal environment for freedom was one that corrupted freedom itself.

Yang wasn't sure anymore. There were too many things in this world that his wisdom left him ill equipped to decide. Would a clear answer ever come to him?

III

Reinhard stepped onto the soil of the alliance capital of Heinessen, welcomed by admirals von Reuentahl and Mittermeier, as well as his private imperial secretary, Hildegard von Mariendorf. Despite it being early summer, a cold misty rain clung to his luxurious golden hair like droplets of dew.

"Long live Emperor Reinhard!"

On this day, May 12, the soldiers mobilized to be the young dictator's bodyguards had originally numbered two hundred thousand, but many off-duty soldiers had also come to get a look at the object of their loyalty and devotion, rushing out of their appointed lodgings in droves and tearing the curtain of rain with their maniacal refrain.

"Long live the emperor! Long live the emperor!"

In a strange twist of fate, those same self-professed patriots who once assaulted pacifists on street corners and filled the air with cries of "Down with the emperor!" now extolled the virtues of their conqueror. Seeing the blond-haired youth waving from the window of his landcar, their cheers grew even louder, tinged with ardor, and enough were moved to tears to form a navy division of their own. Many had died for the sake of this youth to whom they were devoted, and many more would have to die still, but for now such things were beyond the scope of his heart.

Reinhard had arrived at the High Council building a few days later than planned to receive the soldiers' welcome.

Reinhard gathered not only military men, but also administrative experts to hear their opinions on what form the results of this campaign might take. Simply put, it was impossible to rule just after winning and maintaining hegemony, and so they had to come up with a more efficient method.

"We cannot allow ourselves to be stretched so thinly indefinitely. Our navy has already reached the breaking point of its actions. Let's concentrate our efforts on getting territories as far as Phezzan in our grasp before perfecting our rule over the alliance."

"At this point, we can invade alliance territory from the Phezzan and

Iserlohn corridors at any time. If we can guarantee this military supremacy, we won't have to be so particular about sovereignty."

"Besides, our soldiers want to return to their homeland now that they've won. A drawn-out occupation will only intensify their homesickness, if not also arouse dissatisfaction with Duke von Lohengramm."

"Trying to rule twelve billion people brimming with enmity toward the imperial government by statecraft alone is inefficient. Moreover, the alliance's financial affairs and economy are on the verge of bankruptcy, and the prospect of taking all of that upon ourselves, forcing new burdens on the empire's own finances, which have been restored over two long years of reform, is far from ideal."

Von Oberstein reported as much to Reinhard.

"I'm inclined to agree with the prevailing opinion that bringing about the total dissolution of the alliance, even officially, and placing it under direct rule would be premature." To this, the artificial-eyed chief of staff added his own opinion. "That said, I think we should set aside measures to further corrupt the alliance's finances. In any case, once we've reduced military spending, the economy will be restored, so there's no need to treat them like a second Phezzan."

"Of course."

Reinhard tossed the report onto his desk. That desk, used by successive generations of alliance High Council chairmen, had been witness to many clandestine political and military schemes against the empire.

On May 25, the Bharat Treaty went into effect. Reinhard postponed a total merger with the Free Planets Alliance, and before the people could take up armed resistance, they would return to their imperial mainland, where they would be well provisioned. Looking over the terms of the treaty, even someone as particular about total conquest as Reinhard could only be satisfied:

1. The Galactic Empire guarantees that the Free Planets Alliance will retain its name and sovereignty.

2. The FPA will cede the Gandharva star system and the two star systems at either end of both corridors to the empire.

3. The FPA will sanction the free passage of all imperial ships and civilian craft throughout its territories.

4. The FPA will pay a yearly security tax to the empire in the amount of one trillion five hundred billion imperial reichsmark.

5. The FPA will retain its armaments as a symbol of its sovereignty, but all warships and mother ships will relinquish their independent rights. Furthermore, the FPA will consult the imperial government before establishing and improving any of its military institutions.

6. The FPA will establish a national law and put an end to any activities that hinder friendship and conciliation with the empire.

7. The empire will install itself in the high commissioner's office on the alliance capital of Heinessen and have authority to station a military garrison to defend it. The high commissioner, as representative of the imperial sovereign (herein: the emperor), will negotiate and cooperate with the alliance government and be allowed to attend various meetings…

From the eighth condition onward, the reality that the alliance had become an imperial territory was clear to both sides. The alliance's head of state, Job Trünicht, shielded by a thick wall of imperial troops, signed and sealed the treaty. Immediately afterward, he announced that he was taking full responsibility for the defeat and would resign forthwith. Trünicht resigned, while the Defense Committee chairman, Walter Islands, having exhausted both mind and body, was confined to his bed. A gathering of cabinet ministers nominated Trünicht's political opponent, former chair of the finance committee João Lebello, as de facto ruler.

Even as Lebello was worried about the gravity of the situation, he accepted the nomination, but once these stipulations were made public, his friend Huang Rui read them with a critical eye.

"A noose has been tied around your neck, and only your toenails are touching the ground. A tough spot to be in, Lebello."

And if he didn't wake up soon, the other high officials, whose frank expressions were of anything but triumph, would be shedding tears of resentment on his behalf. Why had Ahle Heinessen taken that ten thousand light-year journey so filled with hardship two and a half centuries ago, only to set in motion the events leading to today's disgrace? And by the hands of a representative of its own people, to boot!

As Trünicht had imagined, the people's fury and hatred turned its spearheads away from Reinhard and toward Trünicht for accepting this humiliating treaty.

On May 26, the day after the treaty was signed, Reinhard heard from his private secretary Hilda that Trünicht was seeking an audience with him. Hearing the name of the former chairman, known to all as a walking disgrace, flames of hatred licked Reinhard's white face.

"I refuse to meet him!"

"So you say, but it's not that easy."

Reinhard turned his eyes, gleaming like a stubborn child, toward Hilda.

"After achieving the highest authority on this planet, why must I meet a man I have no desire to meet?"

"Your Excellency…"

"If I could, I'd toss that piece of human trash into the den of the very extremists whose hearts burn with a desire for vengeance."

"I understand how you feel, but you swore on your good name to overlook the crimes of the highest responsible parties. I know it doesn't please you, but if you go back on your word, you will incur distrust in your ability to keep your promises and adhere to the terms of the treaty."

As Reinhard clicked his tongue furiously, he slammed the desk with his palm. Although he left choppy waves on his emotional waterline, he turned his gaze to Hilda.

"So what does that bastard want from me anyway?"

"Assurance that his life and assets, as well as his right to reside in the imperial mainland, are maintained. He says that if he could get some sort of post, then he will gladly work for Your Excellency."

An unpleasant smile adorned the corners of the dictator's mouth.

"Seems like he can't handle living alongside the very people he betrayed. And what makes him think he'd receive my protection by living in imperial territory? Very well, I hereby grant his request. And now that I have, there's no need to meet with him. Send him away."

Knowing it was impossible to compromise further, Hilda made to leave.

As she did so, Reinhard called her to a halt, hesitated for a moment, and then shook it off.

"Fräulein von Mariendorf, I'm aware that I'm a narrow-minded man. And while I know I owe you my life, I cannot bring myself to thank you right now. Just give me a little more time."

Hilda had no objections. In fact, she couldn't help but be touched by the blond-haired youth's awkward expression of gratitude. Beneath that coolheaded, indifferent strategist's mask of his was the face of a boy raised on his elder sister Annerose's gentle affections.

"It's my fault for exceeding my brief. No matter what scolding I receive, it's only natural, but to hear you speak like that makes me embarrassed. If I may be so bold, I do have a request—that you please reward Mittermeier and von Reuentahl sufficiently for their meritorious service."

"Ah, consider it done."

Reinhard raised a hand slightly, and so Hilda took a bow and her leave. When she exited the room, her head of cropped blond hair turned as she cast a glance over her shoulders at the figure of Reinhard reflected in her quickly narrowing field of vision, resting his chin in his hands and giving himself up to contemplation.

When it came to naming a high commissioner to dispatch to the alliance capital of Heinessen, Reinhard considered von Reuentahl as a candidate. The high commissioner would be more than just a diplomatic figurehead and would need to oversee the alliance's national government and champion the empire's interests to the utmost. The commissioner would also be responsible for dealing with resistance and opposition in all forms and suppressing any armed insurrections. While Reinhard's abilities were seemingly sufficient to deal with such things, his chief of staff von Oberstein disagreed. His subordinate Captain Ferner was the only one privy to the real reasons behind his disagreement.

"Von Reuentahl is a bird of prey. It would be extremely dangerous to let him roam free. A man like him should be chained to a place where one can keep an eye on him at all times."

Indeed, future literary works would say the same. In any event, Reinhard struck off von Reuentahl from candidacy and appointed Lennenkamp instead. Because the von Lohengramm dictatorship had essentially institutionalized the political rule of a military man, bringing a civil official into this important office was unthinkable. Naturally, however, the many civil officials among Lennenkamp's followers—including experts in diplomacy, financial affairs, and administration—were assigned to him.

Incidentally, von Oberstein was also opposed to the personal selection of Lennenkamp. The reason was, of course, different from that for von Reuentahl. Lennenkamp was too much the military type, and as such his thinking was far too rigid. And because he'd suffered an infamous defeat against Yang Wen-li, his attitude toward the alliance was inflexible. Hearing this, Reinhard smiled.

"If Lennenkamp fails, I'll cast him off. And if the alliance is responsible, I'll charge them with that crime as well. That's all. There's nothing more to consider."

Von Oberstein bowed and deferred to his master's wisdom. As with the occupation of Phezzan, von Oberstein paid due respect to his young master's genius and magnanimity.

Reinhard further appointed Steinmetz as base commander of the Gandharva star system, now under direct imperial control. It was better for the high commissioner and commander in residence to hold concurrent posts, but that was a matter for a later day, when the alliance was under total subjugation.

The legitimate imperial galactic government, remnants of the old nobles under another name, was naturally looked upon by the Imperial Navy as hostile. Secretary of Defense Merkatz was already purported to have been killed in action at Vermillion, and his death straightened the collars of the Imperial Navy's high-ranking officers.

The legitimate imperial galactic government's prime minister, Count Jochen von Remscheid, poisoned himself to death. This was just after von Reuentahl's soldiers had surrounded his private residence. The heterochromatic admiral paid his respects to Count von Remscheid and gave him enough time to do the deed. And with that, the exile government disappeared as fleetingly as it had formed.

Nevertheless, the child emperor under its care was nowhere to be found. The results of the investigation revealed that Count Alfred von Lansberg, the criminal who'd absconded with the emperor to the imperial capital of Odin and the next in command after the legitimate government's defense secretary, had disappeared along with the eight-year-old boy.

This turn of events sat comfortably with neither von Reuentahl nor Mittermeier, who could only widen their search network. They said as much to Reinhard, but the young dictator didn't rebuke them for their oversight.

"He can go wherever he pleases. When something destined to perish doesn't, whether it's a person or a nation, it's destined to die in obscurity."

Somewhere behind the indifference of Reinhard's voice was a particle of compassion.

"If they want to dream about a Goldenbaum family comeback, then they're welcome to crawl into their beds and shut their eyes to reality. Why should we seriously associate ourselves with people like that?"

Reinhard, in fact, had no time for the delusions of unrealistic romanticists. He had to prepare for his enthronement and coronation, and think through how to plan an imminent merger with alliance territory and the predetermined relocation of the capital to Phezzan. In addition, allocation of human resources following the establishment of the new empire was becoming an extremely pressing issue. Because the new empire would be under direct imperial rule, a prime minister would be unnecessary, but he did need cabinet ministers, and it was also necessary to reform the military. He was warned by von Oberstein to order a search for good measure, but it was thrown into a well of forgetfulness and sealed off.

⁜

Neither could the people of the alliance afford the luxury of fussing over the past while making light of the future. Alexandor Bucock liberated his body from public office and decided to heal his wounded heart by his elderly wife's side.

Yang Wen-li retired from military service, and an unintentional military life of twelve years came to a full and sudden stop—or so it seemed. His rather comfortable retirement had begun, and over the past few days, he had been working out the details of his marriage to Frederica Green-hill, who'd also retired. The fact that he now had the life he'd always hoped for was tempered by the knowledge of the many other human lives that had been sacrificed for this modest fortune—it was a thought that would never leave his brain. But even as he worried about being under the constant surveillance of the Imperial Navy, the practicalities of planning for his future life with Frederica were overwhelming. Indeed, it was as if he had no conceptual ability when it came to the home, and so he was nothing more than a yes-man agreeing with Frederica's modest proposals.

Julian, meanwhile, was secretly preparing to sneak into Terra, deep within imperial territory, motivated by that small bit of information he'd gleaned from Bishop Degsby of the Church of Terra. If there existed a church disciple with enough clandestine power to bring about Chairman Trünicht's anti-coup d'état, then even if Degsby's words—"Everything will make sense once you go to Terra"—were exaggerated, there had to be *some* truth to them. Surely there was no harm in investigating.

Moreover, as he'd declared to Caselnes, Julian had no intention of getting in the way of Yang and Frederica's newlywed life. He knew the two of them wouldn't stand in his way. Although—if not because—he knew this, Julian wanted to disappear for at least six months. His short life on Phezzan had matured him to some extent. And he wanted nothing more than to reunite with the two people he loved most after this journey, more of a man.

The dark-skinned, round-eyed ensign Louis Machungo was preparing to go to Terra with Julian as if it were the most natural thing in the world. When he said, "One cannot avoid his destiny," not one person believed he was being forced to go along with a destiny he didn't want. Both Julian and Machungo had tendered their letters of resignation, indifferent about whether they would be accepted. At any rate, right after returning to Heinessen, Machungo had become a live-in employee at a private residence cohabitated by Yang and Julian on Silverbridge Street, and from then on, even the imperial soldiers who came for inspection believed he'd been living in the Yang household all along.

Yang shrugged his shoulders and accepted Machungo's presence, but had no doubts about entrusting the giant to protect Julian with his life. Besides, Yang was responsible for the social disappearance of Merkatz and the rest, and it seemed impossible to be a total hermit. If the imperial forces knew this, then Yang's position in the new order would become problematic.

Boris Konev, once known to Yang as "Boris the troublemaker," reunited with administrative officer Marinesk, who'd arrived from Phezzan. When he heard about the loss of his beloved *Beryozka*, it was impossible for him to fall back on his usual limitless optimism.

Meanwhile, those remaining on Phezzan gathered in the high commissioner's office, which had lost its legal basis for existence, uneasily sharing with each other whatever scant news they had, but Boris Konev left early to pay a visit to Yang Wen-li's official residence. Imperial soldiers were already guarding the front door, as Yang was under house arrest, but after somewhat exaggerating what a close friend he was of the admiral's, Yang came to the entrance and convinced them to let him in. Konev hadn't seen his old friend in sixteen or seventeen years. Savoring Julian's black tea, he learned that his younger cousin Ivan had died in battle.

"I cannot thank you enough for your help, Julian. *Beryozka*, was it? I hear everyone on that ship owes you their lives."

"The honor is all Marinesk's, so there's no need to thank me. Problem is, that was my ship. The alliance government's as good as gone, and it's not like I can take this up with the imperial forces."

"Leave it to me," promised Yang nonchalantly, turning to his old friend with a knowing smile. "But first, I'm going to need you to do something for me…"

Among the generals who followed Yang back to the capital, von Schönkopf and Attenborough high-handedly submitted their letters of resignation and left government service. Caselnes's resignation was rejected, and he was forced into a position as acting general manager of rear services. Fischer, Murai, Patrichev, and Carlsen were temporarily laid off. Over them all, the shadow of time was moving little by little, but no one knew how long, or how short, the winter would be.

IV

The sun sank into the horizon, and the fading light reflected diffusely in the atmospheric particles, soaking the world in orange waves. The land, which had once promised an abundant harvest as if ashamed of its own barrenness, begged for the wings of night to give it shelter.

This same land, which senility and fatigue had ravaged with deep wrinkles, had once been the heart of this planet called Terra, and indeed the center of the universe. That had been a long time ago, thirty generations into the past.

A man in his prime covered in black walked through an old stone building with a sluggish gait. As he stood before a certain door, a bodyguard bowed and opened it. The inside of the room was filled with a dull, cloudy light. He saw an old man, who seemed to have been a friend of time for much longer, sitting on a sheepskin.

"Grand Bishop…" The man who so reverently addressed the silent bishop continued. "Reinhard von Lohengramm has conquered the Free Planets Alliance."

Upon hearing this, the black-clad bishop lifted his face at last and beckoned the man with an arid hand. The door behind the man was closed.

"And what will he do now?" he said, his voice rasping.

"I hear he has entrusted a man named Lennenkamp with watching over not only the conquered land, but also the grand navy, and he himself has returned to the imperial mainland, accompanied by a certain Trünicht…"

"It seems that man has also served his purpose. Do you intend to use him as a rotten apple within the empire?"

"No, we already groomed someone else in the empire over a year ago. A baron by the name of Heinrich von Kümmel. I just need a little more time."

"I hear he's very ill, but you're sure he'll be of use?"

"If he can just hold out for another six months, our objective will be carried out. Doctors have been dispatched, and if he's jealous at all of von Lohengramm's good looks and health, he won't be difficult to manipulate."

"Very well, then. I'll leave it to you. What will become of Phezzan?"

"Yes, regarding Phezzan, there are still too many uncertainties."

The man's voice for the first time lost its surplus of confidence. An aura of doubt wavered about his jaundiced eyes. The grand bishop inquired of him further.

"Are you in contact with Rubinsky?"

"For the time being. But the depths of that man's heart are unknowable to me…"

Despite the fact that no one was listening, the grand bishop's subordinate lowered his voice and leaned forward on his knees.

"It's not just that I doubt the spirit of his obedience. It's that I have reason to believe he might be harboring some insubordinate ambition toward us. We'll need to be on our guard…"

"I've always known that."

The old man's voice was indifferent.

"I don't care what kind of style he dances, so long as he does it in the palm of my hand. More importantly, what's become of that incompetent fool Degsby?"

"I can confirm that Degsby is dead. The problem is whether he spilled any secrets before he died…"

Far overhead from where these two men were talking in secret about wanting to change the tide of history, the profuse light of the stars began to speckle the sky.

Reinhard, having triumphantly returned to the empire, commenced vigorous activities for formality's sake. Various things that needed to be dealt with were awaiting his judgment and decision.

The first task he carried out was for his own personal duty and timid dissatisfaction. To his sister Annerose, now carrying the title of Countess von Grünewald, he gave the title of archduchess. He decorated Siegfried Kircheis with the posthumous title of archduke and established a medal in his honor. Von Oberstein raised an eyebrow at these measures but was put in his place by being told there was no harm in taking them.

With that decided, Reinhard put on his business hat, focusing his attentions on human resources, organization, and institutions. On the military side of things, von Reuentahl, Mittermeier, and von Oberstein became marshals, and von Oberstein took on the additional role of secretary of defense. Ten admirals became senior admirals, but the youngest, Müller, became their leader as reward for the meritorious service of saving Reinhard from certain defeat at Vermillion. Human resources for civil officials were decided, and Hilda's father, Count Franz von Mariendorf, was nominated as secretary of state. Eugen Richter became secretary of finance, and Karl Bracke the newly established secretary of civil affairs.

On June 20, the father of the child empress and the current head of the Pegnitz family, Jürgen Offer, was promoted three ranks from viscount to duke. Bearing the burden of uneasiness and uncertainty, he was invited through the imperial prime minister's gates. A young noble in his early thirties who'd devoted nearly all his attention to his passion for collecting ivory carvings and his assets, and who had no interest whatsoever in politics or military affairs, Offer was presented with a piece of paper by a coolheaded von Oberstein: a declaration of the empress's abdication. This was followed by a declaration that yielded the throne to Reinhard. In all, the young noble, dripping with sweat, was presented with three pieces of paper, each of which already bore Reinhard's signature. The Pegnitz family's peerage and safety were guaranteed, and it was specified that from now on the empress would be provided with a yearly pension of 1,500,000 imperial reichsmark for the rest of her life. Duke Pegnitz, for the sake of his own relief, dabbed his face with a handkerchief, drenching his expensive clothes with even more sweat. Taking the pen, he signed two documents as the parental authority of the empress, now one year and eight months of age.

And with that, the Goldenbaum Dynasty, which since the time of founder

Rudolf the Great had welcomed thirty-eight emperors on its throne to rule the people over 490 years, came to its demise.

June 22 marked the enthronement and coronation of the new emperor, Reinhard. From this day forward, he would cease to be His Excellency Duke Reinhard von Lohengramm and come to be called His Majesty Emperor Reinhard. The Goldenbaum family, which had once snatched his sister Annerose away from him, had lost everything and had hidden its wretched self away in the territory of the past.

Thousands of high officials of both pen and sword filled the spacious Black Pearl Room of Neue Sans Souci to the gills to pledge their loyalty to the new dynasty. But the two people Reinhard wanted most to see weren't there. The one whose head was golden just like his, and the other whose head was red like a burning flame.

And while cries of "Long live the emperor!" overwhelmed the spacious room, Reinhard picked up the golden emperor's crown nestled in purple silk, and casually, yet with an elegance no one could duplicate, placed it on his own head. The golden crown meshed with his golden hair as he silently proclaimed himself its rightful owner.

The Lohengramm Dynasty had begun.

ABOUT THE AUTHOR

Yoshiki Tanaka was born in 1952 in Kumamoto Prefecture and completed a doctorate in literature at Gakushuin University. Tanaka won the Gen'eijo (a mystery magazine) New Writer Award with his debut story "Midori no Sogen ni…" (On the green field…) in 1978, then started his career as a science fiction and fantasy writer. Legend of the Galactic Heroes, which translates the European wars of the nineteenth century to an interstellar setting, won the Seiun Award for best science fiction novel in 1987. Tanaka's other works include the fantasy series The Heroic Legend of Arslan and many other science fiction, fantasy, historical, and mystery novels and stories.

HAIKASORU
THE FUTURE IS JAPANESE

TRAVEL SPACE AND TIME WITH HAIKASORU!

USURPER OF THE SUN—HOUSUKE NOJIRI

Aki Shiraishi is a high school student working in the astronomy club and one of the few witnesses to an amazing event—someone is building a tower on the planet Mercury. Soon, the Builders have constructed a ring around the sun, threatening the ecology of Earth with an immense shadow. Aki is inspired to pursue a career in science, and the truth. She must determine the purpose of the ring and the plans of its creators, as the survival of both species—humanity and the alien Builders—hangs in the balance.

THE OUROBOROS WAVE—JYOUJI HAYASHI

Ninety years from now, a satellite detects a nearby black hole scientists dub Kali for the Hindu goddess of destruction. Humanity embarks on a generations-long project to tap the energy of the black hole and establish colonies on planets across the solar system. Earth and Mars and the moons Europa (Jupiter) and Titania (Uranus) develop radically different societies, with only Kali, that swirling vortex of destruction and creation, and the hated but crucial Artificial Accretion Disk Development association (AADD) in common.

TEN BILLION DAYS AND ONE HUNDRED BILLION NIGHTS—RYU MITSUSE

Ten billion days—that is how long it will take the philosopher Plato to determine the true systems of the world. One hundred billion nights—that is how far into the future Jesus of Nazareth, Siddhartha, and the demigod Asura will travel to witness the end of all worlds. Named the greatest Japanese science fiction novel of all time, *Ten Billion Days and One Hundred Billion Nights* is an epic eons in the making. Originally published in 1967, the novel was revised by the author in later years and republished in 1973.

WWW.HAIKASORU.COM